MW01268540

Christmas at the Secondhand Bookworm

EMILY JANE BEVANS

CHRISTMAS AT THE SECONDHAND BOOKWORM

DEDICATION

This novel is dedicated to Rosalinda.

CHRISTMAS AT THE SECONDHAND BOOKWORM

CONTENTS

	Acknowledgments	i
1	A CHARLIE BROWN CHRISTMAS	1
2	THE SINGING FATHER CHRISTMASES	34
3	HI-DE-HI AND THE KNUCKER DRAGON	63
4	OF MINCE PIES AND MEN	76
5	SNOWED IN WITH ONLY 27,000 BOOKS FOR COMPANY	96
6	THE SNOWMAN IN THE YARD	116
7	THE GRINCH WHO STOLE THE COLE BOOKS	136
8	ROGER THE ELF	161
9	MR HILL'S UNDERPANTS, THE DUKE AND SHOPPING BY CANDLELIGHT	182
10	THE DISGUISE IN CHRISTMAS TOWN	198
11	THE RAVENS AND THE CHRISTMAS STAFF MEAL	217
12	FELIX AND THE CHRISTMAS FARMERS TURKEY MARKET	241
13	THE SURPRISE AT THE JOLLY CHRISTMAS THEATRE	256

CHRISTMAS AT THE SECONDHAND BOOKWORM

ACKNOWLEDGMENTS

I will always remain grateful for the ten years I spent
working in Kim's secondhand and antiquarian bookshops
on the South Coast of England, which afforded me greater
experience in the world of books.

CHRISTMAS AT THE SECONDHAND BOOKWORM

1 A CHARLIE BROWN CHRISTMAS

Inside a cluttered secondhand and antiquarian bookshop, surrounded by shelves and cases of books, upon books, upon books, a woman stood next to a little oil heater. Her name was Nora Jolly and she was gazing through frosty glass windows into an empty cobbled market square on a cold Monday morning of the third week of December.

Wearing fingerless gloves with a thick woollen scarf wrapped around her neck, Nora was trying to get warm in the front room of The Secondhand Bookworm as she stood behind an unusually tidy, large wooden counter.

Upon the counter stood a computer monitor with a thin layer of dust across its screen; a display of quirky or interesting books in an assortment of stands or flat upon the desk top; a yellow spinner that contained copies of various *Shire Albums*; a till that looked as though it had emerged from the Tudor age; a cash book opened next to a bulging message pad; several pens in a neat row and a handful of pencils standing in a broken mug.

Outside in the square the sky was overcast and the ground was hard and cold. A few flakes of snow danced by, promising the heavy flurries and falls that had been forecast for later on in the week. Several Christmassy stalls had been set up to sell Christmas gifts or little trees as tourists arrived for some special wintry events.

A gust of sleety wind blew against the window.

"What we need..." Nora mused to herself, rubbing her woolly hands together, "...is a lovely open fire in here. But what to burn?" She glanced around at the endless shelves of books and gasped. "Burning books is *criminal*, Nora!" She told herself but shuddered because of the cold.

The windows of The Secondhand Bookworm were thin, single panes of glass. The door let the wind whistle through the cracks around it and sailed in through the jammed open letter box, sounding like the pious ghost of a monk singing Christmas hymns. There were a few night storage heaters throughout the several rooms in the winding three floors of books, but sometimes the weather was just too cold for them to make a substantial difference to the temperature. The additional oil heater was helping, but Nora had only switched it on a few moments ago after she had set up for the day.

The sound of a distant door slamming shut followed by footsteps on the wooden flooring of the back room and then the flagstones of the stairwell came from behind Nora.

"Got them!" Her colleague Cara Hathaway said cheerfully, almost wedging herself in the walkway between rooms as she came through to the front carrying a huge mouldy box.

"Eeeew!" Nora grimaced.

"What?" Cara laughed and dumped it unceremoniously onto the wooden stool behind the counter.

"That looks hideous, Cara."

"Well, it's free of poop." Cara promised. "I'm amazed seeing as it's spent a year in the disused outside loo in the back yard. I thought it might have been ruined from last month's *sewage* adventure but it was on a pile of broken crates, so nicely elevated."

"I hope you checked for spiders." Nora winced.

"Yes." Cara promised. "There were only two…*hundred*."

Nora gave a small shudder. She then swung her leg over the rickety old oil heater, letting the warmth wash up and over her.

"Well they're supposed to be the Christmas decorations not the Halloween ones." She reminded her colleague.

Cara chuckled; wrenching open the damp stained top flaps of the cardboard box. She peered inside and reached in to grab a handful of shimmery gold tinsel.

"This'll do nicely." She decided, pondering the window shelving across the room. "Why didn't we put these up earlier? It's almost Christmas."

"Georgina was reluctant to ruin our window display after she bought a recent substantial library of children's illustrated books. She said she wanted us to hold off filling the prime sale shelves up with tinsel, lights and baubles for as long as possible." Nora explained.

Georgina Pickering was the owner of The Secondhand Bookworm. She had two branches, one in Castletown and one in Seatown. Nora had worked for Georgina for three years and was sort of dating her brother, Humphrey (they had been on four dates and although Humphrey was certainly keen on Nora she still thought him more of a best friend). Georgina currently had the flu.

"Makes sense." Cara shrugged and continued rummaging.

"Brrrr, it's so cold." Nora thought she saw fog come out of her mouth as she spoke.

"What I heard..." Cara mused, pulling out heaps of tinsel "...was that if you stuff paper inside your clothes it acts as a kind of insulation against the cold."

"Oh?" Nora was interested in her theory. "Really?"

Her eyes moved to consider the shelves of books around her again and when Cara noticed she laughed.

"But I don't think we should use books! Georgina will fire us both."

"I could go and get some newspaper." Nora considered. "Oh wait, there's all the packaging from the deliveries of book remainders Georgina recently acquired."

"We'd look like *Michelin* men." Cara said.

"But we'd be warm."

The door opened and a blast of arctic air preceded the arrival of their first customer of the day. Nora reluctantly stepped away from the oil heater and stood before the till. The customer was a large man with two scarves wrapped around his thick neck, an enormous puffy coat, big thermal gloves and a massive blue woollen hat with a bobble on top. He stood on the mat and stared around the room before his gaze rested upon Nora.

"Whew! It's warm in here!" The man said.

His fingers moved to one of his scarves and he eased it from his throat, puffing out some breath and then fanning his face.

Nora's stare followed him as he stomped across the new pink carpet and headed towards the doorway that led into the back of the shop and beyond.

"Really warm." He said, puffing out some more breath and fanning himself again.

Nora smiled politely.

"Can we help you with anything, sir?" She asked.

"No, no I'll just have a browse. Whew. Wonderful bookshop, but quite warm." He said and squashed himself between the wall and the display shelves that led into the back rooms, coming out into the stairwell with what sounded like a pop.

Nora and Cara looked at one another. Cara then watched as Nora picked up a pen and turned towards the wall beneath the alarm pad.

"I'd be warm if I was wearing the entire contents of the mountaineering shop." Nora said in a whisper and drew a line on a sheet of paper to complete a tally. "That makes two hundred and thirty '*it's warm in here*' comments so far this winter."

Cara snorted into the Christmas decorations box while Nora pondered her tally chart.

It had been constructed out of the back of a poster from Castletown Museum advertising an exhibition on teapots that had finished in November, and was covered in a maze of tally charts beneath the title which read: '*THE 'IT'S WARM IN HERE' DOCUMENTATION CHART*'. Nora filled it in as a means of anger management.

When she turned back she pondered a small pile of books on the floor by the Folio Society section, waiting to be put neatly onto the shelves, but was then distracted. It was some moments later and Nora's voice had taken on a very wary and suddenly unnerved tone.

"Er…Cara?" Nora's attention was on the ceiling above her before sliding to what little wall space there was between overflowing bookcases.

Cara looked up from organising baubles into colour groups on the counter.

"Yes?"

"Why is the whole room now *pink*?" She asked cautiously.

"What? Oh! So it is. Hang on. Georgina said she'd asked Humphrey to paint it to match the new carpet. He must have done it overnight as a surprise for you." Cara recalled.

"I didn't even notice until now!" Nora said.

In unison they looked up at the ceiling, then down at the floor, then at one another and they both laughed.

The walls and the ceiling had been covered in a rich pink shade that reminded Nora of squashed raspberries. Not only had the walls and ceiling been painted, but also the beams and the skirting boards too. The new carpet that had been put down at the beginning of December, because of previous flooding and poop-episodes on the old carpet, now matched the room perfectly. Nora had to admit that Humphrey had done an excellent job.

"I'd text him and congratulate him but my fingers are numb." Nora lamented.

"You should make us a round of hot chocolate." Cara suggested, continuing to empty the Christmas box.

"I think I will." Nora agreed. "And then I'll collect all the Christmas books from where we keep them all year on the farthest shelves of the top floor, front room by the window. We can then get to work decorating and changing the window."

"A great plan." Cara agreed.

Before Nora had chance to turn, the door opened once more.

"Where can I buy figs?" A man hollered into the room.

Nora jumped.

"There's a greengrocer shop down Market Street." Cara hollered back helpfully.

"I'll try there." The man tipped his hat, turned, and left, leaving the door wide open.

Nora was about to go and close it when a woman wearing a zebra faux fur bucket hat and a yellow ankle-length woollen coat replaced him.

"Do you have a Santa's Grotto here?" She asked, spotting Nora.

Nora was distracted by her clothes.

"We do. It's in the scout hut all week by the main castle gates. Down by the river." She directed.

"It's not just my granddaughter who wants to sit on Santa's knee. I have a lot of needs this year." The woman shared, turned and set off.

Nora and Cara looked at once another.

"You there!" Another man had appeared.

Nora was alarmed. The town had been empty a moment ago.

He was swamped in an enormous green raincoat, his gloved hands holding several bags of shopping.

"Can I help?" Nora politely asked.

"If you've got any books about the Krampus in there, you can. It's the real meaning of Christmas!" He retorted.

"A horned, anthropomorphic figure bashing badly behaved children with birch rods at Christmastime is the *real* meaning of Christmas?" Nora countered, her brows raised.

"Huh. So you know your alpine legends." The man shrugged. "Well?! Do you?!"

"I'm afraid not." Nora shook her head.

"Forget it then!" His face scrunched in disappointment and he stormed off.

Cara's lips were trembling with mirth.

"We really need that hot chocolate." Nora decided grimly, closed the door and set off for the kitchen.

The Secondhand Bookworm had been seasonally quiet, as always happened each year. December, January and February were often months when Georgina tasked the staff to have a good sort out, clean-up and do mending and tending of certain tatty tomes as well as stock check the 27,000 books in the Castletown branch and the 18,000 books in the Seatown branch. But, because she had the flu, she said she didn't care how many smelly old books she currently had. She had even given them permission to use till money to treat themselves to mince pies from the delicatessen across the road whenever they felt the need and to micromanage themselves. Nora had eaten two dozen mince pies so far.

Cara had left the bunch of internal shop keys in the kitchen door so Nora left them in the lock while she made them a tasty mug of hot chocolate each, grimacing because the kitchen felt like a freezer.

When she returned, Cara was dealing with a customer. The man looked like he was wrapped up in a continental quilt. He wore a black fluffy hat and had blue thermal mittens on both hands so was having trouble examining the book he had requested out of the window. Cara gave Nora a look.

"Hmm, yes, and do you have a book called 'Mr Papingay's ship?" The man asked, frowning over the first edition Enid Blyton held in his mittens.

"Erm…" Cara looked at Nora and shrugged.

"Do you know the author, sir?" Nora asked, placing the mugs of chocolate on the mouse mat.

"Marion St. John Webb." He said.

"Oh yes, she wrote 'The Little Round House'." Nora recalled. "We might have it in the children's room."

"I would prefer a collector's edition."

"I don't believe I've seen a collector's edition of it come in I'm afraid."

"Hmm." The man attempted to turn a page of his book with his mittened hand but ended up shutting it instead. He pretended he had meant to and slid it awkwardly back to Cara.

"I'll leave that thank you. It's too tatty for my liking."

"Okay." Cara smiled politely.

"Do you accept book tokens?" He then asked.

"No, sorry."

"Dear, dear, dear, it was a good job I didn't want that book then." He said, pulled down a thick blue fluffy balaclava that covered his entire face except for his eyes, stared at them for a long moment and then turned, heading off towards the door.

Both Nora and Cara watched him attempt to take hold of the door handle with his mittens, finally yanking it open after six tries and disappearing into the cold, empty street.

"There is a book he might have liked." Cara said thoughtfully.

"What?"

She wheeled herself in the swivel chair over to the rare books shelves and pulled out a Louis Wain illustrated book.

"*The Three Little Kittens Painting Book*?" Nora read the title with a laugh.

"You will be pleased to see your old friends the 'Three Little Kittens'. Here you have a picture to paint of them crying over their lost mittens, and then happy at having found them, and afterwards dancing round their Mummy with the Pie, and lastly you have them washing their mittens. Don't they look dear, merry little kittens?" Cara read. "The young artist must prepare his tints upon a white plate or palette. Begin to paint at the top of the picture and colour downwards."

"He'd have trouble though. I don't think he wanted to take his mittens off." Nora pointed out.

"Georgina might be cross about the four plates being painted, though." Cara said. "That would knock about a hundred pounds off the price. Mad!"

"Louis Wain went *mad*." Nora recalled.

"That's because he was cursed by cats."

Nora blinked repetitively.

"Cursed by cats?"

"Well it says here he pretty much shamed the entire 19th century feline society." Cara said. "Listen to this: *'He invented a cat style, a cat society, a whole cat world. English cats that do not look like Louis Wain cats are ashamed of themselves'*." She quoted H.G. Wells from the back of 'The Three Little Kittens Painting Book'.

Nora chuckled.

"Beware of offending cats."

"They take revenge." Cara warned and while she popped the book back on the shelf Nora picked up her hot chocolate and inhaled it happily.

The door flew open.

Nora paused in mid sip.

"Excuse me! Do you have a book about the legend of the Christmas spider in there?" A slender man wearing a tall fluffy hat cried.

"It's not about a spider that goes around bashing children with birch rods is it?" Cara asked.

The man curled his lip.

"No! It's about a destitute but hardworking widow who lived in a dilapidated hut with her four ragged children. One fine summer day, a single pine cone fell to the earthen floor of the old hut and took root. The widow's children cared for the tree, keen and excited at the thought of having a Christmas tree in their pitiful home by wintertime. The tree grew and grew, but when Christmas Eve was finally upon them, the poverty-stricken family could not afford to decorate it. So, the children went to bed sad and fell asleep. Early the next morning, however, they woke up to find the Christmas tree covered with cobwebs. The Baby Jesus had asked all the spiders in the hut to decorate it for them. When the poor widow opened the curtains, the first rays of Christmas sunlight struck all the webs and turned them into gold and silver. The widow and her children were jubilant. From then on, they never lived in poverty again." He said.

"That's lovely." Nora had listened, captivated.

"Well?! Do YOU?!" He shouted, shattering the magical mood.

"I've never seen it before." Nora admitted.

"Call yourself a bookshop?!" The man hissed and stamped away.

Nora met Cara's mirthful eyes.

"A lovely story, told by the Grinch." She decided.

Nora shook her head, taking a sip of thick, velvety chocolate.

"It's ridiculously cold today. But I do like winter at The Secondhand Bookworm the best." Nora decided, returning to the oil heater with her mug of chocolate. "It's not like summer when all you hear is '*stamps*!', '*stamps*!'…"

"STAMPS!" Cara finished with a laugh. "I'm glad to hear Georgina will stop selling those soon!"

"Agreed."

"Hopefully one day we will be free of postcards, too." Cara pulled a face.

A customer arrived. He stepped down into the shop, closed the door behind him, pulled off his woollen hat and gazed around.

"Merry Christmas." He nodded.

"Merry Christmas." Nora smiled.

"Hello." Cara welcomed.

"Do you have any Peanut comic strip books?" He asked.

"We have a humour section upstairs. It's on the next floor landing." Cara pointed.

"Would you like me to look for you?" Nora offered.

"No thank you. That's kind, but I'll enjoy the browse. Through there?" The man peered.

"Yes, up the stairs, follow it round a few steps and there is a bookcase by the large cookery section. There are usually Peanut comic strips books and Snoopy annuals."

The man tittered.

"Thank you." He nodded, heading off.

"This new pink décor is going to affect the look of the Christmas decorations." Cara frowned, pondering the room as the Peanut customer creaked up the staircase.

"I wonder if anyone will actually notice the colour." Nora gazed around.

"*We* didn't." Cara chuckled, taking more tinsel out of the Christmas decoration box, followed by a gulp of chocolate from her mug.

"We really need a Christmas tree to brighten up the place." Nora decided. "Georgina has given us permission to micromanage ourselves. I don't think she'd mind if we added a tree."

"Can we?!" Cara looked keen. "I don't even have one in my shared flat. My flatmates are like raccoons, they'd destroy it as soon as it was up."

"Well, that's not on." Nora sympathised. "Everyone should have a Christmas tree and a nativity scene for the season. We already have some little nativity figures in the window so we had better get a tree for The Secondhand Bookworm."

"There's a Christmas tree stall on the cobbles." Cara pointed with a blue bauble. "I saw it when I arrived this morning. I was going to visit the Christmas counselling booth run by the Samaritans to speak about my

Christmas blues, but I bought a box of reindeer cookies instead and that cheered me up perfectly."

Nora chuckled.

"I'll go and pick a suitable tree." She decided.

She finished off her hot chocolate, pressed a button to open the till and slipped a twenty pound note out of the drawer.

"That's not going to get us much." Cara remarked with a quirked mouth. "It would be nice if we had a big, pink aluminium tree to match the room!"

"I'll work a Christmas miracle." Nora promised and set out.

It was brisk and sleety outside. Usually, Castletown only put on a few Christmas events over the season, but since the Duke of Cole had returned and rebuilt the sprawling ancient ruins of his ancestral castle into a magnificent stately citadel in his estate behind the rows of rambling shops, Castletown tourism had experienced a boon.

There were now some little Christmas stalls, a Santa grotto, old Christmas movies showing in the town hall and other modest events taking place throughout the week, including the Duke of Cole making his first public appearance to turn on the very large Christmas tree he had donated to the town. It stood by the war memorial looking grand and impressive, awaiting illumination.

A man who looked like a North American lumberjack was manning the Christmas Tree Stall in the shadow of the Duke's tree. There were a few small potted firs and some larger specimens on the table or positioned around him. Nora blinked when she saw the prices.

Her gaze was then drawn to a sad looking small sapling almost hidden behind the rest of the trees. Not only was it labelled at the bargain price of twelve pounds, but it looked in need of a kind home. Nora suspected everyone else would ignore it and it would end up being fed to a wood chipper.

"G'morning." The lumberjack greeted.

"Hello! I would like to buy that tree, please." Nora pointed.

The lumberjack followed her finger. He gave a start.

"*That* one? I mean, certainly madam." He nodded.

"Does the pot come with it?" Nora asked.

"Yep." The lumberjack reached in among the others and yanked it out. He showed it to her, quirking a brow.

"Wonderful." Nora smiled.

Shaking his head, the Lumberjack handed it to Nora. She gave him the twenty pound note. He gave her the change.

"Thank you very much."

"No problem." He watched her head back to the bookshop.

Nora knew he thought she was eccentric but she didn't care. Once it was decorated, it would be perfect.

Cara stared and burst out laughing when Nora returned.

"This will be the *Grinch's Bookshop Christmas*." She watched Nora walk the tree to the space before the bay window.

"Don't listen." Nora told the tree.

"Here." Cara stood and carried a large red bauble over to it.

Nora took the decoration, placed it on the top of the tree and watched as the sapling bent over double with the weight. They both laughed.

"It's a Charlie Brown Christmas." A voice said at their elbow.

Nora gave a start. Cara jumped.

The man who had asked for Peanut comic strip books had returned, carrying an armful.

"A *what*?" Cara asked.

"Shall I be Linus?" The man proposed and stood beside the tree. "Today in the town of David a Saviour has been born to you; he is the Messiah, the Lord. This will be a sign to you: You will find a baby wrapped in cloths and lying in a manger." He quoted the Annunciation to the Shepherds from the Gospel of Luke.

Nora was impressed but confused.

"It's from the 1965 animated television special *A Charlie Brown Christmas*." He said and wiggled his comic strip annuals. "Charlie Brown asked what Christmas was all about. He didn't want commercialism to ruin it. Just keep adding decorations and prop the tree upright and you'll be fine. Merry Christmas, Charlie Brown!" He shouted.

Nora thought she might be in The Twilight Zone again (she often found herself there when in the bookshop).

"Thank you, we will." She nodded, walking around the counter to run the prices of his Peanut books through the till.

The man sighed and shook his head.

"*Millennials*." He lamented.

He piled his choice of books on the counter top.

"We often have a supply of the Complete Peanuts comic strips." Nora shared.

"I find them very amusing." The man nodded, taking out his wallet.

The door opened to admit another Eskimo, this time a woman in a huge white fur coat with an enormous white bobble hat.

Nora placed the Peanut comic books into a blue bag, gave the man his change and receipt and he left as the telephone started to ring. Nora picked up the receiver, leaving Cara to greet their new customer.

"Good morning, The Secondhand Book…"

"Aaaachhhooooo!!" A loud sneeze interrupted, making Nora jump. "Oh sorry Nora, it's this blasted flu, I'll be glad when I'm over it." Georgina Pickering's voice said followed by a loud, unladylike sniff.

"You sound terrible." Nora sympathised, writing down the twelve pound pay out for the tree in the cash book and returning the left over cash to the till.

"I *feel* terrible. I shouldn't even be phoning you, mother has ordered me to stay in bed and not even think about the shops but she's just popped out to get me some lemons so I've dug out my mobile and grabbed the house phone. The very fact that I can lift them now proves I'm on the mend. I even feel like I can face Troy now that I don't look too much like Frankenstein."

Nora bit back a laugh, feeling sorry for Georgina.

"So I'm phoning to," sniff, sniff, "let you know that...aaaachooooo!! Sorry! That there will be a couple of tradespeople coming in this week." Georgina said and loudly blew her nose.

"Does that mean some big sales?" Nora asked.

"Let us hope so." Georgina said in a bunged-up voice. "Hopefully I'll be on my feet again for Thursday; I should think so, aaaachooo! Sorry again! And I'm determined to be well enough for the staff meal on Friday *and* your brother's opening night at The Jolly theatre on Saturday! I expect I will be; I feel like I'm over the worst of this. Mother's not letting me out until Thursday. It's like I'm five years old again."

"You do sound a little bit better." Nora was relieved.

"That's good. Aw, Troy says he's thinking about me all day and is determined to come and see me tonight. I could wrap my head in a headscarf. I haven't washed my hair for a week." Georgina said, reading her text message and referring to her new American boyfriend.

Nora thought quickly back to when Georgina and Troy had first met. Georgina had joined an internet dating site much to Nora's surprise (and concern). Troy, a Texas businessman, who had also had property investment dealings with Humphrey's firm in London some years ago, had responded to Georgina's 'prods', 'messages' and 'heart emojis'. Georgina and Troy had then met up with Mrs Pickering and uncle Orville (Georgina's almost-deaf uncle) at a public event near Seatown for dinner and dancing. They had been dating now for a few weeks.

"Anyway," Georgina paused again, thinking she might sneeze but it passed. "Tall, thin and *unpleasant* Mr Goldfinch is due to pop in tomorrow. He's interested in the half calf binding run of Stand Magazines behind the counter so I said you would be there to show them to him. I shall be meeting a couple of people there on Thursday with some specials too as well as a rep from Penguin about stocking their Penguin book jacket mugs."

"Okay." Nora nodded, watching Cara take some large art books down from the top shelf in the art section to show the Eskimo.

"Has anyone mentioned the pink paintwork yet?"

"No, not yet." Nora glanced around. "Cara said Humphrey did it last night?"

"Yes, he thought it would be a nice surprise for you. I chose it to match the pink carpet. Fluffy, get off my toes!"

Nora heard the sound of a cat meowing.

"Yes, it does match it." She looked dubious. "I wonder if anyone will notice it."

"Probably not. They all have their heads in the clouds over there. Oh dear, now my throat feels sore, I'd better stop talking before mother gets back. Is it busy there?"

"Not really, I'm afraid." Nora grimaced.

"Hmm, typical Monday. It should pick up by the end of the week though, with Christmas almost upon…aaaaaachooooo! Sorry!...us. Agh, I just heard mother's car door! I'd better go. Buy yourselves some mince pies. Byeeee."

Nora said goodbye and hung up just as a figure loomed up in front of the door.

'Post for you.' Phil the postman mouthed, jiggling a pile of letters.

With a smile Nora walked around the counter to the door.

"Morning. Bit fresh today." Phil greeted, handing Nora the stack of letters.

"It's freezing." She agreed.

"They might close the road up the hill because of the ice." Phil explained. "I saw the old town mayor just now, trying not to ski down the pavements, and he told me he was in a meeting in the town hall last night with the Duke of Cole."

Nora blinked.

"Is the Duke here?"

Phil nodded.

"His Grace moved into the castle *permanently* at the weekend apparently. He's on my round now." Phil said smugly.

"That's exciting!"

Nora had read an article in *The Castletown Herald* reporting that the Duke of Cole would be moving permanently into his newly restored castle with a view to being a part of the community, rewilding his lands, working with local businesses and promoting tourism to the town. There had been an editorial about him as well as a photograph (Nora had resisted cutting it out and becoming a stalker).

There had also been a front page headline in *The Castletown Baptist Bugle* that read: *Royal Papist Returns to Town*.

The Duke of Cole was one of England's rare Roman Catholic peers, a cousin of the King of England, and descended from a branch of Catholic aristocrats who had always remained loyal to the Pope, refusing to take the Oaths of Allegiance when King Henry VIII and his heirs broke away from the ancient Faith of England. The Ravenstones (The Duke of Cole's ancestors) had even managed to keep their titles and lands in the wake of the Protestant Reformation.

Nora's family were Catholic so Nora was extra interested in the Catholic Duke, who had told the reporter from *The Castletown Baptist Bugle* he loved and practiced his Faith. For decades it had been a custom in the Catholic Church at the top of the hill to reserve the front, right-hand pew for the Duke of Cole or any members of his family. It was always cordoned off with a heavy blue rope, even if the church was packed to capacity for feast days.

Nora wondered if the Duke of Cole would start attending the local church.

Despite being a thirty year old bachelor, the National newspapers rarely reported on the Duke of Cole, who spent his days rewilding lands, wading lakes, reading books, travelling abroad to work with his charities, overseeing his award-winning architectural firm or climbing mountains by his homes on the borders of Scotland and England. He had never caused a scandal and had never been seen partying. He was known as the *Duke of Boring*.

"You'll probably get to see His Grace on Thursday." Phil told Nora, stepping back for his wheelie post cart. "The town hall booked him to turn on the Christmas tree lights at six. He agreed so they're doing some frantic last minute advertising about it. You're open for late night shopping?"

Nora nodded, pondering the enormous fir tree once more, as well as thinking about the Duke of Cole.

"Yes, until seven."

Phil began to push his cart along the pavement.

"I'm doing a shift in The Duke's Pie that evening so hopefully His Grace will drop in and give me a tip." He winked and walked off.

Phil was a regular about Castletown. He doubled as the local postman and a waiter in The Duke's Pie, a rambling restaurant on the top of the hill more like a smuggler's tavern. He was also a bit of a gossip, collecting the latest news about the townsfolk and repeating it to everyone he met, usually on his postal rounds. Nora suspected he kept gossip journals. Several slanderous old ladies went to him for rumours.

Before she could return to the warmth of the bookshop, a man stopped before her and read the fascia above the door, looked at Nora, looked up again at the fascia and then at Nora again.

"Got any *Questron* books?" He asked.

"*Questron* books?"

"Yeah, you know, the question books that have a battery pen and…"

"Oh!" Nora interrupted. "Yes, I know those. My younger sister Heather recently got into retro toys and books and discovered Questron on eBay. There's a black pen used to reveal the answers to questions in the accompanying book, running it or pressing it along the pages. We did have one randomly come in for stock a few years ago but we no longer have it."

"Yes, I am a nostalgia nerd too." He said. "Do you have any books about the Weebles?"

"*Weebles wobble but they don't fall down*?" Nora quoted the catchphrase with a laugh.

He looked impressed and nodded.

"I'm aware of those too. Mainly from my Generation X uncle who often sings the song. But no, I've never seen any books about the Weebles." She admitted.

"I always ask. Just in case. Do you use eBay?"

Nora shook her head, distracted slightly by the image of a familiar figure plodding down the hill with a brown paper bag and a bleary-eyed red face. He was a local who had once worked in the local Old Inn but had recently been laid off. He had been an avid collector of books and ephemera about Castletown and the county of Cole but had sold off his collection to Georgina not long after losing his job.

His ancient old mother had once told him he was a direct descendent of the first Duke of Cole's closest servant and dung-gatherer, an occupation that many generations of White-Lightning Joe's ancestors had apparently held with pride until the sixteenth century when they had gone up in the world and become chimney sweeps.

"No, we don't sell our books online." Nora replied to the Questron-Man, watching White-Lightning Joe (so called because of the brand of *White-Lightning* cider he drank) thankfully turn left into Market Lane.

"Well if you're interested, my user name is '*Questronseeker76*' and I'm always keen to make new friends."

Nora smiled awkwardly.

"Okay." She said, backing towards the door.

"May the Force be with you." He said, held his hand up like a Vulcan and headed off.

Nora stepped back inside the shop, closing the door and running back to the oil heater with the letters, shaking her head at the man mixing Star Wars and Star Trek together. Her brother Milton would call that *sacrilege.*

Cara meanwhile was punching the prices of two large art books through the till.

"Do you sell many art books?" The Eskimo lady asked, holding her bank card ready to pay.

"Yes we do." Cara said brightly.

"I'm not surprised. Many people enjoy the naked human form." The woman said, holding out her card.

Nora's eyebrows lifted as she placed the post in a post file under the counter on a shelf by the reserved books, most of which was taken up by Matt the Pratt's books.

"I'm sure they do." Cara said cheerfully. "Eighteen pounds fifty please."

"Have you ever modelled for art? I have. I'm in quite high demand for art classes in Little Sea and Seatown. But it can get a bit chilly sitting in the middle of a room with various plants or vegetables placed before your parts for modesty."

Nora turned around and pretended to tidy up the antiquarian section behind her to hide her smile.

"I envisage it would be especially chilly in this climate." Cara said seriously.

"Oh yes, they expect you to have a hide like leather these days and be immune to the cold. Usually the room is rented for the class so they're quite tight about shedding money out for heating and don't spare a thought for the model. It's alright for the budding artists sitting there in their woolly Christmas jumpers and corduroys. But that's the price of modelling." The woman gave a dramatic sigh.

"Have you ever considered taking a hot water bottle?" Cara asked as the transaction took place.

Nora covered her laugh by clearing her throat and was sure she heard Cara do the same.

"I did think about it but there is a common phrase among models. Do you want to hear it? It's *'no pain, no gain'*. I'm happy to suffer in the name of art."

"Yes I have heard of that phrase. It's very admirable. Do you need a bag?" Cara asked.

"Yes please. Thank you, dear." The woman said as Cara passed her the bag of books. "Happy Christmas and a Happy New Year."

"Goodbye." Cara said brightly.

When the woman had left and closed the door behind her, Cara turned.

"Did you see the books that she bought?" She asked, chuckling.

Nora was laughing, shaking her head.

"No. Do I want to know?"

"'*Piet Mondrian: Life and Work'* and a book about Mark Rothko's paintings."

Nora screwed up her nose.

"Aren't they all big coloured squares and straight lines?"

Cara nodded.

"Yes, abstract and abstract expressionism." She said. "The lady was interested in abstract interpretations of the nude body because she said she is made up of lines and squares and she wants the people who draw her to interpret her shape correctly. Oh it was so funny. We didn't have anything specific on abstract nude figures so she said the squares of Rothko and Mondrian looked the most like her."

"Hahaha, she did look a bit like Sponge Bob." Nora noted.

"She did! Well, at least it was a sale." Cara turned around and wrote it in the cash book.

"At the price of our sanity." Nora sighed.

The cash book was a long, thin ledger with several columns on each page and the date written at the top. It was kept as a daily record of book sales and pay-outs. Sometimes the staff wrote detailed accounts down for the book sales, such as the title, colour and condition of a special or random tome (if they were bored), but mostly just a general idea, such as crime, cookery or beer-making.

The pay-out columns were for book purchases, but mainly money spent on sausage rolls or mince pies. Recently, Georgina had bought a computer programme at the recommendation of her accountant, so Cara, who was good with things like that, was copying the pages onto the computer when she had some spare time. They hoped to transfer the method from cash book and pen to computer one day (but it was probably wishful thinking).

"By the way, I just met a space hybrid." Nora recalled.

Cara looked interested.

"Really. What was it?"

"A Jedi Vulcan."

"There's no such thing!" Cara laughed.

"Believe me, there is now. I'll go and get the Christmas books shall I?" Nora suggested, retying her hair into a fresh ponytail. "Then we can get to work on the Christmas window."

"Good idea." Cara nodded.

The Christmas section was all the way up at the farthest point of the bookshop. The staircase was through a walkway and in a small room before the back room. It wound up through three floors, past shelves and shelves, display cases and sections, ending in the attic room that was full of paperback fictions.

Believe it or not, keen book rummagers often found the seasonal themed tomes throughout the year. Nora had once sold a Christmas book of poetry in the spring and a Christmas book of napkin folding in the summer. She wondered if the customers were just being facetious.

She creaked up the first flight, turned right, stepped up two more stairs, continued around, up another case and finally into the big front room where she located the two specific shelves not far from the religion and theology cases.

The books were a variety of shapes, sizes and topics relating to Christmas such as Christmas crafts, Christmas poems, Christmas dating, cookery books for Christmas meals, and the like. It took Nora three trips to bring them down and pile them on the carpet before the bay window next to their new tree (still looking sadly bent over with the weight from the single red bauble). She then stood and looked out of the window, massaging her rotator cuffs.

Two people wrapped up like scientists in Antarctica were examining a map from the box of free maps on the pavement outside the bookshop while a group of old ladies were choosing postcards from one of two spinners Nora and Cara had placed outside when they had opened up.

But Nora's attention was drawn across the square to a shop opposite called 'Marbles'. A large gold statue of a woman stood outside and Stan, the scruffy owner of the shop, was in the process of wrenching a big pink bobble hat onto its head followed by an enormous knitted scarf around its neck. The lights on the Christmas tree that had been placed above his shop door were flashing madly, going through a mixture of sequences that were almost psychedelic.

Penny, who ran a souvenir and knick-knack shop, was shaking her head as she topped up her 'Santa stop here' signs among her windmills and ladybirds on poles outside her shop. Tim and his brother Sam from the butcher shop were each carrying two dead turkeys over their shoulders from a van parked on the cobbles while watching Stan with amusement.

"At least the Woman in Gold will be warm." Nora told Cara with a grin.

"What?" She looked up from threading baubles.

"She's got some nice winter wear on now. But I think Paul from the town hall will be annoyed. Stan's changed the Christmas lights to go through the mad flashing sequence instead of keeping them on the steady setting." Nora explained.

"Can we do that to ours? It is rather boring."

At that moment the door opened. Two frozen leaves sailed in and landed gently on the mat only to be squashed and trampled upon by the old ladies holding postcards. They were talking loudly together, their voices almost drowned out by the sound of a lorry going past behind them.

"Good morning." Nora greeted.

"Oh the step! Watch the step, Mavis, with your bunions." The first lady said loudly.

"Oh yes, yes I see it's a difficult one. Thank you for the warning, Vera. Oh I'd best be careful with this height." Mavis agreed. "I'm not so good with heights because of my bunions."

"I know; it's a long way down, Mavis." Vera nodded. "Here, shall I give you a hand?"

Nora watched as the lady called Vera almost wrapped her arms around Mavis's neck, which Mavis didn't look very pleased about. They both staggered onto the flagstones.

"There now, Mavis. That's protected your bunions." Vera said smugly.

Mavis's lips were pursed as she straightened her padded coat and headed for the counter, leaving Vera to shut the door.

"Hello." Cara greeted cheerfully.

"It's warm in here!" Mavis exclaimed, waving her pile of postcards before her face.

"Yes, very warm in here!" Vera agreed.

The sound of a fanfare indicating a Skype chat message from The Secondhand Bookworm in Seatown distracted Vera and Mavis for a moment. Nora moved to the computer to read it.

"Last of the big spenders." Mavis said, holding three postcards out to Cara.

Cara smiled politely.

"Do you need stamps?"

"Do you sell second hand stamps?"

"No, they're new." Cara assured, slightly baffled.

"No thank you then, dear." Mavis said.

Nora looked at the message on Skype from Seatown which read:

'Morning girls! And what a chilly morning it is too! Please can you have a look for a copy of 'Miss Pettigrew lives for a day' by Winifred Watson in a Persephone Classics edition? Customer telephoned so when you get a chance. Hope you've had some customers. Quite busy here. Thanks. Love Jane xxx'

Nora replied that she would check now, so left Cara with the postcard ladies and ran up the stairs to the paperback room in the attic. Once inside the cosy, slanting area (once a storage room filled with woodlice but converted to the fiction chamber when Georgina bought the property), Nora scanned the many shelves. She was amazed to see the requested copy. Usually paperbacks printed by Persephone Books were kept in immaculate condition by their previous owners so were snapped up within a week from the shelves.

She took the copy from the row of books, feeling suddenly slightly uneasy. Glancing around the room, Nora frowned. Something was different, but she couldn't quite put her finger on it. She walked to the middle where several piles of excess novels stood in tottering columns.

Yes, something was certainly different, certainly odd. But what was it? Hopefully not the arrival of a new ghost to haunt The Secondhand Bookworm (Cara often wished for that).

Frowning, Nora hurried back down the winding staircase to the ground floor. When she returned to the front it was empty and devoid of heat. Cara had decorated the spindly tree wonderfully, even managing to tie it to a stick of wood from the yard at the back of the shop so it was now upright.

The gangly branches were swathed with tinsel and hung with a selection of baubles. A line of battery-powered string-lights had been looped throughout and twinkled nicely.

"The tree is perfect." Nora praised.

"It's a Charlie Brown Christmas indeed!" Cara cheered.

She was taking books out of the window and piling them up on the counter. Most of them belonged on the antiquarian shelves located behind so they would need to make some room to fit them back in.

Before she sat down to Skype Seatown, Nora grabbed a pen and started a new tally on her '*It's warm in here*' chart with a shake of her head.

Cara noticed and chuckled to herself.

"By the way," Nora mused. "Is there something different in the paperback room?"

"Yes!" Cara exclaimed. "I wondered if Georgina had mentioned it to you, but she probably forgot because of her current foggy brain syndrome."

"What is it?" Nora asked.

"I worked with Jane on Saturday and we both noticed the large terrifying poster of Stephen King's novel '*IT*' had disappeared from the ceiling."

Nora stared.

"You're right. In fact, there are NO posters in the paperback room now."

Cara shook her head.

"I think we may have been experiencing bandits."

"I can't believe it!" Nora was shocked.

"I told Georgina she should fit some CCTV cameras around the shop. We can then sit and watch people like security guards and catch any crooks in the act."

"She won't agree to that." Nora knew.

"You're right, she didn't. She said she doesn't want the bookshop experience to be ruined for people when they spot cameras and feel their privacy is being invaded by Big Brother or the Deep State. She's always been against cameras in corners spying on her customers. Shame. It's not like we're voyeurs."

"We had this discussion when we first opened The Secondhand Bookworm in Castletown. I suspected one man with shifty eyes like Gollum from The Lord of the Rings was stealing. She said just to keep an eye on him. It's very trusting of her to allow people to be alone in the rooms, probably sliding books up the fronts of their t-shirts."

"Or down their trousers." Cara grimaced.

"So, someone has definitely stolen our book posters." Nora glowered glumly.

"It appears so. We asked everyone who works here and we came to that conclusion. It's very sad. Jane also felt like someone has been swiping books regularly, but she hasn't got any proof."

"I have to admit I've often looked for a book I was sure we had and found we didn't." Nora mused. "I've then spent some time ploughing through the cash book to see if the specific titles were written down as having been sold, but I put it down to the sales been written down generally. It's not really a good idea to have books priced over thirty or forty pounds on the general shelves. I also think people move the topography books to other sections, too. We had a book about the Duke of Cole's family crests priced at forty pounds. I looked for it for a customer and couldn't find it anywhere. It was back a few days later."

"Weird. I bought some Castletown and Cole books from White-Lightning Joe the other day which I thought we already had. He said he had held onto them but was ready to sell them now. When I marked them up and put them on the shelves I found we didn't have additional copies, so maybe someone moved them or swiped them. Perhaps we should randomly join customers in rooms pretending to be customers ourselves and keep an eye on them." Cara proposed.

"I'm beginning to think that might be a good idea." Nora agreed, grimly.

A man arrived accompanied by a fresh blast of cold air. Nora noticed he wore just jeans, boots and a t-shirt, the latter with an image of Michael Jackson on the front and the word *Bad* in red.

"Howdy. Do you sell paperclips?" The man asked, peering around the front room.

Cara was staring at him too, a long strip of gold tinsel held in each hand.

"No, sorry." Nora shook her head.

"You don't? Do you know where I can get some?"

"Maybe in the Co-op over the bridge?" Nora suggested.

"Oh right. I'll check there. Thanks." He continued to look around in interest. "Do you sell books?"

Cara looked confused.

"Yes. This is a bookshop." Nora nodded.

"Is it? Haha, I could have sworn you were a wine shop. Peace." He said, making a polite 'vee' sign with his fingers, turned around and left, slamming the door.

Cara and Nora looked at each other.

"Since when does an off licence even sell paperclips?!" Cara exclaimed.

"Just looking at him made me feel colder." Nora grimaced and rubbed her woolly hands together again, glad for her fingerless gloves. She started to type her Skype message.

'Yes! We actually have it. It has a painting of two ladies on the front, one with a hat that looks like a fried egg on her head. Priced at £4.50. Perfect condition and with its original bookmark too that matches the pattern on the end papers.' Nora typed.

She saw the pen start moving and a moment later a message appear.

'Wonderful! The customer will be pleased. The author only wrote six novels apparently and was interviewed at the age of 94 by the Guardian newspaper when the book was republished. The headline was something like 'Bodice-ripping fame at 94'.'

Nora snorted with laughter.

'Not something I'd like to imagine!' She typed back.

'My thoughts exactly! Please put in the transfer box for Mrs Jessop, 01243 555111. Thanks, love Jane xxx'

'Will do!' Nora skyped and sat back with a sigh that became a shudder because of the cold.

"My eyes have turned to ice." She told Cara, pretending to be frozen solid for her younger colleague's amusement.

Cara squealed from where she was balancing in the window, one leg out behind her, her head and shoulders squashed around the left side of the bookcase as she stuck tinsel along the front edge of the top shelf facing the glass.

"That's a horrible image, Nora! I love it!"

The door opened and Nora stared as what looked like an enormous snowman stepped down onto the flagstones. He wore an ankle length padded white coat and a white bobble hat. His nose was red and his eyes small and black. He wore a green scarf and glided to the counter as though he was walking in the air. Nora's lips twitched as she thought of the allusion to the depressing Christmas cartoon movie shown every year called 'The Snowman'.

"Good morning!" Nora greeted.

"Merry Christmas!" The Snowman returned. "Odd request, but do you have any books bound in human skin?"

Nora's eyes almost popped. Cara nearly fell out of the window.

"It's not a joke. I am a member of the Anthropodermic Book Project and the practice is called Anthropodermic bibliopegy." The Snowman said. "They're very, very rare, but it is highly probable people in the antiquarian book business would mistake human skin bindings for pig or cow leather."

Nora blinked several times.

"I erm…" She looked warily over her shoulder at the antiquarian and leather tomes. "I sincerely hope not."

The Snowman chuckled.

"Do you mind if I take a look? You never know. This might be my lucky day." He said, rubbing his hands together and moving around the counter.

"Be my guest." Nora watched him with a mixture of horror and fascination.

"Hmm, a nice selection of leather." He observed, macabrely running his fingers over the spines. "But none of these topics would suit anthropodermic bibliopegy. Usually people bequeath their skin for book binding. The most famous of all anthropodermic bindings is exhibited at the Boston Athenaeum in the States. It's '*The Highwayman: Narrative of the Life of James Allen alias George Walton*'. James Allen asked to have his memoir bound in his own skin and presented to a man he had once tried to rob. Allen admired the man for putting up a brave resistance." The Snowman said.

"Lovely." Nora grimaced, glancing at Cara who was peering through the window bookshelves with her face screwed up in disgust.

"Well, thank you for letting me have a look." The Snowman smiled serenely, stepping away from the antiquarian section. "May I leave my card with you, just in case you ever come across something suspicious?"

"Yes, of course."

Nora jumped as he brandished a small *tan* coloured business card and handed it to her.

"I'll pass it on to the owner." She promised, relieved to feel that it was simply card.

"Happy New Year!" The man bade them and left, humming cheerfully.

"Eeeew!" Cara objected once the door had closed behind him.

"I was going to suggest we have a mince pie, Georgina keeps insisting we are well supplied with them, but I've been put off eating now." Nora winced, holding the business card at arm's length.

"How about another cup of hot chocolate instead. With LOTS of sugar."

"A good idea, Cara!" Nora placed the business card into Georgina's post file, shaking her head.

"At least he didn't say it's warm in here." Cara pointed out.

"True!" Nora agreed and headed off for the kitchen, trying not to imagine being surrounded by 27,000 books all bound in human skin and sought after by a rather macabre snowman.

CHRISTMAS AT THE SECONDHAND BOOKWORM

2 THE SINGING FATHER CHRISTMASES

While Cara was on her lunch break early that afternoon, Nora managed to place all the books that had been taken out of the window display back onto the antiquarian shelves, polish the counter, sell some postcards to a group of walkers, deal with two telephone requests, answer some emails and add two baubles to the half-finished Christmas window. She was pleased to feel her appetite had returned after the visit from the Anthropodermic bibliopegy fanatic, so was thinking about what to buy for lunch.

The box of Christmas decorations sat neatly behind the counter on a rickety old brown stool that was often kept along the small walkway leading under the stairs behind them. There was a small area at the very back where boxes of cheap paperbacks were stored for topping up the black boxes outside, as well as excess postcard stock, bags of books people had left for Nora or Georgina to look through and consider buying, a broken shelf, boxes of extra bookshop carriers, an old teapot and some brown paper for wrapping parcels.

Nora was about to have a rummage through the box again when the door opened to admit a waft of ice-cold air, some flakes of snow and a thin lady with a rainbow coloured bobble hat and a long black woollen coat.

"Oh, it's pink in here." She said.

Nora blinked, thinking she should have heard '*warm*' instead of 'pink' and was thrilled because the lady was the first customer to have noticed the new décor.

"Yes!" Nora said, making the lady jump. "We've had a repaint."

"Oh, is it just for Christmas?" The lady asked.

"No, I don't believe so." Nora replied warily.

"I sometimes paint my lounge for Christmas but I choose red and green in keeping with the season." She explained.

Nora smiled politely.

"Is there anything I can help you with?" She asked.

"Yes please. I have a list of books I am looking for." She replied and dug a piece of paper and a screwed up hanky from her coat pocket.

"Wonderful." Nora waited eagerly, pleased when customers knew what they wanted.

"I'm looking for five Mills and Boon novels." She said.

"Oh." Nora's shoulders slumped. "I'm afraid we don't stock those."

"Really? They're perfectly good literature. Why not?" The woman asked, offended.

"Because the charity shops have so many donated to them and sell them at cheap prices. It's just not worth our while competing." Nora said, leaving out the other information that Georgina called them 'old lady tat'.

"Well you've missed out on some sales today." The woman said, folding up her paper and shoving it and her hanky back in her pocket.

"Sorry." Nora apologised.

"I won't wish you a happy Christmas." She said, turned around and stomped off huffily.

Nora arched an eyebrow.

"Sorry about that." She called but the door closed firmly, drowning out her voice.

It opened a second later for the arrival of a very small, slim man wearing a trucker hat.

"Happy Festivities." He greeted.

"Good afternoon." Nora welcomed.

"If you say so." He retorted sharply.

Nora blinked.

"Mind if I browse?" The man then asked, politely.

"Of course not, sir. Is there anything in particular you're looking for?"

"Respect!" The man snapped, confrontationally.

Nora stared.

"What a lovely shop. And such a pleasant smell." He then smiled mildly, gazing around.

"Thank you."

"If you like paper moulds!" The man barked, his eyes round and flashing.

Nora felt like she was on an emotional rollercoaster. She wondered if this was Doctor Jekyll in the flesh.

Fortunately (or unfortunately?) he glided through the walkway that led into the back room. Nora leaned forward to watch him, wondering if he would transform into Mr Hyde.

The door opened once more and admitted a regular customer who stepped down onto the flagstones smiling.

Nora sighed in relief.

"Hello." Nora greeted cheerfully, pleased to see Charles who was one of Castletown's locals with a passion for reading and collecting books.

"Hello, Nora. How's business today?" Charles asked, leaning a tall black umbrella against the wall behind the door.

His blond curly hair was dusted lightly with snow and his cheeks were pleasantly red from the cold. Charles carried an umbrella but used it more as a walking stick or to whack obstacles out of his way.

"A little bit quiet."

"Just how we like it though." He headed for the antiquarian books, casting a curious look at the heavily decorated spindly Christmas tree by the window.

"Absolutely." Nora nodded, reaching for a bag from the reservation section under the counter. "This came in and I thought of you. It's nothing special, but you'd probably enjoy the read. I read it myself some years ago and my brother is currently promoting the works of the author."

"Oh, what is it?" He asked, standing next to her.

Nora slid a book out of a clear plastic reservation bag and handed it to him.

"*The Club of Queer Trades*' by G.K. Chesterton." He read and laughed.

"Queer meaning *peculiar* in this case." Nora explained.

"'Cherub Swinburne and his friend Basil Grant are drawn, via Basil's detective brother Rupert, into the strange case of Major Brown." Charles read the blurb aloud. "Having devoted his half-pay retirement to the cultivation of his beloved pansies, the soldier chances to peer over the wall into next door's garden - only to see that the blooms in his neighbour's flowerbed spell out the words 'DEATH TO MAJOR BROWN'! This is their first encounter with the bizarre Club of Queer Trades - an association of those who make their living by extraordinary and entirely new means - but it will not be the last..." Charles concluded. "I'll take it. Something to peruse tonight."

"It's very amusing." Nora chuckled.

"I look forward to reading it." Charles said and handed it to her. She popped it on the counter, leaving him to browse the antiquarian books as he often liked to do.

After a moment he said:

"Something is funny in here."

Nora saw him look about him with a frown which then lifted.

"The room is pink."

"Yes." Nora confirmed. "Humphrey did it last night."

"Very modern." Charles approved. "The twenty first century comes to Castletown at last."

"It's to match the new pink carpet."

His shoulders shook with a chuckle and he returned to his browsing.

Nora revisited the Christmas decoration box on the stool and removed a long piece of silver tinsel. She draped it over the computer monitor, keeping an ear out for any transformation sounds taking place in the back room from Doctor Jekyll and Mr Hyde.

After a while, Charles showed Nora a copy of *The Natural History of Selbourne*.

"It's the most popular reprinted book after the Bible." He said. "People keep it next to their bedsides to read because they are all letters. You can open it anytime and read something inspiring. I like this edition because it looks like it's seen some action but I already have several copies and my wife will throttle me if I bring back another old book. Hmm, I'll just stick with '*The Club of Queer Trades*'." He decided and walked around to the counter, taking out his wallet.

"Enjoy the read." Nora said after he had paid.

"I'm sure I will. See you later."

"Bye." Nora bade him, watching him retrieve his umbrella and head off with his book under his arm.

After Charles had gone, Dr Jekyll (or Mr Hyde) returned.

"Your bookshop is a total mess. There are submarine books mixed in with books about The Cinderella Boys in the back room!" He exclaimed with glinting, flaring, angry eyes (it was Mr Hyde).

Nora grimaced.

"I'm sorry about that. Books about aircraft should be on the shelves in the stairwell. We recently moved some sections about. I'll make sure it's sorted as soon as possible."

The man smiled, warmly.

"That's very efficient of you. What a wonderful shop." He said, his eyes twinkling.

Nora swallowed hard, watching him walk around the counter towards the door.

"Let's get out of here! It's like the Kingdom of Bloody Boring Hell!" He exclaimed.

"After you." He then said, politely gesturing with his arm to the door.

"I should think so, you blighter!" He shouted, pulled open the door and left.

Nora released her breath, shaking her head as he stomped and then strolled past the window.

"Poor dear." She sighed charitably and collapsed into the swivel chair.

Once the maniac was long gone (Nora had checked by looking up and down the roads to make sure), Nora took a box out of the Christmas decorations, checked it tentatively for spiders and had just opened it when Cara returned.

"Look at this!" Nora exclaimed, holding up a Father Christmas on a parachute.

Cara was carrying a large pizza box acquired from Pizza Express across the road.

"What is it?"

"Jane bought this last year along with the electric candles we need to put in the window for the *Shopping by Candlelight* event. He flies across the ceiling and sings." Nora explained.

Cara burst out laughing.

"Oh we have to put that up."

"I thought you'd enjoy it. I expect it will need new batteries because Georgina confiscated them in the end, it was driving her insane, but since she's off with the flu we can enjoy Santa's songs."

"Until he drives *us* mad." Cara agreed. "Did you have any customers while I was waiting for them to cook my pizza?"

Nora cleared her throat.

"Doctor Jekyll and Mr Hyde. And Charles." She nodded.

Cara blinked.

"I'm especially sad I missed the first two."

"They were actually terrifying." Nora grimaced.

"Poor you." Cara sympathised and gave Nora a hug. "By the way, there's a costume for sale in the charity shop. A big puffy orange ladies costume, like a princess or something."

"Is there? How much is it?"

"Twelve pounds. It looked good."

"I may have to go and get it. Seymour still has me on prop scouting duty and a costume find is a real gem." She said, referring to her younger brother.

"Go on then." Cara urged. "Before someone else snaps it up."

"What about your pizza, Cara?"

"I can eat some slices in between serving customers and then finish it when you come back. It's too cold sit in the kitchen for a lunch break. I'll eat it here." She decided, dropping the pizza box on top of the Christmas box on the stool and unravelling her chunky scarf. "You'd better wrap up though. It's like Moscow out there. The woman in Pizza Express said there will be heavy snow on Wednesday."

"While I love the idea, I actually hope not." Nora sighed, grabbing her coat. "I don't like driving in the snow to get here from my parents' house."

"You're a great driver. Except for that time you almost ran White-Lightning Joe over." Cara remembered.

"That was not on purpose." Nora winked.

She headed off quickly; keen to make it to the charity shop before someone discovered the costume. Once the bookshop door was shut behind her, Nora hurried past the estate agents to the kerb. Loud laughing and overly-posh talking could be heard inside.

"Nora! Oh Noraaaa?" A loud, well-to-do voice called out the opened door.

Nora stopped and saw Jeannette, the head estate agent, filing her long red nails with her huge stilettoed feet up on her desk. The door was open. A large man with ginger hair and a smiling cherubic face was sitting on the other desk where Jeanette's colleague was typing at her computer and sipping coffee.

"Hi, Jeannette!" Nora remained on the doorstep, almost gagging on the cloud of expensive perfume.

"This is my cousin Oliver. He's planning to lease the last shop up the top of the hill by the private castle gates." Jeannette introduced.

"Hello." Nora smiled.

"Hello." Oliver greeted warmly, standing up to shake her hand.

"I was telling Olly that we have your details on file for a small flat in town." Jeannette smiled, picking up her iPhone to read a message.

"Yes." Nora nodded.

"Oliver and his wife Gertie won't be leasing out the flat above, it belongs to the Duke of Cole's estate, and they just want the retail space below. I told them you'd make a nice tenant above them Nora, if you're interested."

Oliver winked.

"I hope you like fudge, Nora. My wife and I are hoping to open a Fudge Pantry."

"That sounds wonderful." Nora nodded, keen to enter the world of a fudge scented apartment with the Duke of Cole as her landlord!

"Perfect, Nora. I'll keep you in mind, then." Jeannette beamed. "If it all goes through I'll be in touch. If not, I'll keep an eye out for any other small flats above the antique shops that come onto the market."

"Thank you, Jeannette. I'm very grateful." Nora nodded. "Nice to meet you, Oliver."

"Nice to meet you too, Nora." Oliver smiled.

Jeannette then howled with loud laughter at her text message and started to read it out to her cousin and listening colleagues. Nora waved goodbye and left, continuing quickly to the charity shop with a fresh skip in her step.

The little road between the estate agents and the barber shop on the opposite corner was called Tree Lane and housed a tiny photography shop and an Indian restaurant called *Castle India,* the latter of which Nora liked to scowl at whenever she saw it.

For years the Indian restaurant had been pouring cooking oil down their sinks, resulting in a build-up of fat in the drain network that caused flooding and explosive sewage sagas. Because the sewage pipes from the restaurant and their flats (in fact, most of the shops and properties in the immediate vicinity) flowed past the bookshop's back alleyway, if there were any blockages further down the line then the waste backed into the bookshop's back yard, bubbled up from all the little drains like a toxic spill and it was Nora who had to deal with the horrifying poop episodes.

A charming man named Max had recently acquired the property but had placed his misogynistic uncle in charge of the Castletown branch of his restaurants. Said uncle had allowed the continuation of cooking oil to be emptied down Max's restaurant kitchen sinks, so another blockage and rancid explosion had occurred just last month. Georgina was in the process of taking Max and his uncle to court to get her money back for having to pay for the unblocking trauma.

Nora passed the barber shop and hurried into the charity shop next door, stepping over a pile of bugle horns in the doorway and several sacks of donated clothes and children's toys.

"Hello, Nora." Annabel greeted from behind the busy glass counter.

"Good afternoon, Annabel" Nora smiled, heading for the racks of clothes. "Cara said you have a costume in here."

"Oh, yes. Are you interested in costumes?"

"My brother owns a theatre and has asked me to look out for anything useful."

Annabel indicated to the rack at the back of the shop between shelves of VHS video cassettes and the doorway into the stock room.

"I'll keep an eye out for you too, then. Is it The Jolly Theatre?" Annabel asked.

"Yes, it is." Nora nodded, spotting the puffy orange dress.

"My husband and I have bought tickets to the opening night performance this Saturday. I heard it was a sell-out. We were lucky to order them early."

"Yes, there's a lot of expectation about it. It's lovely to have it back in use, such a great Art Deco building."

"One of the few in the country that escaped being torn down by the destructive British councils of the nineteen eighties." Annabel agreed.

They examined the costume which was simple yet well-made.

"Mind if I phone Seymour, just to check?" Nora asked.

"Go ahead." Annabel smiled, turning as a group of old ladies entered the shop complaining about the cold.

Hooking the costume onto an ugly oversized blouse embroidered with seals, Nora pulled her iPhone from her pocket and was soon listening to it ringing on the other end.

"Yellope." Seymour greeted, sounding small and distant.

"Are you inside a tin or something?" Nora asked, examining a large Lord of the Rings *Treebeard the Ent* toy on a shelf in front of her.

Seymour's laughter filled her ear.

"I had my head in the trap door on the stage." He said, sounding normal.

"How's it going?" Nora asked.

"Good. Everyone's almost here for a dress rehearsal. The costumes look amazing."

"Speaking of which…ooops." The arm fell off Treebeard when Nora touched it so she bent down to pick it up. "I'm in the charity shop and there's a costume here for twelve pounds…"

"Get it!" Seymour said, accompanied by the sound of loud ticking.

"Don't you want to hear the description?" Nora asked.

"No. Costume and twelve pounds together is too good a bargain to resist, especially when you compare it to the price of the one Harriet here is wearing."

"Hi, Nora!" The distant voice of Harriet, one of Seymour's actresses, called.

Nora smiled.

"Hello, Harriet." She frowned, listening to the loud ticking. "Are you diffusing a bomb?"

"What?" Seymour laughed. "No, it's the grandfather clock set piece. Amazing, eh. It works. Thanks to Billy Bunter."

"Don't let him hear you call him that." Nora warned, referring to Billy who owned Passageway Collectables a few doors down from the bookshop. Billy looked the spitting image of the large, plump, fictional schoolboy character William (Billy) George Bunter that had been created by author Charles Hamilton using the pen name Frank Richards. Billy Bunter featured in stories set at *Greyfriars School*, an imaginary English public school located in Kent. The stories had been published in the boys' weekly story paper The Magnet mainly during the nineteen twenties and thirties. There were often annuals of The Magnet in The Secondhand Bookworm.

"I'll try to remember not to." Seymour said, followed by the sound of a loud hooter.

"I'll let you go." Nora shook her head.

"Wait. Is Cara working with you today?" Seymour asked, lowering his voice.

"Yes." Nora replied, suspicious.

"Is she coming to the opening night?"

"I don't think so. I thought it was fully booked."

"I kept a ticket back for your private box." He revealed. "Can you ask her if she'd like to come, but make it sound like it comes from you, only make out that I'm a benevolent theatre owner and it would be my privilege to have her as a guest as well."

"Hmm. Playing matchmaker for my little brother now am I?"

"Something like that." Seymour's smiling voice returned.

"Okay, I'll mention it to her."

"What's that music?"

"I believe it's *'What a day for a daydream'* by Right Said Fred on the radio." Nora replied with a grimace, heading for the counter with the costume. "I'm still in the charity shop."

"I'll leave you with Sexy Fred then. Thanks, sis!" Seymour said goodbye and they rang off.

Annabel bagged the costume up nicely, said she was looking forward to Saturday night, and Nora braved the cold once more, clutching the bag close.

She ran down to the corner shop quickly to purchase some batteries for the singing Father Christmas, nipped into the delicatessen and bought a turkey, cranberry and stuffing Christmas special sandwich, two mince pies and two cans of '*La Limonata*' lemonade from Alice and hurried back into The Secondhand Bookworm, which smelt strongly of Pepperoni pizza.

The branch of candles had been placed in the front of the window and flickered realistically. Cara had been sticking paperchains all over the ceiling while eating her lunch.

"Sorry I was so long!"

"You weren't." Cara assured her cheerfully. "But you missed two '*It's warm in here*'s' so I added them to your chart."

"Grrr." Nora growled.

She reimbursed herself for the batteries and mince pies from the till, stapled the receipts to the cash book page and wrote down the pay out in the correct column. Then she gently jiggled the *La Limonata* cans so Cara 'ooohed' with delight. Nora set them down on the counter. Rather than go into the freezer-kitchen to eat, Nora decided to munch her lunch in the front room with Cara seeing as it was so quiet.

Just to be safe, she placed a packet of anti-bacterial hand wipes next to the message pad in case they had to handle smelly, dirty old books in between eating!

She turned and shrugged out of her coat and then gave a start.

"Cara. It's your birthday next week!" Nora spotted the writing on the calendar pinned to the electric meter door.

Written in their colleague Chris's slanting penmanship in a box a few days before Christmas (he was a Saturday worker) was:

'Cara's birthday – 22 years old!!! What an old lady. Note: Zimmer frame for present.'

The latter note had been added by Nora. She was joking of course, seeing as Nora was actually four and a half years older than Cara!

"Yes it is. I'm a Christmas baby, remember. My middle name is Elf." Cara smiled, leaning over the counter and taking a large slice of pizza from her box.

"Are you free on Saturday night? This Saturday." Nora asked, realising how Seymour's plan to invite Cara would fit perfectly.

"This Saturday?" Cara repeated, sticking a pin into the ceiling by a network of cracks in the plaster. "Why?"

"Would you like to come to The Jolly Theatre for her opening night of 'The Surprise'? There's a group of us going. It'll be the seven thirty p.m. performance, seats in a private box, and the owner of the theatre assures me he is very benevolent."

Cara frowned with amusement but looked interested.

"That sounds really good. I heard about it on the grapevine but thought it would probably all be booked out."

"There's one ticket left for our private box. A birthday treat."

"Really? Thank you, Nora, I would love to. I don't have any plans for Saturday night yet so it'd be perfect. What is the play again?"

"It's called '*The Surprise*' by G K Chesterton. It has puppets that come to life in it and a Christmas theme. Seymour said it's very clever and highly enjoyable."

"Is Seymour in it?" Cara asked, taking a bite of her pizza.

"Apparently so." Nora replied innocently, opening the packet of batteries.

"I'm working in Seatown on Saturday and you're here." Cara remembered.

"You can get the train straight through to Little Cove station not far from my parents' house straight after work. I expect Humphrey will be picking me up so you could come with us in his car." Nora offered.

"That sounds really good. I'll bring a change of clothes with me." Cara nodded, pleased.

"Wonderful."

"I'm glad you and Humphrey are dating, Nora. He's certainly keen on you."

"He's very nice and he makes me laugh." Nora nodded, lifting up Father Christmas's large gold and white fur coat. "I can't help thinking of him as another brother, but don't tell him that!"

"Let's hope you see how delicious he is. For a thirty year old!" Cara winked.

Nora laughed.

"I don't really think it appropriate to shove batteries up Santa's bottom." Nora then said.

Cara choked on her pizza, both of them laughing as they continued to decorate the front room of The Secondhand Bookworm in time for Christmas, and ate their lunch.

Castletown fell dark at about half past four. As Nora placed the missing shepherd from the little nativity figure scene in the window (discovered at the very bottom of the mouldy old Christmas box) she noticed a muscly man jogging down the hill in the sleet.

"Terminator alert!" She warned Cara, who was watching Father Christmas parachute across the ceiling between the paperchains singing Jingle Bells in a high pitched voice.

"Hide!" Cara warned, disappearing behind the counter.

Nora didn't have anywhere to hide so flattened herself against the Folio Society books. She watched Harry run past the bay window, staring inside.

"I don't think he saw us." She sighed with relief.

"He'll be back." Cara said in an interpretation of Arnold Schwarzenegger.

Harry was a local resident in his early thirties who had been given his nickname by The Secondhand Bookworm the first time Nora had met him. He had swaggered into the shop looking exactly like The Terminator, with his dark glasses and black tight t-shirt over his bulging muscles and, after flirting for five minutes, had told Nora he would *be back*. He considered himself the local heartthrob, often visiting the ladies in the bookshop and conducting vanity runs about the town.

Usually they had to endure five minutes of push-ups, squats and bicep curls while he asked for Beano and Dandy annuals for his nephew. Although he was certainly ripped, he was annoying.

The door suddenly opened.

"Eeek." Cara said.

For a moment she and Nora thought it might be Harry after all, but another regular stepped inside instead.

"Any new regimental histories?" Don asked with a glance at Father Christmas parachuting past his head.

"Not since you last checked on Friday." Nora said politely.

"I'll have a look in the back, just in case." He wiped his feet on the mat.

"I'm quite sure we haven't had any fresh stock in that section over the weekend." Nora assured him.

"I'll look anyway, though."

"We don't come across regimental histories that often for stock." Cara added.

"No harm in checking, just in case." Don beamed, strolling through the walkway.

Nora pursed her lips.

Cara shrugged.

He had left the door slightly ajar so Nora went to close it but paused when she heard some terrible singing outside accompanied by an out-of-tune guitar. She noticed a scraggly looking, toothless man dressed as Father Christmas walking along the street opposite, singing Jingle Bells while strumming. The singing competed comically with the parachuting Santa in the shop which was currently enjoying its circuit around the ceiling singing loudly.

Cara was adding up the day's takings to get a head start at closing time and paused.

"What on earth is *that*?" She gawped.

Nora's lips trembled with mirth.

"Castletown's unique brand of carol singers."

"Let's hope he doesn't come here." Cara grimaced.

"Hello!"

Nora jumped when a woman appeared before her.

"Hello."

"Ae you still open for business?"

"Yes, we are, for another half an hour." Nora stood aside so the woman could enter The Secondhand Bookworm.

"Where are your art books?" The lady peered around the front room, keenly.

"Just there." Nora indicated with her right hand, closing the door with her other.

"Thanks." She hobbled to the art section with a slight limp, chuckled at Father Christmas, placed her hands behind her back and started to browse, singing along to Jingle Bells.

The door opened again, letting in some more frozen leaves with a gust of sleety wind and the form of a man in an enormous striped bobble hat. He remained standing on the step.

"I wonder if you can help me!" He begged, looking distraught.

"Are you searching for a book?" Nora asked.

"No, I'm hunting for my wife."

Nora glanced at the lady browsing the art section.

The man leaned in.

"No, that's not her. My wife is large with blond hair and will be wearing a pink beret." He said in a panicky voice.

Nora stared.

"I haven't seen her come in." She assured him.

The man screwed up his face.

"You have to help me. Can you check around your shop, please? I think she's having an affair. I saw her calendar on the fridge when I got home early from work this afternoon and it had a note for today that said '*Bookshop, 4:30p.m, Brett*'. I think she's meeting this Brett here for an affair."

Nora wasn't sure if she was being '*Facejacked*' (*Facejacker* had been an irreverent British comedy pranking series years ago, a follow on from *Fonejacker*

51

– Nora was certain she was regularly the victim of the latter at The Secondhand Bookworm!).

"Well, have you got the right town?" She asked, looking around for a camera crew outside.

"I think so!" He looked wildly around, too. "Please, please check your bookshop."

"You're welcome to come in and have a look yourself." Nora invited. She squinted at his face to see if it was a prosthetic mask.

"No, I daren't. I don't know what I'd do if I saw them holding hands while reading books together." The man lamented. "Oh, Angie!"

Nora had the sudden urge to burst out laughing.

Cara was standing behind the counter, listening with bafflement.

"Please! I think she might leave me! For Brett."

Nora finally nodded.

"Okay, I'll check our whole bookshop for you." She relented, aware of Cara snorting and coughing to cover up her laughter.

"Oh thank you! I'll be out here trying to get her on her mobile phone." The man nodded frantically, held up his iPhone, dropped it so it clattered to the ground and picked it up with a sob.

'*What is this?*' Nora mouthed as she walked quickly around the counter, past Cara who was wiping tears from her eyes.

"Can you check your CCTV history too, in case she arrived with Brett early?" He shouted at Cara.

The woman by the art section turned and stared.

"Okay." Cara decided to humour him.

Nora left her pretending to access their (non-existence) CCTV footage on the computer by hitting random keys on the keyboard.

Quickly, Nora leaned into the back room. It was empty. She ran up the stairs, leaned into the next floor front room and made a man reading a gardening book jump.

"Sorry." Nora apologised.

"How much is this book?" The man asked.

Nora entered the room and took it from him.

"Our prices are in pencil here, on the first page." She pointed.

"Seven pounds fifty?! It's used!!" The man exclaimed.

"Yes." Nora nodded.

"I thought it would be fifty pence!"

"We're not a charity shop." Nora said bluntly.

"No a *rip-off* shop." The man muttered, taking the book back. "I'll leave it then. Is there a charity shop in town?"

Nora sighed and politely gave him directions. She then went and checked in the children's room for Angie and Brett. It was empty.

As she climbed the final staircase, Nora heard a giggle coming from the room ahead. She stopped in her tracks.

A text message arrived on her phone, giving her a start. Nora quietly drew it from her pocket while listening for any other sounds in the shop. She then walked loudly into the top floor front room, clearing her throat.

A woman was at the craft section, flicking through a book about quilting while shaking her head and giggling.

"The loopy hearts and the wobbling spiral stitches. Classic." She said to herself.

Nora's shoulders relaxed and she checked her text message, turning to visit the last room, which was the attic. The message was from Cara.

'He's gone! He got hold of Angie! Apparently she was in Wall Town selling some Victorian photo albums

to the owner of a shop. The owner was called Brett. Lol xx'

Nora shook her head.

'We were just Facejacked!' She sent back.

Nora heard Cara's laughter sailing up the stairs.

She checked the attic room anyway so she would have an idea of how many customers were in the shop around closing time. Finding the attic empty, Nora made sure the windows were firmly closed for the night. She shook her head, glaring at the empty spaces where the book posters had once been, unsettled about having a thief on the loose in The Secondhand Bookworm. She then examined with interest the ice ferns creeping eerily over the glass, before turning around and walking all the way down the winding staircase to the bottom, feeling dizzy as she stepped onto the ground floor flagstones.

"I won't come in because I've got rabies." A man was telling Cara from the doorway.

Nora gave a start.

"Really?" Cara called out to him, alarmed.

"Yeah. A rabid dog bit me while I was on holiday in Italy. Don't worry, I'm not rabid myself."

"Ooeer." Cara grimaced, sounding like Nora's cousin, Felix.

"If you think you've got a copy of Matt Brolly's *The Bridge* then I'll take it, love." He said, mopping his very sweaty forehead.

Cara stood up from the swivel chair.

"I'll have a look in the crime fiction section for you."

She and Nora exchanged wary looks.

As Cara started up the creaking staircase, the singing and guitar-playing toothless Father Christmas reached the bookshop. Nora winced as his rendition of Jingle Bells clashed horrifically with the one currently parachuting about the ceiling.

The man with rabies turned and stared as Toothless Father Christmas stopped behind him, singing loudly.

"...on a one horse open sleeeeeiiigh!" Toothless Father Christmas crooned.

"...on a one horse open sleigh." The high voice of the parachuting Father Christmas parroted, whizzing past the top of Nora's head.

Nora winced.

Toothless Father Christmas leaned in past the man with rabies, holding his guitar in mid-strum while grinning horribly. He held still for a long moment, until Nora clapped tentatively.

"Thank you, love, thank you." He bowed, almost falling inside. "Merry Christmas to you and yours and..." He paused, noticing Father Christmas parachuting past him. He then blinked, turned around and set off up the hill again, this time singing 'Ding, dong, merrily on high'.

Rabies-Man watched him go, bewildered.

The woman still browsing the art section now seemed oblivious.

Nora cleared her throat, starting to find it amusing.

Cara was heard running back down the stairs in no time.

"I'm sorry but we don't have anything by Matt Brolly in stock at the moment." She said, ducking as Father Christmas sailed past her head.

"Thanks for looking." Rabies-Man nodded and left, leaving the door wide open.

"You missed the toothless Father Christmas." Nora told her grimly.

Cara gasped and hurried to look out the door for a glimpse of him just as the woman by the art section approached the counter. Reluctantly Nora moved away from the oil heater.

"That didn't take me too long." The lady said (even though it actually had). She held a big book about the artist Degas open at the last few pages. "I'm researching *that*; the Russian dancers. He did five of them!"

Nora leaned in.

"How lovely."

"I'll have this book then, please." The woman decided, dropping it on the counter and rummaging for her purse.

Nora watched when she started to remove endless objects from her handbag. It was like The Tardis, or Mary's Poppins' carpet bag. There was a fantastic array of pens, a roll of dog-poop bags, a pack of bent straws and a plushie in the shape of Scooby-Doo's head, a pair of scissors and an empty mustard jar, two bottles of fizzy water, a bobble hat, some orange lipstick, a hairbrush, a pack of handkerchiefs, a notebook, three newspapers, a bag of crisps, two black lightbulbs and a peach coloured tea light. Nora stared at the pile on the cash book blankly.

"Six pounds please." She finally said, typing the price into the till. "Would you like a bag?"

The woman didn't hear her because Father Christmas sailed between their heads, singing loudly.

"My daughter-in-law is studying Degas at Night College and wanted me to find anything I could about his Russian dancers, as soon as possible. I searched the whole internet using *Ask Jeeves* for ages and couldn't find anything, but my neighbour Cyril told me there were five of them and they are exhibited in New York and Milan and goodness knows where else. Cyril suggested I come down to you here in the bookshop. Apparently, according to Cyril, Degas painted the Russian Dancers and the Woman with the Vase, the latter of which is his best one, so I'm so pleased I found this book." She blathered, all the while making a very loud noise while shaking her coin section in her purse.

Nora unhooked a blue carrier. She didn't think the *Ask Jeeves* bit of the story was true because Ask Jeeves had finished years ago, way back in 2005. She assumed the woman just didn't use the internet so had made up that part of the story.

"That's great." Nora smiled, slipping the book inside.

"I've got to keep in with my daughter-in-law because she's the mother of my lovely grandchildren. I wouldn't want her to hide them in the cupboard from me every time I visited, pretending they were still at school." The lady handed Nora a ten pound note. "She'll think I searched the earth for this."

"It is a lovely book." Nora agreed, taking the money. She counted out four pound coins in return and held them out.

The woman took an age and a half to return all the objects to her bag.

Nora held out the change for so long her arm started to ache.

"I'm so happy! Thank you, dear." The woman finally took the change, the bag with the book and set off, leaving Cara scanning the street with her iPhone torch app shining brightly (as if that would help) for just one glimpse of Toothless Father Christmas.

Parachuting Santa sped past Nora's head.

"I'm beginning to understand why Georgina took the batteries out of *him*." Nora grimaced, reached up and turned him off!

At ten to five Nora and Cara brought the two (frozen) postcard spinners, empty free map box and black boxes full of cheap (frosty) paperbacks into The Secondhand Bookworm.

The Christmas stalls had all been packed away, leaving just the Lumberjack loading a few leftover trees into the back of his van. Nora didn't expect he would be back again because he had sold most of his wares.

The town looked cheerfully seasonal with twinkling Christmas trees above most of the shop doors. Nora thought the Duke of Cole's Christmas tree would be a spectacular edition once the lights were turned on.

Cara placed the last black box onto the floor.

"I'll lock the door against the evil vapours of the night." Nora told Cara, taking her keys out of her pocket, but stopped suddenly dead, stifling a sudden gasp.

Cara turned and yelped.

A tall, imposing old man had appeared silently on the step. He wore a thick, heavy Russian knee-length shuba coat with a heavy fur trim around the collar, cuffs and hem, and a Russian fur hat. He looked like a Soviet military intelligence officer from the 1940's.

"Do you happen to have a copy of *The Fir Tree* by the Danish author Hans Christian Andersen?" He asked. "I wish to read it to my grandchildren over Christmas. They've got too big for their boots, wanting to grow up and give me lip well before their time."

"Er…" Nora stared.

"We don't I'm afraid." Cara apologised. "I looked for anything by him earlier and we appear to be out."

"That's a shame. *The Fir Tree* tells the story of a fir tree that is never satisfied. As a young tree in a forest it is simply *not* content with the sunlight and the wind it receives, or with its forest friends. Rather, the tree constantly wishes to be old and tall (and give its grandfather lip)." The man explained as if deciding to lecture them instead of his grandchildren. "Eventually it gets its wish and is cut down and taken to the home of a joyous family for Christmas. It listens to stories and is adorned with light. But gradually, the fir tree fades and shrivels, is taken into the garden, chopped up and burned, wishing it had enjoyed its youth and childhood while it had the chance, and not acted older than its years, giving lip."

Nora cringed.

Cara grimaced.

"Nope?" The Russian from the Red Army shrugged. "Okay then, Merry Christmas." He turned and left.

"What a cheerful story." Cara said sarcastically.

"Don't listen." Nora called over to their tree as she turned the 'OPEN' sign to 'CLOSED'.

Once they had locked up, turned off the shop lights and counted out the till float, Cara tallied their final figure.

"Three hundred and five pounds today." She said, closing the cash book.

"Not too bad." Nora said, checking her text messages by the bay window.

There was one from Humphrey.

'Hi Nora, how was your day? I'm staying in my apartment in London tonight and am currently heading down to my car from the office (strange to be back here again). Been thinking about the great time we had on Saturday night Xx. I hope it didn't smell too strongly of paint this morning (Georgina's Sunday afternoon mission for me!). Looking forward to Friday – Humphrey xx'

Nora smiled.

'Hi, hope you had a good day back in London. No, it didn't smell of paint at all. In fact, it took me a couple of hours to notice your extremely proficient work. Thank you, Humphrey. The shop is beautiful. Looking forward to Friday, too xx'

"Texting with your *extra* brother?" Cara asked, her green eyes twinkling playfully.

"Ahem." Nora lowered her iPhone. "Maybe."

"When's your next date?" Cara asked.

"The staff meal on Friday night." Nora grimaced.

Cara laughed.

"Ooooh, how romantic, Nora!"

"Hush. I'm taking our dating slowly, remember."

"It's not as if you have all the time in the world. You're almost heading into middle aged madness." Cara half-teased.

"Cheeky!" Nora looked down at another text alert. "I'm only twenty-six."

"Old lady!" Cara insisted.

Nora shook her head.

"You're welcome about the painting. Not too sure about the colour though, but Georgina insisted. Have a good evening. Drive carefully xx' Humphrey had written.

'You too xx' Nora sent back, thoughtfully.

Cara watched her, bemused.

"Obviously your calendar is filled with dates if you can't see him until the Christmas staff meal." She said, sarcastically.

"Humphrey's up in London and is very busy." Nora deflected with a shrug.

"All week?" Cara quirked a brow.

"Oh look, is that the time?" Nora pointed to the clock, changing the subject.

Cara snorted.

They Skyped goodbye to Seatown (who didn't answer), turned off the computer, put on all their winter clothes, grabbed their bags (including the orange, puffy costume for Seymour), Cara set the alarm and Nora spoke kindly to their spindly Christmas tree, turning off its battery lights.

"See you tomorrow." She told it.

Cara snorted.

"I've parked along by the castle moat today." Cara said while Nora turned her key in the door.

"So have I. I'm not risking sliding up and down that icy hill top if I can help it." Nora said, slipping her hands in her pockets and burying her face in most of her scarf.

"I did well today. Normally I spend my month's wages on books but I resisted buying a single one." Cara was pleased.

"Me too." Nora nodded.

They walked together, crossing the little road between the estate agents and the barber shop and pausing to look at some children's Sylvanian Family figures in the charity shop window, staring at three sets of the Hedgehog family all positioned around a tree house.

"It must have been fun to be a child of the eighties." Nora chuckled.

There was a book on display in the window too. It was about the history of the Dukes of Cole. Nora cleared her throat.

"Did you hear the Duke moved into his castle at the weekend?" She asked Cara as they continued past the remaining shops.

They turned the corner in front of the post office and set off past the towering main castle gates (large black bolted doors set between two gatehouses and high walls), where tourists used to pay and enter to explore the castle ruins and where they would now be paying and entering to visit the magnificently restored fortress come April.

"Oh yes! I haven't seen him yet, though." Cara nodded.

They walked alongside the small moat by the banks of the new castle, which towered beside them on the Duke's estate.

EMILY JANE BEVANS

"Apparently he's turning the Christmas tree lights on
in the square on Thursday night. I'm staying late with
Roger for late night shopping in Castletown. It's usually
a bit of a flop but you never know this year."

"You'll have to take a photo of the Duke and show
me." Cara suggested, wondering if the duck floating
beside them on the water was frozen solid.

"I'll try." Nora agreed. "You know, I think I might
have nightmares tonight about books bound in human
skin."

Cara shuddered, taking out her keys.

"I hope we never have the misfortune to buy in one
of those!"

Nora agreed.

They said their goodbyes at Cara's car, Nora walking
the short distance to where she was parked by a glaring
swan.

Once inside her little blue *Toyota*, Nora turned her
heater on full blast, warmed up her engine and followed
Cara's green *Ford Fiesta* to the little roundabout where
they both stopped to let a lady named Iris cross the road.

Iris was from the Antique's Centre down Market
Street and ran a room containing several thousand
teacups and saucers. On her head she wore a home-made
hat, comprised of a large piece of white card with the
message '*Jesus loves you!*' painted on it in bold letters.

Both Cara and Nora watched Iris head off over the
bridge, passing her as they drove out of town.

Smiling to herself, Nora turned right towards her
parents' home in Little Cove (she was staying back there
until she found a new place to live – hopefully above the
upcoming fudge pantry, or at least in a flat with a view
of the Duke of Cole's castle and some pious ghosts in
her attic) and Cara turned left to head for her shared flat
in Piertown, leaving Castletown shivering in a cold
December night.

3 HI-DE-HI AND THE KNUCKER DRAGON

It was bitterly cold on Tuesday morning when Nora opened The Secondhand Bookworm, well prepared to face the day by wearing multiple layers of vests, t-shirts and blouses beneath her Christmas jumper. Her colleague Agnes, who worked whenever she was back from university, was due in at eleven o'clock, so Nora had an hour to deal with any bookworms by herself.

Although it was freezing, the ground was sludgy with snow that had fallen lightly overnight and had then started to melt. The met office had predicted a big freeze that night followed by heavy snow showers on Wednesday, but today it was sloshy and uncivilized.

The first customer of the day, a man with a big bushy beard, orange bobble hat and oversized green parka, trod snow purée across the floor as he made his way into the back room. Nora leaned over the counter, grimacing at the nice new pink carpet.

"It's warm in here!" A woman said after throwing open the door and brandishing a handful of postcards from the outside spinner.

Nora had been rearranging the tinsel on the spindly Christmas tree so turned to smile politely.

"Good morning." She greeted, walking around to behind the counter.

The lady plodded towards her, leaving wet footprints on the flagstones.

"Do you sell stamps?"

"Yes. Worldwide and first class." Nora nodded.

"A pack of twelve first class stamps and these twelve postcards." She said, waving them in front of Nora like a fan before opening her handbag to put them inside.

"Do you mind if I count them out? Sorry, I've been told to count out the postcards as I run them through the till."

The lady paused.

"I ain't no thief!" She defended snottily.

Nora looked awkward.

"No, of course not, but it's not my shop…"

"What rot." She lifted her chin and held the cards out to Nora, who took them with an apologetic smile. "Count them aloud then! Just so's the world can hear I ain't no con artist."

Nora assumed the lady thought she might be on livestreaming CCTV, but the room was empty even of other customers.

"Okay." Nora nodded and carefully counted them aloud onto the cash book.

"See!" The woman smiled in triumph as Nora finished on twelve.

"Three pounds sixty for the postcards." Nora rang the price through the till. It opened and crashed against her hip. With a wince, Nora sorted out the stamps too, charged the lady for the completed sale and popped everything into a brown paper bag.

"Where is there a nice place for a cup of tea?" The lady asked, squashing the bag of postcards and stamps into her handbag.

"There are some good cafés down Market Street." Nora shared, writing the sale down in the cashbook. "I would recommend The Flowery Teacup."

"Thank you." The lady fixed her with a withering look and walked off towards the door as it was flung open.

Nora stared as a lady with flashing Christmas tree earrings and a flashing Rudolph the Reindeer jumper entered the shop.

"Where are your books about basket weaving?" She asked.

"We have a section on crafts on the next floor." Nora explained.

"Oh I don't do stairs." The woman decided, turned around and left, shutting the door hard.

The temperature had already dropped to what felt like minus two, so after Nora had added a line to her '*It's warm in here*' tally chart she wheeled herself over to the oil heater, sitting next to it in the swivel chair as she planned what to do that day.

Because Georgina had been off with the flu for two weeks there hadn't been any calls days so there was only a bit of new stock that Nora, Cara or Roger had managed to buy from some people who lugged in carrier bags and boxes full of books to sell.

Humphrey had dropped in some lingering stock from Georgina's garage over the weekend too. But the Saturday staff had managed to put everything away and the shop was relatively tidy.

Nora decided to get out her Kindle and read it sneakily and was about to get up and reach for her bag when another lady entered The Secondhand Bookworm. She was tall and neat with black hair tied up in a bun, a black scarf wrapped around her neck and a big warm coat.

"Hi-de-hi!" She greeted cheerfully.

"Good morning." Nora returned.

"I'm from Butlin's and I have five hundred pounds to spend on books for our new restaurant by the Skyline pavilion!" She exclaimed. "Anything will do, as long as they're real books. Oooh, Hi-de-ho! What are those?"

Nora blinked, watching the lady hurry over to the walkway between the front room and the stairwell in the back.

"Oh, those are Heron runs of Agatha Christie, Charles Dickens and Catherine Cookson." Nora explained tentatively. "They were published in the seventies and eighties by a company called Heron Books."

"They're perfect!" The woman cheered.

"Oh, really?" Nora tried to hide her excitement at the prospect of selling them all. Georgina despised Heron runs of books. They smelt of plastic and were boring, very common and quite ugly, but she had purchased several sets from someone a few weeks ago and told Nora to squash them on the shelves in the walkway with bright, tempting signs. Sometimes they put them in plastic crates on the pavement in the summer for a pound a book.

The woman picked up a red Agatha Christie and flicked through the thin pages quickly.

"These are perfect for our shelving." She nodded, reading each sign that had been tacked to the shelf that each set stood upon.

The run of Agatha Christies were priced at seventy five pounds the set, the green Dickens at one hundred and ten and the green Catherine Cookson at one hundred and twenty the set.

"Hmm, that's about three hundred pounds for those; I suppose I should add some others for variety. What are they?"

"Oh, they're a set of Rudyard Kipling books." Nora replied.

"They're smaller, very cute. I'll have those too."

The set was comprised of small, slim, dark blue bindings with gold effect edging and lettering.

"Are those *Nazi* symbols?" The woman then noticed on each spine.

"Yes. The swastika was an ancient religious icon before the 1930's when the Nazi party adopted it as their main symbol." Nora explained, awkwardly.

"How interesting. Certainly a talking point in the restaurant. I'll take those too. Hmm, I like those. What are they?"

"Cloth bound classics published by Everyman's Library." Nora said.

"How much each?"

"Between eight and ten pounds a book I believe."

"Alright, we'll round up the budget with a selection of those too and we're done! Marvellous, that only took five minutes and they gave me the morning to do it so I can go and do some Christmas shopping for myself now." The lady enthused.

Nora smiled, heading for the counter.

"If you could do me a printed invoice on those I'd appreciate it, and box them up for me; I'll come back with my colleague in a couple of hours and off we go! Will you take credit card?"

"Yes, of course." Nora nodded, standing by the till to start running the prices through.

They put the prices of the four sets through the till and added a selection of boring Everyman's Classics until the total was four hundred and ninety six pounds.

The lady paid, left her name and number and headed for the door.

"That's me done then. Hi-de-hi!" She exclaimed. "We don't use that catchphrase at Butlin's of course. My manager would kill me if he heard it, but I've been watching old reruns of the nineteen eighties TV show and love it! Merry Christmas!" She chuckled and went off cheerfully to do her own shopping about the town.

When she had gone, Nora heaved the sets all off the shelves, added the classics and made a large ugly pile that in her eyes was now beautiful because her takings were over five hundred and thirty pounds and it was only ten thirty.

During the next forty minutes, while Nora boxed the books up in empty paper towel or loo roll boxes that were stored in the kitchen, she also sold twenty more postcards, three cheap paperbacks, two Christmas books from the window, an art book about *Seurat*, a local book about Walltown, two old ordnance survey maps and some theatre books from the room above.

A woman arrived and Nora held still, staring. She wore a tiny red velvet Santa outfit with white buttons down the front, white fur edging on the cuffs and hem, red leggings, red high heels, a red Santa hat and carried a selection of brightly coloured paper bags. A little scruffy, grey sausage dog trotted at her heels.

"Merry Christmas!" She greeted cheerfully, closing the door behind her.

"Hello." Nora replied, leaning across the counter to see the dog.

"Oh, this is my little helper." Lady-Santa smiled. "Twinkle."

"Hello, Twinkle." Nora greeted.

Twinkle ignored her and waddled off to sniff the bottom shelves of the Observer books.

"My name is Sherrie and I am from Kiddies Boutique down Market Street. We opened last month. Are you a mother?"

"No, I'm not."

"But you have little nieces, nephews, baby cousins?" She asked enthusiastically.

"I do." Nora admitted.

Lady-Santa was delighted.

"Well, this week I shall be about town with some wonderful Christmas promotions. Would you like to see? I have some magnificent items in my bags at special festive prices such as baby shoes, baby bonnets, cute little Christmas baby-grows. Twinkle! Don't eat the books."

Nora glanced at Twinkle as he shuffled towards the art section and licked the spine of a copy of 'Vincent Van Gogh's Letters'.

"I don't think it would be worth your while showing me. I already have my Christmas gifts." Nora admitted.

"Do you have any work colleagues who might be interested?"

"No, not today."

"Oh well, as I said, I am about town this week so I shall pop in another day." Lady-Santa announced cheerfully. "Merry Christmas! And if you ever find yourself…with child…you know where to find us. Come on Twinkle!"

Nora stared, blinking as Lady-Santa strolled out of the shop with Twinkle at her heels and set off up the street, causing numerous male heads to turn as she wiggled past them and an old man to drop a crate of beetroots in the road.

Two customers replaced her.

"Hello." Nora smiled.

"Hello." A man acknowledged. The younger man with him ignored her.

The man stood and made a show of breathing in the scent of ink, paper, leather bindings; moulds, damp and grease. He sneezed.

"Bless you." Nora said.

"Thank you." He blinked. "Here we are, Callum. What about art books?" The man pointed.

"Dull." Callum sighed.

Nora turned to the computer, observing them out the corner of her eye.

"Mind if I have a browse at these Folio Society books?" The man asked Callum.

"Knock yourself out, dad." Callum shrugged and focussed on his iPhone.

He didn't last very long.

"Can we *leave*?" Callum whined literally a moment later. "I'm surrounded by dusty boredom."

Nora was offended.

His father sighed.

"Let's go." He nodded and they left.

"Excuse me! Where can I buy wrapping paper?" A woman leaned in and shouted.

"The post office?" Nora suggested.

"I just passed it. Thank yooooou!" She sang and left.

Nora had just printed the Butlin's invoice out to add to her neat stack of boxes behind the counter and was contemplating the singing Father Christmas who was immobile in his parachute looking down at her, when the door opened and her colleague arrived.

"Hallloooo!" Agnes greeted cheerfully, stepping into the shop accompanied by a strange rustling sound that was similar to the sound made by the Ravens, two notorious ladies who plagued The Secondhand Bookworm with a deluge of bags and black sacks.

"Hello, Agnes. How are…" Nora stopped in mid-sentence and blinked when she noticed Agnes's feet.

"I'm fine." Agnes paused for effect.

"What are they?"

"Plastic bags."

"On your feet?"

"It's like Sludge-City out there and I don't have waterproof shoes so I wrapped my feet in Tesco carrier bags to walk down." Agnes explained cheerfully. "It worked! My shoes are perfectly dry."

Nora chuckled, watching Agnes drop her bag beside her and begin to unwrap her feet.

"Aren't you cold?!" She asked, noting Agnes's slip-on ballet pumps, thin black tights, short gold skirt and small Christmas jumper as she unbuttoned her coat.

"No." Agnes assured her and headed behind the counter, carrying her plastic bags.

Nora shivered just looking at her.

Agnes was nineteen and had a riot of red curly hair, big blue eyes and a cheerful, bouncy disposition. She was studying at Cardiff University and seemed immune to the elements.

"What are these?" She asked, squeezing past the stack of boxes.

" I just sold all the hideous Heron sets."

"Bonanza!" Agnes approved.

The phone started to ring so Nora picked it up while Agnes threw her belongings behind the stairs and stood before the computer monitor to read the Seatown Skype chat messages, which were few and far between.

"Do you buy books?" The crackly voice of a man asked over the telephone line once Nora had greeted the caller.

"Yes we do." Nora said cheerfully.

"My dad died and he was hoarder. Subscribed to loads of book clubs, something called *Reader's Digest*." The man explained.

"Those wouldn't be for us, I'm afraid." Nora apologised.

"Oh." His crackly voice grumbled. "What shall I do with them?"

"You could try a charity shop but I don't think they find them saleable either." Nora suggested with a grimace.

"I could burn them on Christmas day." The man then said. "We've got an open fire and will need something to burn."

"Well, burning paper does create a lot of *ash*." She said warily.

"I'll just shovel it all over my garden plot as we go along. Give my fat grandkids something to do. Yeah, I'll do that. Thanks for the suggestion. Bye." He said and hung up, leaving Nora frowning over his plan to burn a library of Readers Digest books on Christmas day.

"Seatown are looking for any Agatha Raisin novels." Agnes said once Nora had hung up. "Where would they be?"

"In the crime fiction section, at the top of the top floor staircase." Nora replied. "They're by M.C. Beaton."

"Okay. I'll have a look!" Agnes said and ran off, creaking lightly up the stairs in her soft ballet pumps.

The door opened, letting in a whistle of North Pole wind and Monica, a guide up at the new castle. She wore her usual black beret, black coat and a shiny black handbag over her arm, exactly the same get-up she wore in summer. Like Agnes, Monica seemed immune to the elements.

"Good morning, Nora." Monica greeted grandly, stepping inside and carrying a cheap battered paperback from the black bargain boxes clipped either side of the front door.

"Hello!" Nora greeted fondly.

"A good find. What a gem. Agatha Christie's first novel, 'The Mysterious Affair at Styles'. I read it as a young girl and that's when I fell in love for the first time. Poirot was my first love, I admit it. He's why I remained single all my life. No man ever competed with Hercule." Monica said, stopping at the counter. "The novel was written as the result of a dare from Ms Christie's sister Madge who challenged her to write a story. And what a story."

"Fifty pence please." Nora smiled, punching the amount into the till.

"How are you my dear?" Monica asked as she placed her bag onto the counter. "Not too cold, I hope."

"A little." Nora grimaced.

"I expect you've heard that His Grace is now in residence in the new castle? I'm not on duty there until it all opens in April next year but I've several meetings coming up. I met His Grace yesterday, a charming young man, a rarity. If I hadn't given my heart to Hercule, His Grace the Duke of Cole would have stolen it there and then."

Nora chuckled, taking Monica's pound coin.

Monica opened the tatty paperback.

"The setting of this novel is also the setting of Hercule Poirot's last case, *Curtain*." Monica explained. "Oh, I shall enjoy reading this. I'm staying in The Old Hotel up the hill, in my favourite room. I'll settle down tonight with a cup of cocoa and begin a new affair with my old love."

Nora handed Monica her change.

"How is it up at the castle?"

"Almost complete." Monica nodded, slipping the paperback into her handbag. "And it is magnificent. Breath-taking. The Duke is a genius, and has such love and care for his heritage. We are most fortunate to have him here. The town will change for the better, mark my words."

"Will you be here for the turning on of the Christmas tree lights on Thursday?"

"Not on your nelly!" Monica refused aloofly, although her dark eyes twinkled. "All those people, and in the dark too. I despise crowds. Oh no. I shall be back at home in Three Bridges watching television in my apartment. Tell me, dear. Any luck with '*our dragon*'?" She asked, referring to her longstanding request for a book about a local mythological dragon, also known colloquially as a Knucker.

"No, not yet." Nora told her regretfully.

"Ah, the *dragon* of the knuckerhole." Monica sighed, setting out to repeat what she said almost every time she saw Nora. "The infamous Knucker of Cole. There are several variants on the legend of course, but here is one of the town ones. Long ago, in Little Bay near Castletown, there lived a dragon whose home was in a bottomless hole. The hole is known as a Knuckerhole in local legend and is a curious place. It will never freeze over in winter and will never evaporate in the summer. The Knucker (dragon) would emerge from the Knuckerhole and seize unwary farmers and livestock, flying away with them to the hills for a tasty snack. There are several knuckerholes on the Duke of Cole's estate. Let us hope a wicked Knucker doesn't emerge and gobble up His handsome Grace. Well, in our legend, eventually a young knight slew the beast and brought an end to the Knucker's reign of terror. Ah, such a tale of chivalry and heroics, not like today's lesbian stories."

Nora watched Monica walk away.

"One day we'll find '*our dragon*', Nora. Goodbye."

"Goodbye, Monica." Nora smiled.

Agnes returned with an armful of paperbacks.

"I found all these!" She said, pleased.

"Well done!." Nora moved over for Agnes to sit and Skype the titles through to Seatown. "Shall I make some hot chocolate?"

"Bonanza!" Agnes agreed with a grin.

Preparing to venture into the ice-box/kitchen, Nora added her scarf from where it hung over her bag under the stairs and set off to put the kettle on, thinking about The Knucker-Dragon and wondering if his Knuckerhole was located in the yard.

4 OF MINCE PIES AND MEN

Lunchtime arrived quickly. Because she was only working between eleven and four, Agnes said she didn't want a lunch break that day. She had brought a bag of hardboiled eggs with her which she said she would nibble at in between serving customers.

Nora braved the sloshy pavements to collect a Christmas sandwich from the delicatessens. It was manic inside. Philip was selling boxes of cigars and bottles of expensive brandy to two loud, snobbish women, while Alice cut up cheese and weighed olives, bagged up slices of cake and counted out mince-pies for a chattering mass of people at the deli counter. The little walkways between the shelves of produce located deeper in the shop were teeming with people who looked angry and were using their elbows as weapons against each other.

Nora decided to remain at the front so waited her turn by the savouries and then used the tongs to slide the last hot sausage roll into a white paper bag, grab another '*La Limonata*' from the fridge, which she regretted being completely addicted to, and joined the queue where Alice's son, Gray, was serving at a small till.

"It's a little bit mad in here." Nora handed Gray a five pound note.

"Tell me about it." Gray grimaced. "How are things in the bookshop?"

"Quiet. Maybe we should start stocking cigars and sausage rolls." She took in the scene enviously.

Once Gray had given Nora her change she squeezed through the dense new arrival of a crowd of men in yellow cords and wax jackets. Out in the street her legs almost skidded apart in the snow slush. She grabbed hold of someone's arm to stop herself flying into the road and was relieved when she saw it was Spencer Brown, one of her regular customers.

"Steady there, Nora." Spencer warned, helping her straighten up. "This place is lethal."

"Thank you, Mr Brown!" Nora noticed his hair was growing quickly after a recent severe haircut he had had. The pure white, wispy locks were already returning to his signature white flowing mane.

Cara sometimes called him Gandalf the White.

Spencer Brown collected occult books, mostly from libraries Georgina discovered in strange or haunted houses on calls days. He lived in a large dwelling at the top of the hill with a gothic tower where he kept his library and wrote articles for esoteric or UFO journals and magazines. Nora was convinced he was a vampire because he often lunged for her neck. Once she had seen a bat following her to her car and thought it might be him.

"I'll try to come in this week." He said, peering at her from his round blue eyes. "I'm researching the local gnome population so I'd like to check your shelves for any fairy folk books. Anything new come in for me?"

"No, Georgina's had the flu so she hasn't been on calls for a couple of weeks. We've just had general stock brought into us."

"That's a shame. I hope she feels better. I'll bring my friend into the bookshop in the New Year. He'll be staying with us over *Mōdraniht*. That's *Christmas* to you Catholics but we pagans or mediums use the *olde English* term."

Nora wasn't completely sure that was true about the mediums, but spencer Brown also fancied himself a bit of a ghostbuster (and gnome-catcher) as well as a pagan.

"I do hope you won't be conducting any sacrifices." Nora frowned, recalling Saint Bede's *De temporum ratione* work in which the historian had written, '*when we celebrate the birth of the Lord...that very night which we hold so sacred, they used to call by the heathen word Modranecht, that is, mother's night, because (we suspect) of the ceremonies they enacted all that night.*'

"Only on night-gnomes or witch-fairies." Spencer winked.

"How lovely." Nora smiled politely.

They said their goodbyes and Spencer set off, holding out a whirring metal device he had once explained to her detected phantasms. She shook her head, baffled, walking carefully back to the bookshop in the sludge.

When Nora returned to The Secondhand Bookworm, the sound of 'Jingle bells' greeted her ears and the parachuting singing Father Christmas flew over her head. Nora quickly ducked.

Agnes had a whole boiled egg in her mouth and tried not to grin.

"It was too quiet and lonely so I switched on his posterior." She said as she chewed.

"He'll soon drive you mad." Nora decided. "Ah, the Butlin's books have gone."

"Yes, two people came and picked them up in the short time you were out." Agnes nodded.

"That's typical. I hope it wasn't too fiddly for you."

"It was fun. I gave them the invoice and receipt and they were really pleased."

"Great." Nora smiled.

Nora removed her coat but kept her scarf and hat on for a while, snuggling up to the oil heater to eat her sausage roll and watch Father Christmas flying happily around the ceiling between the paper chains. Nora and Agnes chatted, managing to eat their lunch and make another round of tea before their next customer arrived.

"Oh, it's pink in here." The woman said, stepping into the room and looking around.

Agnes did a double take, noticing it for the first time.

The woman became aware of the sound of high-pitched singing as Father Christmas parachuted towards her. She ducked and headed for the counter. She was wearing a large green and red knitted bobble hat and a huge knitted cardigan, carrying a basket of shopping and a big gold handbag.

"Can we help?" Nora asked.

"I hope so." The lady replied. "I would like to buy a book for a Christmas present for my daughter. She doesn't read at all, either lazy or prejudice, I don't know, but I'd like something that might get her interested or spark a new-found hobby for her."

"Okay, how old is she?"

"Nineteen."

"What are her interests?" Nora next asked.

"Game of Thrones. She's always going on about it."

"She may like Robin Hobb, perhaps her *Live Ship* series." Nora mused. "We do have a first edition here of *The Ship of Magic*. It's a lovely copy and is a collector's edition so something special. It's priced at forty pounds."

The woman gave a low whistle.

"That's certainly an investment."

"Yes, it will retain its price and, being a first edition, your daughter will be more inclined to read it. My sister has read the series; it's a trilogy, and she says they are brilliant. The genre is fantasy and the author of Game of Thrones praises the books."

Nora ran her fingers along the spines of the first edition shelf until she reached the copy of the thick book and eased it carefully out. The lady looked through it; ignoring the singing Father Christmas as Santa circled around her head.

"You've convinced me." She decided impulsively.

Agnes glanced at Nora, impressed.

"Wonderful. I'm sure she'll like it." Nora smiled, pleased.

"Better than the case of Prosecco I was planning to get her." The woman nodded, reaching for her purse.

Nora placed the book in a brown paper bag followed by a blue carrier and completed the transaction.

"Now, as it's Christmas and you've found me a nice present, please have a mince pie. They're from the delicatessen over the road."

"Thank you." Nora reached into the paper bag.

Agnes eagerly took one too; nothing could beat the mince pies from the delicatessen in Castletown. The lady bade them a happy Christmas and left.

"If only all sales were that easy!" Nora said to Agnes as she bit into the crumbly pastry.

"We'd be millionaires." Agnes agreed, biting into hers, too.

They had just finished eating when the phone rang. Nora picked up the receiver, just as the door flew open and crashed against the wall. The group of yellow-corduroy-trousered men entered the shop, talking loudly.

"Good afternoon, The Secondhand Bookworm." Nora greeted and held still at the sound of heavy breathing.

"Who's that?" A familiar voice asked, followed by more heavy breathing and a few coughs.

"It's Nora, Mr Hill." Nora grimaced.

"Oh, Sarah? It's Mr Hill." Mr Hill said wheezily.

"Nora." Nora corrected.

"Hello, Clara."

"Hello, Mr Hill." Nora said tightly, aware of Agnes gasping as she recognised the name of their most notorious regular customer.

"Nora, in the back room of your shop, left hand side, fourth shelf down, would you happen to have a copy of '*Eleanor: April Queen of Aquitaine*' by Douglas Boyd?" He asked.

"I'll have a look for you Mr Hill." Nora moved away from the counter.

"Can you see it?!" Mr Hill demanded in Nora's ear so that she edged the receiver away.

She frowned at the history section, counted four shelves down and saw the title on the spine of a shiny black book.

"Yes, I have it Mr Hill." Nora said, pulling it out.

"And how much is it?" He asked.

Nora opened the front cover. The whole first page was almost like a work of art made of swirly rubbed out pound signs and prices from the many thousands of times Mr Hill had bought and sold that very book over the years. He was a regular customer of The Secondhand Bookworm and made it his mission to buy and sell the same group of books almost every week in a never ending mind-altering Twilight Zone saga.

"It's priced at ten pounds, Mr. Hill." Nora replied.

There was the sound of spluttering and rapid heavy breathing and Nora arched an eyebrow.

"Ten pounds is it Nora? Ten pounds you say? Oh right. I think I shall leave that purchase today thank you. B-bye." He wheezed and hung up.

Shaking her head, Nora pressed the button on the phone to end the call and remained where she was, holding the book and telephone in expectation. When a few moments had passed and Mr Hill had not phoned back, she popped the book back on the shelf and returned to the front room, squeezing through the group of men who made loud apologies and bowed her through the walkway.

There were several more people in the shop and Nora grimaced at the carpet which had a snail-like trail of wet from the flagstones through to the walkway. Agnes was serving a customer so Nora helped bag up some walking books and sell a few postcards and stamps, casting glances at the noticeably empty shelves where the Heron runs of books had been.

When a few customers disappeared into the depths of the shop, Nora suggested displaying some art books on the shelves in the walkway, so Agnes chose a pile, arranged them nicely and typed out, printed and cut out a variety of signs, singing along to the parachuting Father Christmas who was making Nora's eye twitch.

"Do you have any humour books?" A German lady asked, standing with her husband before the counter.

Nora was in the process of switching off the singing Santa. She nodded.

"We do, on the next floor landing."

"Yes, we Germans do have a sense of humour." She said, heading off towards the walkway.

Nora stared as the woman stomped past.

A man dropped a book on the counter and stood smiling at Nora with his wife. They were wearing matching bobble hats with different single letters knitted into each.

"It says eleven pounds fifty." The man said, smiling. "Can you do it for ten?"

"I'm so sorry but I can't change the prices." Nora apologised, opening the front of the book.

"How much for cash?" He asked, still smiling.

Nora glanced up.

"I'm afraid I'm unable to do discounts, even for cash."

He smiled continuously, without seemingly moving a muscle and Nora began to fear he was an android.

"If you're wondering what the letters stand for on our bobble hats," his wife began to say, smiling serenely, "they're the initials of our children."

"Oh. That's nice." Nora said warily, taking a chance and running the price of the book through the till.

"We were going to go for 'Thing 1' and 'Thing 2' from '*The Cat in the hat*' by Doctor Seuss but Janet chose to honour our children instead." The man smiled.

Agnes was watching them with her mouth slightly open and when Nora noticed she cleared her throat.

"That's eleven pounds fifty for the book." Nora said.

"Oh, I won't be paying that." Thing 1 smiled. "It's far too expensive."

"A lovely shop though." Thing 2 said and they both turned around in unison and walked away, heading for the door which opened to admit a man in a bobble hat with reindeer antlers.

"Maybe I should start a '*bobble hat*' tally chart." Nora said to Agnes out the side of her mouth.

Agnes agreed, watching the man in the reindeer bobble hat look around.

Nora cancelled the sale, handed the book to Agnes with a look and she turned around to put it on the display shelves she was working on.

"Do you take American Express?" The new customer asked, stamping his feet loudly on the flagstones followed by the carpet as though attempting to clean his footwear.

Nora looked down at his boots, which were sloshy and muddy.

"I'm afraid not." She said, resisting the urge to glare.

"Excuse me!" A man with an enormous handlebar moustache shouted into the shop.

Nora jumped.

"Hello." She greeted.

"Do you have any maps of Castletown? You've run out. You only have maps of Seatown!"

"They fold out and the map of Castletown is inside." Nora explained patiently. "It's small."

"Oh, they fold out and it's inside? It's small?" He repeated and opened the map in the doorway as what little heat Nora had been basking in was sucked outside like the victim of a hoover.

A tall, thin man pushed past the man in the doorway, almost squashing him against the door frame. Nora saw that it was Mr Goldfinch, Georgina's trade customer.

"Excuse me!" He said aloofly, gliding into the room.

The man who had asked if they took American Express was absorbed in a book on the counter, muttering to himself, and the man with the handlebar moustache was hidden behind the free map on the doorstep. Nora greeted Mr Goldfinch politely.

"I won't be stopping long. Georgina said you would show me the Strand." He said.

Nora nodded, always feeling intimidated by him.

"Yes of course, it's just here." She showed him the row of books which were tall and relatively thick, half bound in calf leather, polished and in very good condition with gilt stamping on the spines.

"What can you tell me about them?" He asked.

Nora thought carefully, watching him pull out a volume.

"It is a set of volumes one to twenty four." She said, having swotted up about it before he was due in. "They comprise of numerous Sherlock Holmes adventures, until 1893 where there followed an eight year break. After public pressure, Sir Arthur Conan Doyle released The Hound of the Baskervilles in the 1901 and 1902 volumes, here." She touched a finger to both books, knowing that the Strand Magazines with Sherlock Holmes in were of extra value and interest. "Internally they are firmly bound with minimal foxing. There is only a little rubbing on the spine of volume eight. They are priced at eight hundred pounds to you."

Mr Goldfinch frowned over the set carefully so Nora left him to it to help Agnes with a couple of postcard sales. The map-man was shooed politely away, the door closed behind him and the man who had asked about using his American Express card returned the book to the counter and headed off for a wander about the shop.

Nora turned back to look at Mr Goldfinch, wondering if he would go for the sale. He was examining each book, flicking through the pages and then placing it back on the shelf. Finally, he gave Nora a nod.

"Do you have a box for them?"

"Yes." Nora asked Agnes to fetch a nice clean banana box that Georgina had sent over with Humphrey's delivery a few days earlier.

"Good." He said and walked around to the front of the counter. "I'll pay by card."

"Thank you." Nora smiled, pleased that the days takings were very good considering the cold weather and snow slosh deterrent in the town.

When Agnes returned from the kitchen they wrapped each book in tissue paper and placed them carefully in the box. Mr Goldfinch left to collect his car, pulled up on the double yellow lines outside the bookshop, ignored the beeps and glares from passing traffic, picked up the box and left with a dry 'thank you'. When he had gone,

Nora let Agnes write the sale in the cash book where she added miniature drawings of balloons and party poppers.

"We can go home now." She grinned.

"If only." Nora chuckled.

Later that afternoon, Agnes disappeared to the paperback room to salvage the sci-fi, fantasy and horror section after it had had an abusive rummage through by a group of Goths, one of the walkie-talkies clipped to the waistband of her skirt.

Nora used a pack of paper towels to dry off some of the carpet, laying them flat and walking backwards and forwards over them until she had two customers who gave her a funny look.

"Just those for you?" She asked, moving behind the counter.

"Yes please." The woman said, sliding a pile of theology and religious books towards Nora and sending the cash book sailing to the floor. "Ooops, sorry dear."

"That's okay." Nora smiled, opening each book and finding the pencil prices. "Thirty seven pounds altogether please." She grimaced as the woman handed her two twenty pound notes while holding a snotty tissue which she then placed to her nose and blew into with a variety of loud snorts.

"Thank you, dear." The woman said, taking the bag.

"Don't you want your change?" The man with her asked, looking at Nora's hand which held out three pound coins.

"I had to blow my nose because it was tickling." The woman said.

"Oh, I thought you were being generous. For a change. Giving out Christmas bonuses."

"Don't you crack your jokes now!" The woman tittered and took the pound coins. "Merry Christmas." She said and they left.

At that moment, a customer dressed in biking leathers appeared with an armful of books on motor biking and the Grand Prix.

"Hello. These please." He said, placing them on the desk and reaching into his leather trousers for his wallet.

Nora rang the prices through the till.

"Would you like a bag?" She asked him.

"Yes please or they'll be flying over the A27. You take cards don't you?" He asked.

"Yes, we do."

While the sale was rung up and Nora placed the books in one of the bright blue carrier bags, the door opened to admit a familiar customer. Nora groaned inside. The young man was local and purchased a lot of art books from The Secondhand Bookworm, but he always bought them when he was either drunk or high, and he seemed to be both as he staggered into the shop.

"Thank you, have a nice day." The biker said once he had paid for his books and picked up his bag.

"Thank you, bye." Nora bade and turned to the computer.

'*Drunk-boy!!!*' She typed, followed by a sad faced emoji.

He didn't acknowledge her this time but made his way to the art section where he stood clasping a wad of notes and browsing the shelf, throwing her the occasional glance, sipping from his can of coke and dropping his bag twice.

'*We have three copies of IT by Stephen King. Shall I bring one down to put in the transfer box for Seatown?*' The disembodied voice of Agnes crackled over the walkie-talkie followed by a beep.

The drunk-boy looked wildly around him before staring at Nora with wide eyes. He watched her pick up the other walkie-talkie from the cradle next to the till.

"Good idea!" She said.

'Bonanza!' Agnes replied, followed by a beep.

The drunk-boy grinned in understanding and delight, laughed into his collar, slurped his coke and belched loudly.

"Sorry, sorry, haha, sorry about that." He said, covering his mouth with the hand that held his pile of money.

"Pardon you." Nora said with a straight-face, checking through the cash book to make sure they had written down all of their sales.

After she had sat scowling and lamenting the thievery of the Stephen King *'IT'* poster for a few minutes (not that it probably mattered seeing as they had three copies on the shelf so it hadn't inspired customers to purchase a any!), Drunk-Boy drew her from her ruminations.

"Do you have any books about David Hockney?" The Drunk-Boy asked.

"Erm…if we did they would be there." Nora said politely.

He frowned suddenly at her lack of enthusiasm.

"You should…" He began and pointed with his coke so that some slopped out the top and spilt on the floor. "…ooops, sorry, haha, sorry."

"You shouldn't have drinks in here." Nora said, trying not to smile.

"There's rules for everything in this Mickey Mouse town." He glowered irritably and went back to browsing while muttering, slurping his coke and burping.

Nora shook her head, adding up the takings as the phone began to ring.

"Good afternoon, The Secondhand Bookworm."

"It's me." Georgina's miserable voice returned, followed by a sniff.

"Oh hello. How are you?"

"Bit better. Sick of honey and lemons but mother's right, it does help. And I've stopped with the aches now so I'm definitely on the mend."

"Good-oh!" Nora smiled.

"How's it been there? Miserable?"

"No. We're on…" She checked her final figure. "…one thousand three hundred and ninety four pounds."

"Whaaaaaaat?!" Georgina exclaimed hoarsely followed by an onslaught of coughing and blowing her nose. "Well done!"

Nora told Georgina about the lady from Butlin's, Mr Goldfinch and various other customers, watching the drunk-boy pull out several large books and shaking her head at him as he placed his can of coke on the top shelf, dropped all his money, gathered it up laughing to himself and, muttering, picked out another book.

"That's good news for Castletown this time of year." Georgina said croakily. "Buy yourselves some mince pies with money from the till."

"At this rate I will become the shape of a mince pie!" Nora lamented.

Georgina made an intermittent crackling sound that Nora supposed was hoarse chuckling before sneezing loudly. They bade their goodbyes and Nora hung up just as the drunk-boy came to the counter.

"These please." He said in a slightly slurred voice.

Nora looked at the books; three large art tomes.

"Are you sure?" She asked, always uncomfortable that he came in and spent lots of his money on art books when he was tipsy or trippy.

"Wha'?" His jaw seemed to unhinge as he stared at her amazed, mouth open stupidly. "Why would I not…listen 'ere, I appreciate these artists, I mean, Hockney was *insane*, he's considered one of the most influential artists of the twentieth century and a significant contributor to the nineteen sixties Pop Art movement, look, look here…"

Nora watched as his twenty pound notes scattered over the counter while he fumbled with the book.

"…you seen his 'we boys together clinging'? Look it's far out there; painted while men loving men was still illegal in England, from Walt Whitman's poem of the same name."

Nora gathered up his notes.

"Are you going to buy them then?"

"Why wouldn't I?" He asked in amazement.

With a sigh Nora rang each book through the till.

"Seventy five pounds please." She said.

He handed her the wad of notes, she counted them out and asked if he wanted a bag.

"No!" He glowered. "You and your plastic bags…"

He took his change, picked up his books and staggered off, leaving his empty coke can on the top art shelf which Nora removed with a sigh, hearing him walking up the street while loudly asking Billy from the Antiques Centre if he liked the art of David Hockney.

Nora and Agnes were taking a break with a cup of hot chocolate each when a man stepped into the bookshop accompanied by a crisp packet and several frozen leaves that dropped onto the mat.

"Good afternoon." Nora greeted the customer, both hands wrapped around her hot mug.

"Hello, I'm looking for a book." He peered around. "Oh. Are these all secondhand?"

"Yes, we have a few new books."

"Oh, I don't buy secondhand books. If anyone's like me they pick their nose while reading and turn every page. Can you imagine what the pages of all these used books contain? It makes my skin crawl thinking about it. Secondhand books are like passing on your used underwear; I won't be buying any of these!" He said, all the while walking backwards towards the door whereupon he left and closed it behind him.

For a long moment Nora and Agnes just stared. They didn't have a chance to say anything because a large lady replaced him.

"Hello! Oh it's lovely and warm in here. And it's pink! Wonderful!" She gushed, stepping on the leaves, crisp packet, flagstones and carpet.

"Good afternoon." Nora greeted, wanting to laugh about their previous customer.

"Have you tried the mince pies in the delicatessen on the corner there?" The lady asked, taking a white paper bag from her shopper. "They are delicious! Please, have one each, share the joy!"

"Thank you." Nora accepted eagerly.

With a grin Agnes took one too. The lady kept one out for herself, returned the bag and took a large bite.

"I'm looking for a book about Tiffany glass and lamps." She said through her mouthful.

At that moment the telephone started to ring, so while Agnes took the lady to the section where the books about glass were kept, Nora grabbed the receiver. She paused to swallow her mouthful of mince pie and almost choked on it when she recognised the familiar sound of heavy breathing.

"Hello? Hello?" Mr Hill's wheezy voice called.

"Hello, Mr Hill." Nora said between coughs. "Excuse me, I just have something in my throat.

"Who's that?" Mr Hill asked.

"It's Nora, Mr Hill."

"Oh, Flora. It's Mr Hill."

"Yes. Hello!" Nora said tightly, taking a gulp of tea.

"Nora. The book I inquired about earlier called '*Eleanor: April Queen of Aquitaine*' by Douglas Boyd? Do you remember? Nora?"

"Yes, Mr Hill."

"Well, I would like to purchase it." He said. "Could you put it by for me please? I shall come in on Thursday by bus to collect it."

"Okay. I'll put it by for you." Nora assured him, trying to sound enthusiastic.

"Oh you would? Thank you very much. So, I will arrive in Castletown on Thursday to collect the book and pay by postal order. B-bye." He said and hastily hung up before Nora could challenge his choice of payment method.

Nora shook her head, hung up too and replaced the telephone as Agnes sold a book about the art of Tiffany to the mince-pie lady. When the lady had left, they sat down to finish their tea, rather relieved that the town was almost deserted now that it was growing dark and starting to get very cold.

Four o'clock arrived at last. After Agnes had topped up the box of free maps from the supply box under the stairs she wrapped her ballet pumps in plastic bags and rustled to the door.

"Hopefully *I'll* get home before the big freeze." Nora said optimistically as she joined her, dragging in a frozen solid postcard spinner.

The town was empty and she didn't expect to have any more tourists before she closed.

"Hopefully I'll be able to get up the hill before it becomes a ski slope!" Agnes grinned.

"If I don't see you before Christmas, have a lovely time." Nora said.

"I'll be at the staff Christmas meal on Friday." Agnes reminded Nora.

"Oh, yes! Of course. See you then!"

"Bonanza!" Agnes nodded and Nora waved.

Agnes waved too and rustled off up the sloppy street, Nora staring at her feet which looked strangely bright on the dark wet pavement.

There weren't any more customers over the next hour.

Sneakily, Nora slipped her Kindle from her bag and sat reading a novel she had downloaded at the weekend. It was a gripping thriller so at one point she was so absorbed she forgot she was in the bookshop. She became aware of a man standing at the counter so gasped and threw it quickly on top of the reservation books.

"I'm sorry, have you been there long?"

"No. Do you have any film ephemera?" The man asked, rolling tobacco into a thin, brown cigarette.

Nora shook her head.

"Not at the moment, but we do stock some when they come along. The last item we had was a Vintage Austrian film program for the 1933 US film King Kong."

The man balled his fist.

"Son of a nutcracker!" He exclaimed in frustration and bashed the cash book. "I wish I had known."

Nora edged back.

"Sorry." She apologised, warily. "I can add your name a telephone number to our database. When we get some more film ephemera in we can let you know."

He cleared his throat, straightened the knot of his scarf and bowed his head.

"I'd appreciate that." He said in a controlled voice.

She heard a message arrive on her iPhone as she tapped his name and number on the computer keyboard.

"There we are Mr Goggins. We'll be in touch."

"Where can I buy an ice pick?" He asked.

Nora blinked, having the sudden thought he was going to hack her to death in revenge for selling the King Kong movie ephemera.

"Erm…perhaps in Seatown."

"Thank you!" He turned and stomped away.

Nora grimaced, watching him go.

The text message was from Humphrey.

'Hi Nora, how has your day been? I'm driving back from London. Currently stuck behind a broken down snow plough. Thinking of you – Humphrey x'

Nora smiled.

'Hello! What a jolly experience for you. I hope it's mended soon! A typical bookworm day today. How was London? – Nora x' She typed and pressed send.

Nora had just picked up her Kindle again, after glancing carefully around, when Humphrey replied.

'Busy up here. I knew I'd be called up occasionally to help with some deals but this one was tough. My former partners were having a hard time with The Lodbrok Syndicate, headed by a ruthless Viking whose parents once owned The Secondhand Bookworm – long story. I know he's got it in for me. I'll tell you all about it when I next see you. Looks like the snow plough is about to move xx'

Nora was interested. She remembered the previous owners of The Secondhand Bookworm, a Mr and Mrs Lodbrok who had specialised in Norse mythology, but she hadn't been aware they had a son.

'Look forward to it. Drive carefully. Speak soon x' She sent back and turned off her Kindle.

Humphrey replied with a couple of '*x*'s.

Nora smiled, placing her phone in her bag.

As it was ten minutes to five, Nora brought everything in from outside and locked up. She turned off the light upstairs, locked the kitchen, switched off the candles in the window, went through the cashing up procedure, said goodbye to the Seatown branch via Skype, dressed up like a Muscovite, set the shop alarm and left The Secondhand Bookworm without any incident.

It was already starting to turn icy as Nora walked tentatively along the pavement to her car which she had parked along the road next to the moat beside the castle. She paused to examine the new buildings which loomed magnificently in the darkness. One lone light was shining out of a room in the largest tower. She wondered if that was where the Duke was and tried to imagine him inside, surrounded by his beautiful heirlooms and stately finery.

Five minutes later, Nora drove out of Castletown, passing Iris from the antique centre who was heading for the train station wearing her 'Jesus loves you' hat.

5 SNOWED IN WITH ONLY 27,000 BOOKS FOR COMPANY

The next morning, Nora sensed something was different when she woke up. She threw open her bedroom window curtains and blinked in astonishment when she saw the amount of snow that had fallen overnight. Her parents' back garden looked beautiful; truly a Christmas card picture.

"If you can go in Nora, I'd really appreciate it." Georgina said when Nora answered her iPhone once she had showered and pulled on leggings, jeans and three jumpers. "Cara's going over to Seatown. It'll be just you in Castletown. Park in the first car park by the swimming pool and reimburse yourself from the till. And buy some mince pies from the deli with money from the till to keep you going, too."

"Okay." Nora grimaced; dubious about driving into town and doubtful there would be any customers.

The drive over to Castletown was easy enough but slow going. Although the gritters had been out overnight, banks of snow lined either side of the dual carriageway. There was hardly any traffic at all. The roads felt slippery beneath her tyres, so Nora took extra care heading into Castletown.

Nora turned into the first car park by the outdoor pool and almost burst out laughing. There was not a single other car. The only vehicle parked in the middle was a bright yellow snow plough. Shaking her head, Nora stopped in the first place by the entrance, stepped out of her car and almost did the splits. She walked tentatively over to the pay machine and dropped in a pile of pound coins. The machine groaned and whirred in protest as it printed her ticket. A moment later, Nora skidded the whole length of her car, grabbed her wing mirror and managed to steady herself before she popped her ticket on her dashboard inside.

She grabbed her bag and set off in the muffled silence out of the car park and along the road, pausing to look at the magnificent view of the river as she crossed the bridge, and to gaze at the new castle. It looked like a fairy tale; ledges and turrets and great sprawling rooftops covered in heavy snowfall; so she snapped loads of pictures with her iPhone to load onto Facebook, Instagram and Twitter, as she continued into the main street.

A great big sign was in the process of being placed in the middle of the road by Hugh the road sweeper. It read: TOWN CLOSED.

Nora slowed to a stop.

"What you doing 'ere?" Hugh hailed in surprised, his voice echoing around loudly in the silence.

"Morning to you too." Nora answered, continuing towards him and nearly sliding into the gutter.

"You better watch out. The whole place is lethal." Hugh warned, shaking his head. "Are you actually going to open up the bookshop?"

"Yes. I'm anticipating a brilliant day of sales." She replied sarcastically.

"Mental." Hugh muttered, continuing to position the road sign. "Well, the whole country's gone on strike. No other shop is stupid enough to open today."

"You are very rude." Nora pointed out, grabbing a lamp post outside the charity shop to stop herself skidding over.

Hugh stared at her and then laughed.

"Yeah. But I'm saying the truth."

"You probably are." Nora agreed with a wince, wondering if she would make it to the bookshop without falling flat on her face.

"Do you need a hand?"

"No thank you!" Nora assured him.

Hugh watched her cross Tree Lane and pass the Estate Agents. When she reached The Secondhand Bookworm, Nora peered around the square. Hugh was right. No one else was in. Even the delicatessen was shut, she noticed with a groan, thinking of all the lovely homemade mince pies they were depriving her of, and then deciding that was probably a good thing.

Nora sighed and opened up, not even bothering to close the door behind her.

"Blimey!" She exclaimed.

The room was like a freezer and this time Nora didn't imagine the frozen fog coming out of her mouth.

"It looks colder in there than it is out here." Hugh's voice sailed loudly into the room, as if he was speaking through a megaphone.

"It is!" Nora agreed, running around the counter to turn off the alarm.

Hugh remained on the doorstep, reading the title of a book on a nearby shelf.

"You won't be staying here for long. Waste of time." He told her smugly.

"Hmm." Nora turned on the lights and switched on the oil heater.

"Don't bother putting out your postcards and crap." He advised thoughtfully.

"Who works here?" Nora asked him pointedly.

He shrugged and headed off.

"This will probably be a very lonely day." She said to herself, starting to fill up the till. "Brrr. This is torture. At least I have you for company." She told the books on the shelves and then ran up to the next floor to turn on the upper lights.

It was just as freezing on the next floors. In fact, Nora thought it might be worse. She checked each room and took a photo of the view of the yard which looked impossibly beautiful covered in snow, with snow on the numerous window ledges of the surrounding flats, the roof of the outside toilet, the orange cone and the little kitchen roof. All memories of past sewage disasters disappeared from her mind. She ran down the stairs, checked no one was in the front of the shop, grabbed the internal shop keys and unlocked the kitchen door.

After Nora had filled the kettle up with freezing water, pleased the water pipes hadn't frozen, even though it felt as though it was flowing from a glacier, she put it on to boil and unlocked the yard door.

"Oh, if only I could make a snowman." She sighed to herself, watching a yellow wagtail hopping about.

She locked the door and headed into the front, shivering. The oil heater was making little sounds as it attempted to warm up so Nora stood over it, staring into the deserted street. It actually seemed as though the air from the street was warming up the front room so Nora decided to keep the door open. She then put a postcard spinner outside to show any people who ventured into town that The Secondhand Bookworm was open for business. And hopefully she would pinch everyone else's, seeing as they had abandoned her to trade all alone, and without any mince pies too!

By half past eleven, Nora had browsed through every art book they had about surrealism, read a book about walking the South Downs trail, prayed the mid-morning liturgy of the hours on her iPhone app (a selection of psalms and short readings), skimmed through three Egyptian history tomes, including how to read Hieroglyphs, read the highlights in a brand new copy of 'Bradshaw's Handbook' (it was still boring), looked at all the coloured plates in the fairy tale Folio Society books, speed read the complete works of Jane Austen, turned the singing Father Christmas on for five minutes and then off again, and polished the till.

There had been *no* customers, visitors or phone calls. Nora had had several amusing conversations with Cara in Seatown on Skype, even exchanging 'Skype Art' designs across the Skype chat made out of emoticons, until Cara had been deluged with customers and gone quiet for an hour, sending the occasional angry faced emoji.

Nora was about to eat her squashed and soggy tuna fish sandwich out of boredom when her mobile phone began to ring. She smiled to see Humphrey's handsome profile picture.

"Didn't you get any of my texts?" Humphrey asked when she answered.

"No. How many did you send? Hang on a minute…" The sounds of numerous text messages arriving almost deafened her.

"That'd be them, then." Humphrey said.

"The signals in Castletown can be intermittent." Nora reminded him with a smile.

"And the main phone line wasn't connecting either. I was insanely worried about you, Nora. When Georgina told me she had sent you off in this weather I almost tipped her hot lemon and honey on her head. What was she thinking? I bet you haven't had a single customer?"

"No. The only person I've spoken to is Hugh the street sweeper."

"I'm coming over to you, Nora." Humphrey decided.

"Really?"

"Well, I can't have you alone in a town with just Hugh for company."

"Are you jealous?" Nora teased.

"Immensely." He admitted.

Nora gulped.

"I would have been there earlier but three people needed their cars dug out with our neighbour's snow plough. I'm heading over now."

"In a snow plough?" Nora joked, hoping to cheer him up.

"No." Humphrey snorted.

"Drive carefully." Nora warned.

"I will." He promised and hung up.

Feeling more positive now Humphrey was on his way, Nora organised fresh glacier water in the kettle and popped a teabag in each of two mugs. When she came back into the front of the shop she shut the door and opened Humphrey's text messages. She blinked when she saw there were seventeen! The first one was a reply to the message she had sent him in reply to his last text when she had woken up:

1)   *'Yes, I enjoyed our chat last night too. I hope you're not going into work today! I miss you and want to see you xx'*

2)   *'Georgina said she sent you in. I'm very cross with her. Are you there yet? xx'*

3)   *'Did you get into town alright? Xx'*

4)   *'Are you there? Xx'*

5)   *'Answer your phone Nora! I've tried the bookshop number but it's not connecting Xx*

6)   *'I'm really incredibly annoyed with Georgina x!!'*

7)   *'Answer me before I really worry xx'*

8)   *'I just accidently ran over a snowman and upset some kids because I am stressing about not hearing from you xx'*

9)   *'I'm hoping you are extraordinarily busy and haven't had a chance to check your messages yet, but let me know how things are over there xxx'*

10) *'Are you okay? Xxx'*

11) *'You're not having an affair with the Duke are you?! xx'*

12) *'Okay you're probably sulking because there are probably no mince pies in the deli xxx'*

13) *'Please let me know you're there, I'm really worried now xxx'*

14) *'Answer your phone!! Bookworm landline is still not connecting. Xx'*

15) *'You're going to think me the most devoted and concerned man when you finally get all my messages and that's true, I am. I'm also still incredibly worried about not hearing from you. Please reply xx'*

16) *'I've decided not to let you out of my sight ever again after this xx'*

17) *'I'm heading over! Will keep trying to call Xxx'*

Nora sent a whole text message of *'xxxxxxx's* to Humphrey along with a profuse apology for not checking her phone. Since resigning from his high powered multimillion pound business in London recently, and returning to the county of Cole to move in with his sister (Georgina spoilt her little brother terribly) while he sorted out a new flat or house, Humphrey had been helping out friends and relatives (including his sister) while he enjoyed his early retirement (even though he was only thirty years old) from his *very stressful* corporate job. This saw him doing a variety of odd jobs (in between popping back to his company to help with the occasional project). He and Nora had been friends for years, but only dating for a month or so. Nora was quickly learning that Humphrey liked to now keep in touch with her regularly. Grimacing guiltily, Nora read a few more messages, several from Georgina:

1) *'Humphrey is furious with me for sending you in. Let me know when you arrive! Xx'*
2) *'I think the main phone line has been knocked out in the snowfall. I keep calling it but it's dead. Call me on your mobile. Xx*
3) *Hoping you are okay. Lock up at about three if the town is dead Nora xx*
4) *Call me when you get these. Humphrey just chewed my ear off, he can't get hold of you xx*
5) *I can't get hold of Cara either. The snow has affected main lines and mobile signals here. I think Cara's mobile is out of credit anyway xxx*
6) *I'm sure everything is okay but if I don't hear from you by lunchtime I'm sending Troy over xxx*

Nora replied to Georgina, explaining she was probably right about the snow affecting the phone lines and mobiles and that Humphrey was on his way. She told her it was also like a ghost town. She then picked up the shop telephone receiver and was surprised to hear the dial tone. Pleased everything now appeared to be connected, she hung up, slotted all the books she had been reading back on their shelves and had a tidy.

Phil the postman trudged past in his civvies. He stopped when he noticed the postcard spinner outside the bookshop, peered in the window and waved when he saw Nora.

"I can't believe you're open today! Even the P.O is closed." He said, amazed.

"It does seem to be rather pointless." Nora sighed, peering around the square and seeing that every other shop was shut.

"Do you need anything? I'm heading up to The Duke's Pie but only for lunch with Cathy. His Grace might pop in tomorrow when he turns on the Christmas tree lights so she wants everything perfect and we're planning some specials. I can bring some pasties down for you."

"No, Humphrey's due over so I'll be fine. Thank you though, Phil." Nora said with appreciation.

"Ah, yes, you've been getting quite chummy with Georgina's brother lately." Phil said, looking interested.

Nora blinked.

"Well, we've been on a few dates if you must know." Nora glared.

Phil winked.

"Word is the snow will start melting this afternoon. Temperatures are already rising so you might get a few visitors, aside from *Humphrey Pickering*."

"Ahem. It's a shame if the snow does melt. Castletown looks just like a Nordic Christmas card. And I *was* hoping to go tobogganing." Nora joked.

Phil smiled.

"Give me a call if you want a pasty." He offered, still looking at her with piqued curiosity.

"Thank you, Phil." Nora nodded.

At that moment the shop phone began to ring so Nora headed off to answer it while Phil set off carefully up the street.

"Good morning, The Secondhand Bookworm." Nora greeted.

There was the sound of heavy breathing.

Nora's eyes widened when she realised who her probably *one and only* caller was that day.

"Who's that?" A familiar voice asked.

"It's Nora, *Mr Hill*!" Nora replied, realising she was strangely pleased with even a call from Mr Hill after a morning of solitude.

"Aroura, it's Mr Hill." He said, breathing and spluttering.

Nora grimaced, deciding she preferred the solitude after all. She was sure he got her name wrong on purpose!

"Hello, Mr Hill!"

"Aroura, I put a book aside for collection, it's called '*Eleanor: April Queen of Aquitaine*' by Douglas Boyd, can you see it? It will be under the counter in a reservation bag for me. The lady I spoke to put it by for me yesterday."

"That was me, Mr Hill!" Nora said, reaching for it.

There was a profusion of breathing, spluttering and coughing and Mr Hill chose to ignore that fact.

"Do you have it?" He asked quickly.

"Yes, I have it here." Nora said.

"Oh you have it there do you. Well, I'd like to cancel my purchase of '*Eleanor: April Queen of Aquitaine*' by Douglas Boyd please. So could you put it back on the shelf for me for another customer? I won't be coming in to collect it after all. B-bye." He said and hung up.

Nora remained holding the book for a long moment before shoving it back, shaking her head. She was about to return the phone to the cradle when it rang again. Nora answered it.

"Nora, it's me." Humphrey's warm voice responded. "I thought I'd try the shop line in case your iPhone didn't have a signal again."

"It did, but it's gone once more." Nora noticed. "I read all your messages, Humphrey. I'm sorry I didn't check before."

"Hmm. Don't you think I'm the most devoted and concerned boyfriend you've ever had?" He chuckled, huskily.

"Are we calling you that now then?" Nora chewed her bottom lip, smiling slightly.

"I think we're almost there." Humphrey decided. "We've been on several dates."

"Yes and you certainly have been devoted and concerned. And, to be honest, you're not as obsessive as Braxton." She added, grimly. "But should you ever get like that…"

"Are you referring to your ex who proposed to you about ten times?" Humphrey recalled.

"Hmm." Nora nodded. "But that was years ago. He and I had only dated a few months."

"I can understand his obsession, though." Humphrey said, flatteringly.

"Why thank you, kind sir." Nora laughed.

"But don't worry, I shan't be dropping to one knee the next time I see you." Humphrey promised with a smile in his voice.

Nora chuckled, sitting down in the swivel chair behind the counter.

"Glad to hear it!"

"Huh." He seemed slightly put out.

Nora grimaced.

"By the way, Georgina was trying to phone you on the shop phone earlier. Apparently the main lines have been down in the Castletown area. They were reconnected about half an hour ago." Humphrey said.

"That would explain the lack of phone calls." Nora realised. "I didn't even think to check it. I replied to her text messages so hopefully she'll get those."

"Are you alright on your own for another hour or so? Mum just informed me she has a doctor's appointment and I'd feel happier taking her when the roads are like this rather than have her risk life and death in a taxi."

"Of course!" Nora assured him quickly. "I'll ask Phil to bring a pasty down from The Duke's Pie. He just offered."

"I'm getting rather jealous, and not just of the pasties." Humphrey grumbled.

"I'll ask him to bring a plateful down."

"I'll be as quick as I can." Humphrey promised. "The doctor surgery is only a five minute drive from Georgina's and I doubt they'll be too busy today."

"Okay, speak soon."

"Bye, Nora."

Phil was more than pleased to bring Nora a plate of the restaurant's famous pasties and delivered it five minutes after she had phoned him. The plate was hot and the pasties smelt delicious. Phil refused payment.

"There are two 'turkey, sage and onion with cranberry and port sauce' from our Christmas menu." He explained as Nora inhaled the delicious scent. "Also two 'chicken curry' pasties and two 'Irish stew lamb and vegetable'."

"Oh my goodness, wonderful!" Nora appreciated.

"You can reheat them in the microwave if they go cold by the time Humphrey arrives."

"Thanks, Phil."

"Enjoy! Merry Christmas." He bade and set off into the deserted town, heading back up the hill.

Nora decided to wait until Humphrey arrived but she had to practice extreme self-control. Her mouth was watering because of the delicious smell of hot, tasty food. Instead of relenting and devouring them all, she occupied herself by putting Mr Hill's book back on the shelf in the history room, pulling out some more books from the many shelves that surrounded her and perusing volumes of art books and topography and then venturing into the railway, shipping and motoring books from the bookcases in the stairwell.

The shop was still cold but the oil heater was throwing out some nice heat now so Nora made herself some tea, munched her soggy tuna sandwich and enjoyed the peace and quiet, left alone with 27,000 books.

It turned out the doctor's surgery was heaving so Humphrey was going to be longer than anticipated. He sent Nora photographs of the miserable people blowing into assorted handkerchiefs in the waiting room, along with Mrs Pickering's withering and impatient frowns, and promised to be with Nora by two o'clock (hopefully contagious free – but he suspected it was just a bout of the snow-chills).

Nora continued to resist the pasties and was absorbed in a book about *three-wheeler Morgan motorcars* when she noticed the Skype Chat flashing. She leaned forward to read.

'Georgina Pickering wishes to join this chat. Do you accept?' A Skype message asked.

Cara had pressed accept so Nora did the same.

'It's me! Troy has set up Skype on my laptop and found the bookworms for me.' Georgina wrote.

'Hallllloooooo!' Cara replied.

'Hello!' Nora typed.

'How is it going?' Georgina asked.

'Dead!' Nora replied.

'*One mad hour or so but now DEAD here too*!' Cara typed.

'*Close up at three.'* Georgina wrote.

'*Yay*!' Cara replied.

'*Okay.*' Nora typed.

'*Nora? Can you let me know what play we're seeing at your brother's theatre on opening night on Saturday? I could Google it but I'm being exceedingly impatient with the loading time on my laptop!*'

Nora chuckled, amused that Georgina had booked up a play without knowing what she was going to see.

'*It is called 'The Surprise' by G.K. Chesterton.*' She typed.

'*I'm going too!*' Cara sent.

There was a pause as Georgina typed back.

'*Lovely! Is your brother in it, Nora?*'

'*Yes'.* Nora replied.

'*And what is it about?*' Georgina asked.

'*I'm not entirely sure but I think it's the story of a master puppet-maker who longs for his clockwork creations to be made free. When his wish is granted, he gets far more than he bargained for! The dialogue is very witty. I've heard some of Seymour's lines.*' Nora wrote. '*He chose it because he studied Chesterton's plays in college and says they need to become well-known.*'

'*Look forward to it!*' Georgina Skyped back.

'*Me too!*' Cara agreed.

Georgina asked for numerous files on the Seatown computer so Nora left them Skyping for the next five minutes until they all said goodbye and Georgina logged off. Cara and Nora chatted for a while until Cara said she was going to the kitchen to microwave some gravy and mashed potatoes. Nora glanced longingly at the plate of pasties.

Hugh walked past, shaking his head mockingly at her as he went by the windows, so Nora glowered at him. She then noticed another human being over the road so got up and peered out, smiling to see a regular customer named Mr Rutler walking along with his camera. When he noticed her he headed cheerfully over.

"Strewth! What are you doing here, Nora?" He asked, joining her at the door of The Secondhand Bookworm.

"I've been asking myself that same question since I arrived." Nora smiled.

"You look bally freezing. Have you had any customers?"

"Not a single one yet."

"Holding on to hope are you?" He chortled fondly.

"Well, I'm hoping I'll sell at least a couple of books to cover my wages and the cost of the heating." Nora admitted. "Are you taking photos?"

"Ah yes. It's not often we get a snowfall like this and the town museum will appreciate a record of it all. Looks like I'm the only resident foolish enough to venture out though. I'll try and drum you up some business if I pass anyone."

"Oh thank you!" Nora nodded.

"Get back inside now by your heater." He ordered, walking away.

"Bye." Nora waved and closed the door. She had considered coaxing him inside by tempting him with their newly organised section of architecture books but he seemed preoccupied with his photography.

"Brrr, too cold." She grumbled to the spindly Christmas tree, attempting fruitlessly to close the jammed open letterbox that let in cold air. It was, as usual, stuck fast, as it had typically been for the past few weeks. With a sigh she hurried back behind the counter and practically sat on the oil heater to warm up again.

As she waited for Humphrey, Nora rearranged the window, turned on the branch of candles and placed the figures of the Nativity scene in a more prominent place between two books relating to the meaning of Christmas. She then put an album of Christmas carols on from her iPhone and pondered the empty cobbled square covered in snow.

The fountain next to the war memorial was obviously iced over because a flock of pigeons were plodding about in the circular stone pool and there was no water flowing out of the top. She felt sorry for the stone effigy of the eighth Duke of Cole in the centre, which looked very cold.

Suddenly, Nora noticed another person walking down the path of the street opposite. He was a tall, well-dressed man in a dark heavy wool double-breasted coat, gloved hands behind his back and a thick cashmere scarf around his neck, probably only a few years older than her. He was pausing to peer into the windows of the closed shops and gaze around the square. When his eyes skimmed over The Secondhand Bookworm they met with Nora's through the window, locked and held. Nora then saw him begin towards her.

"First customer of the day?" She hoped, interested.

She watched him cross the cobbled square and then stared with dawning realisation. Her mouth was still agape as he stood and examined the window display, continued to the door and opened it.

"Hello there." The Duke of Cole greeted Nora.

"Er….erm….er…." She stuttered and then cleared her throat to drop down in a clumsy curtsey. "Erm…hello, your grace."

The Duke closed the door behind him.

"I must commend your dedication to small businesses, the written word and to the town." He said, smiling. "You realise you are the only shop open today?"

Nora smiled slightly.

"And you are my first customer, Your Grace." She nodded.

He grinned, handsomely.

"Well, I simply could not resist exploring the town while it is abandoned." He confessed, looking around the room. "Such a rare opportunity for me to get to know the shops without causing a nuisance to the shopkeepers with all the rules of engagement and propriety."

"I can see the appeal." Nora admitted, watching him.

"So you are rare and antiquarian books?"

"And used and secondhand." Nora agreed.

"Most interesting." He considered the Cole section closest to him and chose a book. "You must come to my castle and see my own library when everything is complete up there." He invited.

Nora's mouth dropped open again.

"Er…" She closed it with a snap of her teeth but the Duke politely continued to peruse the book in his hands. "That's very gracious of you, Your Grace."

She thought she saw his lips twitch slightly but he regarded her with a practiced and polite smile.

"A very nice section about Cole." He approved. "I am interested in this book." He looked around. "Ah, you have three floors? May I browse?"

"Of…of course!" Nora nodded eagerly.

He closed the book in his hands and placed it on the counter as he passed.

"Thank you." He smiled and Nora watched him head off towards the walkway, moving deeper into the shop.

She gulped, blushed and then shook her head, fanning her face.

"Get a grip, Nora!" She told herself firmly, leaned backwards and saw the Duke browsing the aviation section in the stairwell.

His blue eyes met with hers and he smiled, warmly.

Nora smiled back, returning her attention to the front of the shop.

"Get a grip? That's impossible." She whispered to herself and promptly headed to the computer to let Cara in Seatown know who her first and only customer of the day happened to be!

When the Duke of Cole returned almost half an hour later he carried a small stack of books.

"Now, I did not catch your name. Very improper of me not to ask but I was distracted by such a delightful shop." He said.

"Oh. I'm Nora." Nora blushed, drawing the books towards her. "Miss Nora Jolly."

He smiled.

"Good afternoon, Miss Nora Jolly. You may call me James."

"Oh, I simply couldn't, Your Grace." Nora exclaimed with widened eyes.

"But I insist." He said, reaching for his wallet. "We have met in very special circumstances and that calls for very special privileges, Nora. It is not often I can sneak out of my own house and spend a happy half an hour alone in such a treasure trove. Of course, in company we will have to follow decorum, but now we are friends and when friends are alone they do not have to abide by such rules."

Nora grinned.

"Very well, Your Grace." Nora accepted, still unable to bring herself to call him 'James'!

James smiled, warmly.

"Now, if I remember rightly, you are the manager here?" He asked.

Nora's stomach loop-di-looped. The Duke of Cole seemed to already know of her existence!

"Yes, Your Grace. The proprietor is Miss Georgina Pickering. She also has a shop in Seatown." Nora rang the prices of his books through the till; two clean, bright tomes about mountaineering, one of which was about free-climbing, and two unusual books about bird watching in Scotland.

"Ah. And you run this branch for her." He appeared to already know.

"Yes, Your Grace." Nora nodded, adding the Cole book.

"A very fine job you have done too." He complimented. "I meant what I said about your visiting my library. When the last of my building work is complete I would be honoured to give a fellow bibliophile a tour."

"I would be honoured to accept, Your Grace."

"James."

Nora just smiled and glanced at the final figure.

"Forty three pounds altogether." She read.

He handed her two twenty pound notes and a ten pound note.

"Thank you. Would you like a bag?"

"One of those bright blue ones?"

"Yes."

"Yes please." He nodded.

With a smile, Nora bagged up the Duke's books and handed them to him. He took them with a small bow.

"Now are you well supplied, Nora? Warm enough?" He asked.

Nora blushed that a Duke was asking after her well-being.

"Yes thank you, Your Grace. My friend is due here any moment with supplies and I am well prepared with some lunch." She indicated to the covered plate beside the computer monitor. "May I recommend the restaurant up the hill named for one of your ancestors as an excellent place for pasties?"

He grinned.

"I shall certainly bear that in mind." He nodded. "And now before this snow all melts, which I am told it will start to do so within the hour, I must continue my incognito exploration of Castletown and return home before I am missed." He smiled at her warmly, bowed once more and Nora walked him to the door. "Will you be attending the lighting of the Christmas tree tomorrow evening, Nora?"

"Yes. The Secondhand Bookworm will be open until seven for the traditional *Shopping by candlelight*."

"Then I look forward to seeing you tomorrow evening. Good afternoon, Miss Nora Jolly."

"Good afternoon, Your Grace." Nora smiled.

His eyes twinkled slightly at her persistent propriety, he stepped up into the street and Nora watched him head off along the road, tall, handsome and very Duke-ey.

After a while she closed the door and headed back to the counter, deciding to keep the details of his visit to herself. She dropped into the swivel seat, wrote down his sale and then leaned back with a sigh, already beginning to dream of visiting a vast, endless library in the castle of a Duke.

6 THE SNOWMAN IN THE YARD

Humphrey arrived at two fifteen. Nora was still dreaming about the castle and the Duke's library when she saw him walk past the window, peering in. Tall, handsome and dressed casually but smartly, he still bore a resemblance to the dashing businessman who, until recently, had co-headed a top international corporation in London. Imogene, who ran the organic shop over the river, referred to Humphrey as Harvey Spector from the TV show *Suits* (she had a crush on both). Nora thought he was more of a Neal Caffery from *White Collar*. His dark hair was swept back under a black beanie hat but poked out and brushed the collar of his chunky, navy blue designer sweater. He also wore jeans, boots and a fine-wool scarf tied in a Parisian knot. He threw open the door.

"Are you warm enough?" Humphrey asked Nora.

"Well that's a first," Nora chuckled, thinking of her *'It's warm in here!'* tally chart.

He was still frowning as he closed the door behind him, his blue gaze locked with hers.

"It's deadly out there. What was Georgina thinking, sending you over here in this? If you catch a chill she'll never hear the end of it from me." He glowered, headed around the counter and wrapped Nora in a bear hug.

"Oh that's much better." Nora buried herself against his wonderfully woollen sweater. "Although you're quite cold yourself. Where's your coat?"

He swung a leg over the oil heater, drawing her to it too.

"I'm fine." He dismissed, rubbing her gloved hands and bare fingers with his.

"Men." She sighed, shaking her head.

"What's that delicious smell?" Humphrey sniffed the air.

"Phil dropped some pasties in." Nora indicated to the plate on the counter. "I'll heat them up in the microwave; that'll warm us both up."

"No, I'll do that." Humphrey insisted, placing a kiss on her cheek.

"Bread. Toast. Kisses. Everything is just that little bit better when it's French." She prodded his Parisian scarf knot, speaking with a French accent.

"Ah, *oui, oui*. So, French is it?" He arched an eyebrow meaningfully, glancing at Nora's lips.

"*Non, absolument pas*!" She prodded him backwards.

Humphrey scowled playfully and rubbed his nose against hers instead.

"So we really are Eskimos, now." Nora realised, untangled herself from him and sat back down on the swivel seat as he picked up the plate of pasties.

"These look perfect. I'm starving." He rubbed his flat stomach hungrily.

"How is Mrs Pickering? Is everyone in Piertown alright?" Nora remembered, concerned.

Humphrey nodded, heading for the kitchen.

"All fine. Mum was just having her cholesterol checked. Everyone else just had the sniffles and a few bunions. Tea?"

"Yes please." Nora smiled.

Half an hour later, Humphrey and Nora were on the last two pasties, having devoured two each with a mug of steaming tea. As Humphrey bit into his curried chicken pasty, Nora drained her mug.

"So, who do you think my one and only customer was?" She asked, nodding her head at the cash book.

Humphrey leaned forward, chewing his mouthful. He shrugged and mumbled something Nora couldn't make out.

"Yes, that's right." She nodded, pretending he had guessed it. "The Duke of Cole."

Humphrey choked on his pasty and reached for his tea. Since he had finished it, Nora had to run and make them a fresh cuppa after hitting, patting and rubbing his back until he was able to breathe again.

When she returned five minutes later, Humphrey had finished his pasty and was eyeing hers.

"You can have that one too if you like." Nora placed his mug before him. "Believe it or not, I'm finally full."

"Thanks" Humphrey took a bite from the last pasty, the other curried chicken.

"Four pasties. How do you keep so trim?" Nora teased, rubbing his stomach playfully.

He almost choked again so Nora handed him his tea.

"So, tell me about the Duke." Humphrey said when he had finally finished coughing and eaten the last of his pasty. He leaned his elbow in the counter top, searching her gaze suspiciously, and took a sip of tea.

Nora watched him fondly.

"Oh. You would have been insanely jealous, Mr Pickering. The Duke of Cole is *very* handsome, tall, polite and a great bibliophile who has invited me to a private visit of his library when his castle is finished and insisted that I call him James."

Humphrey's eyes narrowed as he listened.

"Hmm. Well I hope you told him I would be coming along too." He frowned.

"No." She said innocently. "But I shall insist."

His frowned lifted and he smiled broadly, dimples appearing each side of his mouth.

"That's okay then." He said and leaned forward to kiss her cheek again.

Nora let him, seeing as the town was deserted and it was unlikely they would have any more customers.

"By the way. Do you think you can close that letterbox? I can feel the cold from here." Nora suddenly remembered.

"What's wrong with it?" He squinted across the room.

"It's been jammed open for the last few weeks. I can't close it."

"Well, we can't have that." Humphrey stood up. He stretched, rotated both arms and then headed over to the door just as it opened, surprising them both.

"Merry Christmas!" A cackling voice greeted, followed by out of tune guitar playing and the beginning of '*Jingle Bells*'.

Humphrey stood stock still, staring mutely as the toothless Father Christmas from the day before leaned in and performed his carol out of tune and strumming so hard that one of his strings broke. Nora covered her mouth with both hands, trying desperately not to laugh.

The carol lasted for an excruciatingly long time but Humphrey seemed spell-bound. Towards the end Nora joined Humphrey, standing next to him and watching the performance until it concluded and the toothless Father Christmas bowed low, almost falling down the step.

Humphrey and Nora clapped.

"Thank you, kindly. Ah, thank you." The toothless Father Christmas appreciated, took off his red and white Father Christmas hat and held it out.

For a long moment Nora and Humphrey were distracted by his shining bald head. Humphrey then dug a hand into the pocket of his jeans.

"Thank you, sir." Humphrey counted out some change. "A welcome festive break from all our bookselling."

The toothless Father Christmas stared at him incredulously as Humphrey dropped some pound coins in his Santa hat.

"This 'ere town's abandoned." Toothless Father Christmas said. "No one else 'ere ta listen to me carols. Doubtful you got any customers. Shall I give ya ano'ver tooon?"

"Erm…thank you but we won't overwork you, sir." Humphrey smiled, ushering him onto the street. "Plus I have a letterbox in need of unjamming."

"Wha'?"

Toothless Father Christmas glanced back at the door.

"Merry Christmas then folks." He said, leered horribly at Nora and set off, strumming his out of tune guitar.

Humphrey shut the door, his shoulders shaking with laughter.

"What a lovely voice he had." Nora said with a smile. "And his carol was beautiful."

"Have you been at the Christmas sherry?" Humphrey winked.

"I would if we had some."

"I'll need to grab a few things from my van." Humphrey said. "Then when we close up I'll follow you home. What we having for dinner tonight?"

"You just ate four pasties!"

"And?" Humphrey shrugged, heading out the door and to his van.

Nora shook her head, checking the clock. It was almost ten past three and the light would be gone in an hour and a half. Georgina had said to close at three o'clock and Cara had already Skyped them a goodbye message which read:

'I'm outta here! Rubbish takings, my fingers and toes are numb and a drunk man just proposed to me. Have a great evening! Byeeeeeeeee. Xxxxxx'

Nora wasn't keen on driving home in the dark, even though she had noticed the snow was melting noticeably outside and Humphrey would be following her. The streets were beginning to look slushy and the roofs were dripping as the snow melted. Hugh was up the hill with his broom, examining the pavements on the opposite side of the square. Nora watched him attack some melting snow and sweep it furiously along to the kerb where it slopped unceremoniously into the gutter.

Humphrey reappeared with a box of screwdrivers and a can of WD40.

"It looks like Hugh is attempting to beautify Castletown." Nora pointed out.

"I'm not sure it will all melt before *Shopping by Candlelight* tomorrow but lingering snow will probably add to the Christmas charm." Humphrey said, crouching down before the door and locking it.

"Who knew you were so poetical?" Nora mused.

Humphrey huffed out a laugh.

"Thank you once again for the lovely paintwork, Humphrey."

"I wasn't convinced about Georgina's colour choice but it works." He admitted.

"I like it." Nora nodded, straightening a book called *'Cole Privies'* on one of the side shelves.

"Well that's what matters." Humphrey said seriously, squinting at the letterbox.

Nora smiled as she watched him, taking out her iPhone and putting on some more carols. She left him fixing the letterbox while whistling along to *'O come all ye faithful'* and made them both another cup of tea. In the kitchen she opened the door to the yard, noticing that none of the snow was melting in it since it was very sheltered and like a Victorian ice well.

While she stood pondering it, Humphrey appeared behind her, hands in the pockets of his jeans.

"Admit it. You really want to build a snowman." He said.

Nora turned.

"Alright. I do."

"Come on then." His lips stretched in a handsome smile.

"Really?"

"It's not often we get snowfall on the south coast of England these day, and at Christmas time too." He paused to take a sip of tea and passed Nora hers. "And it's been years since I've built one. Who cares if we're almost middle aged?"

"Speak for yourself." Nora chuckled. "We don't have any carrots, though."

"We'll improvise."

They drank their tea, examining the yard and discussing a plan of action. Humphrey then placed their empty mugs into the sink behind them and watched Nora step out onto the snow. It was at least four inches deep and made that delicious crunchy sound when her boots sunk partially into it. He followed her out and watched her gazing around in the muffled silence.

A snowball hit Nora's shoulder and she gasped.

"I see!" She exclaimed, watching Humphrey bend over to make another one, his shoulders shaking with silent laughter.

She quickly gathered handfuls from the snow at her feet and made a ball, ducking when Humphrey threw a second. Hers was a perfect aim to his chest.

"Right." He bent down for another.

Quickly, Nora made a second ball and moved backwards away from him.

He missed her again and she laughed at his expression of surprise, taking advantage of his shock at her quick deflection to throw her snowball at his stomach.

"You forget that I grew up with three brothers and a sister and we had numerous snowball fights. We still do." Nora reminded him.

"Is that so?" Humphrey walked towards her determinedly. "But I bet none of them did this."

"Did what?"

She gasped when he reached her and easily swept her up into his arms.

"Humphrey, that's cheating!" She objected as he dropped her into a snow drift.

He ducked when she lobbed a handful of gathered snow at him.

"Okay. You won." He said, holding his hand out to her.

She took it and with a jerk pulled him down so he fell in the snow beside her.

"Now we're equal." She dumped snow on his head.

"Unbelievable." He pulled her down and wrapped his arms around her, holding her close.

"I bet you're glad you left London and your high powered job for this." Nora was amused to see him on his back, covered in snow, in a mossy old yard at the back of his sister's bookshop.

Humphrey shrugged his strong shoulders, gazing up at the sky, thick with snow clouds.

"I wouldn't miss it for the world." He confided, seriously.

Nora smiled.

They finally decided it was too cold (and they were too *old*)to lay making snow angels on the snowy ground so clambered up and set to work making their snowman. The snow was beginning to melt in the yard now, dripping off the surrounding roofs and guttering but the fall on the ground was still perfect for shaping.

It took them a good half an hour to build a five foot tall snowman. Humphrey found two broken pieces of brickwork for eyes and a stick of wood for a nose. Nora added a row of stones for a smiling face and six down the front for buttons. A bush was growing in the corner of the yard so Humphrey sawed off two branches with his Swiss Army knife from his pocket and stuck them in the body for arms.

"It looks a little macabre." Nora admitted when they stood back to admire their work.

"Let's hope it won't become animated by the Great Intelligence." Humphrey said, referring to a Christmas TV special of '*Doctor Who*'.

Nora grimaced and nudged his arm.

"He needs a hat and scarf." She decided.

"He's not having mine. Nor yours." Humphrey said.

"We might have one in the lost property cupboard in the kitchen. I'll take a look."

When Nora returned, Humphrey had rearranged the stones in the snowman's mouth to point downwards, like an unhappy emoji.

"I found these." She said triumphantly.

Humphrey watched her place a red and yellow bobble hat on the snowman's head and a ladies flowery scarf around its neck.

"Truly hideous." He snorted, taking several photographs with his iPhone.

Nora posed beside the snowman and then she snapped several of Humphrey with it. They also took a couple of selfies with all three of them in the shot.

Laughing, they returned to the kitchen and closed up the yard.

"If I find him melted tomorrow I shall feel like the boy from Raymond Briggs' *The Snowman*." Nora knew.

When they returned to the front room, a man was peering into the shop through the door window. Nora unlocked the door.

"You have a book in the window." He said. "'*Christmas Books'* by Charles Dickens."

"Yes. It's a new copy. A Wordsworth edition."

"How much is it."

"Two pounds ninety-nine."

"I'll take it." He said. He followed Nora into the shop and nodded a hello to Humphrey behind the counter. "Afternoon."

"Good afternoon, sir." Humphrey smiled.

Nora reached in to the window display and picked up the book. She passed it to him and then leaned back in and switched off the electric branch of candles.

"My mum will enjoy this. She's just had an operation to remove a wart from the end of her nose. This will cheer her up." The man said.

Nora stared at him.

"I'm sure it will, sir." Humphrey agreed with a look at Nora.

"Have you been busy?" The man asked, digging in his pocket for his wallet. "Whew. It's warm in here."

"Yes, we've been very busy." Humphrey said, taking the five pound note.

"That's good to hear. The town is pretty dead out there but the pub's open now. That's the main thing."

Humphrey gave the man his change and handed him the book. When the customer had bid them goodbye and left, Humphrey grabbed a pen.

"Allow me." He said, leaning towards Nora's tally chart.

"Our only other customer." She sighed, shaking her head. "And he utters the magic phrase."

"What's your goal?"

"What do you mean?"

"Are you aiming for a specific total?"

"I hadn't thought of that."

"How about," Humphrey mused, his dark, straight eyebrows forming a serious line while he added a stripe to a tally, "if you reach five hundred before Christmas Day, you treat yourself to a mince pie."

"Humphrey. I must have eaten three dozen mince pies in the last two weeks!" Nora objected.

"Alright then. How about, if you *don't* reach five hundred before Christmas Day, you and I have to join the Christmas Midnight Swim in the outdoor pool by the car park."

"Are you out of your mind?!" Nora gaped.

"No." He turned back to her. "Not only will it make you welcome as many '*it's warm in here*' comments as possible between now and Christmas Eve, but I'd love to see your face if you lose. And your lovely curves."

"Those people are *crazy*, going swimming in the outdoor pool in the middle of winter."

"It's heated." Humphrey pointed out.

"The water might be. Not the surrounding *air*." She shuddered.

"I dare you." He challenged seriously.

Nora sighed.

"Alright then. *Sadist*." She muttered.

Humphrey looked pleased.

"Excellent. The game is afoot."

"Whew, it's warm in here." Nora said, fanning out her jumpers.

He gave her an ironic look and she chuckled.

"You're right though. It will reverse the effect."

"No cheating." Humphrey warned.

"I promise."

At that moment, the door opened again, letting in a blast of cool air and a frozen 'Monster Munch' crisp bag (Hugh was obviously too busy battling snow to clean up the local litter). Nora turned.

"Hiiiiiiii!" A familiar voice greeted smoothly.

Nora groaned inside when she recognised The Terminator but then she smiled brightly.

"Harry." She greeted cheerfully, watching him step inside, closing the door behind him. "Hello."

"Hi Nora!" Harry returned eagerly.

Humphrey looked bemused.

"Hello, Harry."

"Alright, Humphrey." Harry nodded, his attention remaining to Nora.

"How do you find the temperature in here, Harry?" Nora asked innocently.

Humphrey choked on a laugh which he covered up with a cough.

"Oh, a welcome break from the cold." Harry said.

"Hmm." Nora mused. "And how would you describe it?" She persisted, ignoring Humphrey pointedly clearing his throat.

"Lovely and toasty." The Terminator said, slightly bemused. "Is your heating playing up or something?"

"No." Nora sighed and joined Humphrey behind the counter.

"How can we help, Harry?" Humphrey asked.

"Any new Beano or Dandy annuals?" He asked, standing at the counter with his chest sticking out.

Nora shook her head.

"Sorry, no, not since last week."

"My nephew's collecting them." Harry told Humphrey, still not looking at him.

"So I heard." Humphrey said with a small smile.

"We have you on our database. If any come in we'll let you know." Nora assured Harry.

"Thanks, Nora." Harry appreciated, picking up a large tome from the counter and flexing his bicep with it.

Nora arched an eyebrow.

"Are you open late tomorrow night for *Shopping by Candlelight*?" Harry asked, flicking through the book he held.

Nora saw him grimace at the full page plates showing intricate medieval autopsy examples.

"Yes. Until seven." She nodded.

"Excellent. I shall be down for the lighting of the Christmas tree. They're handing out mulled wine. I can bring you a glass if you like."

"That's nice of you Harry but I shall be doing that." Humphrey said meaningfully.

Harry smiled and shrugged his broad shoulders.

"I can bring you one too, Humphrey." He offered.

"Or I can bring *you* one." Humphrey returned, pointedly.

They stared at one another. Nora looked between them.

"Oh! Is that the time?!" She exclaimed, making Humphrey jump. "I'm sorry Harry but we need to close up and get going before it's dark." She said, drawing his attention from Humphrey.

"Do you need a lift home?" Harry asked, watching her walk around the counter.

Humphrey stared at Harry disbelievingly.

"No thank you. I have my car and Humphrey will follow me to Little Cove." Nora glanced back over her shoulder at Humphrey and winked.

"Okay." Harry shadowed her to the door which she opened. "Have a nice evening." He said, staring at her as he stepped up. "*I'll be back.*"

Nora bit back a smile, waved him off and closed and locked the door behind him.

"Is he always like that?" Humphrey glowered.

"Pretty much." Nora admitted.

"I'll have to keep an eye on him."

Nora admired the fixed letterbox which was now firmly shut.

"Lots of admirers you have here." Humphrey mused, grimly.

"All the *maddos*." Nora pointed out, although she thought fleetingly about the Duke of Cole and her lips stretched in a secret smile.

While they cashed up, Nora allowed the singing Father Christmas to parachute a circuit around the ceiling much to Humphrey's amusement. They said goodbye to their snowman in the yard, turned off all the lights, not including the Christmas tree lights on the tree attached to the outside front of the shop (Georgina said they should keep that on), unplugged the oil heater, grabbed their belongings, turned off the electric branch of candles in the window, set the alarm and left the shop, locking up behind them.

"A nice day after all." Nora decided, turning the key in the door. "It's a shame bookshops can't just be places where the owner or manager sits and reads all day."

"That's not how it works, sadly." Humphrey grinned, taking hold of her gloved hand.

Nora snuggled against his arm as they walked a few steps along the road. She shivered a little, worried he wasn't wearing a coat, despite Humphrey looking quite at ease and comfortable sporting just a thick navy blue designer sweater and jeans in the freezing cold.

"What are your plans tonight?" He asked her.

"Home, bath, dinner, reading. Don't let Georgina know the latter will take place on my kindle." Nora winked.

Hugh was in the process of removing his 'ROAD CLOSED' sign and stopped when he spotted them.

"Was it worth opening up your daft shop, then?" Hugh asked mockingly.

Nora and Humphrey looked at him.

"Yes!" Nora defended.

Hugh shook his head disbelievingly.

"*Books*." He scoffed, shrugged and turned back to his sign, dragging it to the kerb while muttering.

Nora and Humphrey glanced at one another.

They stopped at the estate agents to peer in the illuminated window.

"Anything catch your eye?" Humphrey asked.

"They're all lovely but well out of my price range." Nora nodded. "They have my requirements on file. Jeannette said she'll let me know if one of the smaller flats above an antique shop up the hill comes on the market. Possibly in the new year." She decided not to mention the possible acquisition of the Duke of Cole's flat above a future Fudge Pantry. Humphrey might turn a Grinch-shade of green!

"That'd be good." Humphrey nodded. "Your own place again."

"You should find a place of your own in Cole, too." She reminded him.

"All the while my sister cooks for me and washes my clothes?"

"Fair enough." Nora shook her head, chuckling.

"Once my apartment in London has sold I'll purchase something local." He gave Nora a thoughtful look.

"There are some nice properties in Piertown if you plan to settle here."

Humphrey remained still, watching her thoughtfully as she continued on, until she stopped and held her hand out towards him, smiling.

"Sounds great." He mumbled, catching up in a couple of easy strides, encircling an arm around her shoulders before threading his fingers with hers.

They continued along the short street to the kerbside, crossing the small road and casting a customary dark look at the Indian restaurant as they did so. Memories of the many blocked drain events due to the restaurant workers pouring oil down the drains would forever linger.

"I like the idea of living just up the road from The Secondhand Bookworm." Nora mused, her thoughts lingering on the delightful idea of a little fudge-smelling lounge by the private castle entrance. "It would be nice to be within walking distance of the Catholic Church at the top of the hill, too. I enjoy popping in and lighting prayer candles. I also find the shrine of the Duke of Cole's Elizabethan Catholic martyr ancestor a source of admiration. The Earl preferred to have his head lopped off than denounce the ancient Faith. It's like he's lying there, holding his head, saying, *when they come for you, Nora, just let them swing.*"

Humphrey nudged her arm.

"You and your future plans for martyrdom." He chuckled. "Well, being within walking distance from The Secondhand Bookworm too also means you can nip down and borrow a book if you wake up in the middle of the night and can't get back to sleep."

"In my pyjamas?" Nora pulled a face.

"Or a fluffy white onesie with bunny ears?" He wagered a guess.

Nora's mouth quirked.

"Plus, no more driving along the dual carriageways every day back to Little Cove, especially in weather like this." Humphrey pointed out, frowning.

"Aw, you're sweet when you worry about me."

"*Sweet*?!" Humphrey looked insulted.

"Alright. *Dashing*." Nora amended.

He kissed the tip of her cold nose.

"Now that I like, Nora." He decided, cheerfully.

They reached the corner at the end of the street, passed the closed post office and crossed the road towards the bridge.

"Incoming." Nora grimaced.

Humphrey stared at the lone figure ahead of them.

"Another admirer?" He asked, sarcastically.

She prodded his stomach.

White-Lightning Joe spotted them. He was plodding over the bridge that crossed the river, having topped up his supply of White Lightning cider from the Co-op.

"Hee-looo Nora." He greeted wearily.

Nora's attention was drawn to an enormous Benedictine crucifix hanging from his neck and in the middle of his chest.

"Hello, Joe. How are you?"

"Oh I'm sick of Kenny in the Co-op. He's such a git." Joe grimaced bitterly. "Said I could only have one bottle of cider because that *hag* Jenny has put a limit on what I buy now." His bleary eyes then brightened hopefully. "You wouldn't do me a favour would you? Can you buy me a bottle of cider?"

"Er…sorry, no." Nora shook her head.

"Oh go on Nora. Be your best friend forever." He persisted, glancing at Humphrey suspiciously.

"I'd best not. Georgina would have my head."

"You're not on the clock though are you?"

"I'm afraid so." Nora fibbed, making to continue on.

"What about your brother? Would you lend me a quid?" He asked Humphrey eagerly.

"I'm not her brother." Humphrey pointed out.

"Oh. Haha. Yeah I was looking at the way you were cuddling and I thought…*incest*? Hahaha." Joe sniggered.

"I'm Nora's boyfriend." Humphrey said firmly.

Joe's shoulders drooped.

"Yeah, I was afraid of that." He said and his bottom lip trembled. "All the good ones are taken."

Humphrey and Nora watched him turn and stare woefully over the side of the wall into the fast running waters of the river beside them.

Fearing he was about to launch himself into the water, Nora tugged on his sleeve.

"That's a lovely crucifix, Joe." She pointed out hastily.

"What?" White-Lightning Joe looked down and shrugged. "Oh, yeah. Protects me from evil." He nodded. "Huh. Might be nice if it protected me from hags like Jenny and gits like Kenny."

Nora could tell Humphrey was desperately controlling his urge to laugh so she smiled politely.

"Well, we'd best be off."

"Okaaaaay." Joe sighed glumly.

Although Nora was reluctant to leave him pondering the murky waters of the river, her toes were numb and Humphrey's lips looked like they might turn blue, so she waved goodbye and they turned away to continue on.

"Hey Nora?!" Joe's voice sailed after them.

Humphrey and Nora glanced back.

"I've got some books to sell. Can I bring them in tomorrow?"

"Okay. That should be fine." Nora nodded.

Joe grinned stupidly and stuck up both thumbs, forgetting he was carrying a brown bag of cider. It dropped to the floor with a thud and began to roll towards the kerb.

"Thanks, Nora!" He called as he plodded after it swearing.

Humphrey snorted, shaking his head. Nora sighed.

"You attract all sorts don't you?" Humphrey teased.

"It seems so." She said with a poke in his ribs.

Humphrey laughed.

"Poor fellow." He looked back to see Joe retrieve his bag and shuffle away, stooping.

"Yes. It is sad. Joe was always a little odd but being made redundant from his job recently seems to have sent him right over the edge. He needs another job really but can't get one." Nora explained.

"I wonder if there's anything I can find for the little Grinch." Humphrey mused.

Nora looked at his handsome side profile.

"That's kind of you." She said and kissed his cheek.

"I'll have to suggest finding employment for more madmen." He decided, kissing her back.

Nora laughed, threading her gloved fingers with his.

The short term car park was as empty as it had been when Nora had arrived that morning. Even the snow plough had gone. Most of the snow had melted on the tarmac but Humphrey scraped off the ice on Nora's car windows while she heated up the engine. He checked her wheels and lights.

"I'll follow you to the turn off into Little Cove and continue on to Piertown." He said, leaning his elbows on the door at her opened window.

"Thank you, Humphrey."

He looked as though he wanted to say something, but changed his mind.

"Speak to you tomorrow." He said, leaned close and pressed a lingering kiss on her cheek.

"Have a good evening."

"You too."

Nora watched him turn and jog back to where he had parked his van while she waited and warmed up her car. He pulled into the car park five minutes later and Nora set off first.

The drive to Little Cove was slow and careful with banks of melting snow lining each carriageway.

Nora smiled every time she glanced in her rear view mirror and could make out Humphrey's silhouette in the front of his van. He was like a dashing, devoted bodyguard. She grimaced to herself, wondering if she would ever think of him as *more* than a brother or a best friend. She had better make her mind up soon!

Because of the threats of snow and ice there was hardly any traffic on the roads from Castletown to the turning that wound down into the seaside village of Little Cove.

As she approached it she pressed her hazard lights as goodbye, Humphrey flashed his full beams and she manoeuvred down the road, just as it started to snow.

With a thoughtful smile Nora remembered the snowman in the yard of The Secondhand Bookworm and hoped it would live throughout the night.

7 THE GRINCH WHO STOLE THE COLE BOOKS

Cara arrived at The Secondhand Bookworm the same time as Nora the next day. They stood together outside on the mushy, half-frozen pavement while Nora rummaged in her bag for her keys. Cara, who had a big, healthy appetite, munched an enormous cookie she had bought on her way over to Castletown.

"Where are they?!" Nora frowned as her hand became buried under her purse, two Twix bars, her Kindle, a pack of tissues, three books, her iPhone, a bag of sweets and various other unnecessary objects she carried about with her (typical late-twenties woman).

"Mmm, mmm, mmm?" Cara asked as she chewed.

"What?" Nora laughed, finally holding up the keys in triumph. "Found them."

They unlocked the door, hurried inside to turn off the alarm and Nora flicked on the lights. It was freezing. Nora fired up the oil heater, popping her iPhone into the pocket of her jeans.

"Oh my goodness. How are we going to survive today? It's like Iceland." Nora grumbled.

"Don't you mean *Greenland*?" Cara corrected.

"Greenland?"

"It's a common mistake. Iceland is actually warmer than Greenland." Cara said, taking off her coat. "Greenland is nearer to the North Pole than Iceland."

"So Father Christmas comes from Greenland?" Nora deduced.

"He must do."

They both looked up at Santa, motionless in his parachute above them.

"Perhaps we'll let him sing one song. *Later*." Cara decided and they laughed.

"I must go and check on mine and Humphrey's child." Nora then said, grabbing the shop keys and heading off to the kitchen.

Cara gawped, following quickly.

"What's this?"

"You'll see." Nora opened up the kitchen.

A blast of cold air hit her. Because the kitchen was simply a very small, cheap extension with a Pyrex roof there wasn't a shred of insulation.

Nora cringed.

"Lunch in the front today, I think."

"I doubt we'll have many customers." Cara agreed.

"And usually '*Shopping by Candlelight*' here is a bit of a flop. But Georgina is persistent." Nora unlocked and opened the door to the outside yard. They both peered out. "Oh dear." Nora said sadly.

"What the…?" Cara grimaced.

The yard was a terrible slush-fest. Where Nora and Humphrey's snowman had stood was a two foot high lump of snow, with sticks and branches on the wet, mossy floor around it and the bobble hat, scarf and stones unceremoniously on top.

"I'll inform Humphrey. He didn't make it." Nora sighed, digging out her iPhone.

"I'm sorry for your loss." Cara commiserated.

They returned to the front where Nora shrugged out of her down Parka jacket, reluctant to relinquish its snug fur hood but confident her many layers beneath would keep her relatively warm. She had dressed in a selection of her skiwear that day, revealing a black and white fur lined ski hoodie on top of a thermal sweater and a fleece jumper. Cara wore two knitted jumpers and thermal leggings under her jeans.

"It's going to be a long day and a cold evening staying open until seven tonight. I hope Roger dresses warmly enough." Nora frowned with concentration, typing a text to Humphrey.

"He's due at eleven?"

"Yes."

"I'll head over to Seatown when he arrives." Cara nodded, starting to fill up the till with the various denominations of money.

Nora pressed send, swiped her screen off and placed her iPhone back into her pocket.

"I'll turn on the lights upstairs, check the shop is all as it should be and then start putting the goods outside."

Cara nodded, throwing a bag of five pence pieces into the till tray.

Apart from the rest of The Secondhand Bookworm feeling like *Greenland*, everything was indeed as it should be. Nora had a nice look around, enjoying the peace.

Humphrey replied to her text.

'I'm in mourning xx'

Once she was back in the front room, Nora opened the front door.

"Morning, Nora Jolly."

"Hello, Mr Howard." Nora greeted one of Castletown's councillors.

Mr Howard was a large, shuffling, squat man in his seventies who had once served as mayor for Castletown. He had a bushy white moustache and small round black eyes, an olive complexion, wore a small green hat and reminded Nora of '*Mr Slow*' from '*The Mr Men*' books by Roger Hargreaves. He was accompanied by Mrs Redworth, the current Events Coordinator for the town.

"Would you be able to put this poster in a prominent place in your front window please?" Mrs Redworth asked hopefully.

"Yes that should be alright."

"It has information about all of the events taking place in Castletown leading up to Christmas." She explained.

"The Duke will be turning on the Christmas tree lights this evening and we hope our flash advertising about that on every form of social media will have the desired effect and draw many more people here. Then they can see all our posters and signs about the town advertising the rest of our Christmas festivities."

Nora took the poster and examined the contents.

The roads leading into Castletown were due to close at one o'clock that lunchtime to accommodate the 'thousands of people' who usually attended '*Shopping by Candlelight*'. More were expected this year due to the Duke now in residence and making his first (or second, Nora thought smugly) public appearance.

There was a lantern-making workshop in Market Street from five o'clock that evening and those who made lanterns would follow a nativity procession to the square for the turning on of the Christmas tree lights. Children would be able to enjoy traditional Victorian rides including the chair-o-plane and hook-a-duck by the river and meet Father Christmas to receive gifts.

Nora knew from experience that with all the outside festivities taking place, people didn't seem to want to enter a musty old bookshop. The same would happen on Saturday which advertised an eclectic feast of music, shopping, theatre, visual arts, Christmas lights and outdoor activities for the whole family.

There would be carol singers, a hog roast, a live nativity and the 'Christmas Farmers Turkey Market' all day in the square which stole all the book punters. Over fifty stalls included products such as handmade festive soap, bespoke brooches and scarves, jewellery, bed linen and books (the cheek!) as well as live turkeys and fresh farming produce. Nora grimaced to see the Morris Dancers and a local Mummers drama group had been booked for the whole of Saturday too, fortunately down Market Street. Her cousin Felix was due to start working with her that day and she expected he would be delighted.

"Lovely." Nora nodded politely.

"Do you need any tac?"

"No, we have plenty." Nora assured them.

"Thank you. Have a good day." Mrs Redworth smiled and Mr Howard tipped his hat.

Nora watched them scurry off to the estate agents next door.

The sound of distant, slightly muffled clip-clopping caught her attention and Nora looked up to see Sherrie, the Lady-Santa from 'Kiddies Boutique' down Market Street, heading towards her with Twinkle the dog at her heels. She wore the same get-up as before with her short fur-edged Santa dress that caused a man driving past to almost swerve and squash a pigeon.

"Hello, again!" Lady-Santa greeted cheerfully.

"Hello." Nora smiled; amazed Lady-Santa was wearing stilettos on the icy paths and hadn't fallen over.

"Any work colleagues in today who might be interested in some wonderful Christmas promotions on baby clothes?"

"Er…"

"Oh, hold that thought! Evie from the estate agents has just arrived and her sister had a baby last month. Back later. Come on, Twinkle!" She sped off at an impressive speed, following Mr Howard and Mrs Redworth next door. Twinkle shuffled slowly after her, pausing to sniff a pile of snow-slush.

Nora considered the poster from Mrs Redworth.

"Morris dancers." She groaned, rolled her eyes heavenwards and then held suddenly still.

She froze, staring up, as an ice cold feeling doused her from head to toe and the hair on the back of her neck stood on end. Without speaking, she backed into the shop, turned around and ran silently towards Cara.

Cara looked up from writing the date in the cashbook as her writing squiggled in all directions from Nora shaking her arm.

"What are you doing?" Cara laughed. Seeing Nora's expression, her eyes widened. "What is it?"

Silently, Nora pointed towards the door, finally finding her voice.

"S…s…s…spider!" She gasped.

"Whaaaaaaat?!"

"SPIDER!" Nora repeated in horror.

"Where?" Cara winced.

"In the corner at the top of the door…on the left…uuuuughhhhh!" Nora pulled the fur hood of her ski-hoodie over her head, wrapping her arms around herself while shuddering.

"Is it big?" Cara watched Nora climb onto the swivel chair.

"That…is…an…*understatement!*" Nora drew her legs up from the floor and closed her eyes. "As you can tell, I have arachnophobia!"

Cara walked around the counter and headed to the door to investigate. A moment later she was back beside

Nora, grasping her upper arm so hard that Nora squealed.

"That is *MASSIVE*!" Cara cried.

"What are we going to do?" Nora gasped.

"I don't know!!" Cara wailed and they held onto each other grimacing and shuddering.

"Good morning! It's warm in here." A man's voice exclaimed.

Nora and Cara turned to see their first customer stroll in through the open doorway. When he saw them behind the counter clutching each other, he stared.

"Do you mind spiders, sir?" Cara blurted out.

The man blinked.

"*Spiders*?" He repeated.

Both Cara and Nora nodded, mutely.

"No." He assured them, bemused.

"Would you mind getting one for us?" Cara implored.

The dipped his head.

"My pleasure, ladies. Where is it then?"

When Cara let go of Nora, Nora spun slightly around in the swivel seat before she moved her feet back to the ground and, still clutching each other, they moved slowly around the counter, pointing to the door.

"Top right hand corner of the doorway." Nora pointed.

"Alright. I'll deal with it."

Cara and Nora held onto each other, Nora wincing at Cara's grip on her upper arm. They watched the customer walk back to the open door. He squinted upwards, held still and stared.

"Okay. That's quite a monster."

Nora and Cara nodded.

"It sure is!" They both said in unison.

Not wanting to look as petrified as them, the customer squared his shoulders and scooped up a large black spikey lump, disappearing with it in his hands out into the street.

"How could he?!" Cara exclaimed.

"Insanity." Nora shuddered.

"I have to see what he does with it." Cara dragged Nora over to the door.

Nora remained hidden in her hoodie, cringing and grimacing. They peered around the side of the door and saw the man ushering the enormous black creature along the path. The spider scuttled up onto some lingering snow at the edge of the kerb and then plopped down into the gutter. The man came back, wincing.

"That was big." He said.

"You're very brave, sir." Nora shuddered, walking backwards into the shop.

"Thanks." He shrugged and stepped down, closing the door behind him. "Glad I could be of some service."

"I don't know what we would have done all day with *that* sitting there." Cara said.

"It could have dropped down my neck." Nora lamented.

"Eeeeeew!" Cara squealed and they returned behind the counter.

Nora kept her hood up, digging out her iPhone when she heard a text message arrive. Cara spoke with the customer who had saved them from the spider as he requested any books about 1930's film directors.

While Cara took the customer upstairs, Nora sat back in the swivel chair, still shuddering. She read a new message from Humphrey, messaged him back with the spider story and then turned on the computer in case Seatown had sent any Skype messages. She grabbed one of her Twix bars from her bag, taking out the bag of sweets too.

Cara found Nora munching happily, the sugar having helped her recover her disposition, while typing to Seatown when she came back downstairs.

"*Spiderman's* lost in the film section." Cara said, helping herself to some sweets.

"Hopefully he'll buy a few books." Nora nodded and held up a piece of paper. "Some book requests from Seatown. I'll go on the hunt."

"Okay." Cara nodded and pulled Nora out of the chair to take her place. "Take a walkie-talkie in case I need you to look for something while you're up there."

"Good idea." Nora nodded. "Ugh, that spider."

"Ugh, I know." Cara grimaced.

Popping the last of her second Twix finger into her mouth with another shiver, Nora grabbed both walkie-talkies and handed one to Cara. They switched them on.

"…AND THE CUSTOMER REQUIRES BEING PICKED UP FROM THE CORNER OF MARKET STREET. OVER!" A loud voice shouted out of the walkie-talkies, making them jump.

"ROGER THAT! I'VE PICKED HER UP BEFORE. SHE'S A HARPY." Came the reply.

Nora choked on her Twix mouthful. Cara shook her head, changing channels on their devices so only static could be heard.

"Blooming taxis." She sighed, handing Nora one.

"I wonder who the harpy is." Nora mused.

Cara pulled a worried face.

She turned to the computer to check the emails leaving Nora heading off into the back room to look for two nautical book titles. The room was lovely and tidy. Yet another text message arrived so she read it as she walked in front of the nautical section of books, hunting for the titles.

'Poor you!' Humphrey had written in reply to her spider escapade story. *'I'll be over at about six to take your mind off it xx'*

Nora smiled.

'See you then x' She typed quickly, popped her phone away and checked the last few nautical shelves.

"No, didn't think so." She said to herself and set off for the staircase to hunt for a few gardening books in the front room of the next floor.

When Nora returned empty handed ten minutes later, Cara was putting the second postcard spinner outside on the pavement to join the other. The free maps box and black cheap paperback boxes had been topped up and put out too and the flickering electric branches of candles turned on in the window.

"We sold some postcards." Cara called in through the doorway.

"Wonderful!" Nora nodded. She dropped down into the swivel seat. "No luck on any of those book requests."

"Shame." Cara shrugged. "We should have some weights for these spinners. I'm always worried the brakes will fail and they'll roll into the road, or a gust of wind will blow them over."

"I agree." Nora nodded, typing to Betty and Jane who were working in Seatown that day that she couldn't find any of their requests. "Oh, I've got an idea!" She hit send and spun around to face Cara who had her hand up the parachuting Santa's shorts. "Please don't."

"Just one song?" Cara begged, switching him on.

Nora groaned as Father Christmas set off across the ceiling among the paperchains, singing.

"What was your idea?" Cara asked.

"Hmm." Nora glared at Santa but continued. "One of the sandbags split a few weeks ago; all the hessian had rotted. So I dumped the sand in a bucket under the worktop in the kitchen. We could fill up a few blue carrier bags with the sand and use them as weights on the legs of the postcard spinners."

"Oooh, *sand puddings*!" Cara agreed enthusiastically. "I like it!"

Nora chuckled.

"I'll make some now!" Cara decided, unhooked a few shiny blue carriers, grabbed some packaging tape and headed off for the kitchen. "I'll make some tea, too!"

"Thanks!" Nora appreciated with a smile.

Her smile faded as the door opened, swung against the wall with a crash and a cider-scented blast of arctic air preceded the arrival of White-Lightning Joe. He was crumpled, stooped and bleary-eyed as usual, carrying a white carrier bag and smiling oddly.

"Heeee-loooo, Nora." He greeted, shuffling down the step. "Eeeeep!" He staggered slightly. "Always misjudge that one. Ha-ha."

Nora remembered he had told her he intended to come in that day to sell some books so she smiled warily, bracing herself.

"Good morning." She greeted.

"Hehehe. Mind if I er…erm, eeeep…have a browse?" He asked, eyes darting to the Cole section opposite the door.

"No, of course not." Nora said, surprised, and watched him shuffle over to his old regular haunt.

For several years White-Lightning Joe had collected books and pamphlets about Castletown but had sold most of them to The Secondhand Bookworm after he had been made redundant. Before then, he had always annoyed Nora several times a week by lingering in the Cole section, occasionally purchasing a new arrival or telling her about local history and purchasing for his collection of books when he had money to spare. Nora supposed he was now back to reminisce.

The Cole section was presently packed with some interesting titles with almost a shelf of Castletown history (albeit about twenty-five duplicate town guides took up a lot of room from a collection of several thousand Georgina had purchased from the tourist information centre when it had closed in November). So Nora left Joe browsing.

After a few moments had passed she almost jumped out of her skin when White-Lightning Joe suddenly darted towards the door, yanked it open and ran away, slamming it shut behind him hard.

"What on earth?" Nora was momentarily baffled.

She remained staring at the door for a long moment until it opened again. A woman stood on the step, wrapped in several shawls with a large pink bobble hat squashed on her head.

"It's warm in here!" She exclaimed loudly.

Smiling happily, Nora turned and drew another line on her tally chart, wincing slightly at the thought of a horrific midnight Christmas swim. She remembered 'Spiderman' had said the phrase too when he had arrived so she quickly added another.

"Good morning. Can I help?" Nora asked the lady politely.

"I doubt it. I've got Cotard delusion." She said morosely.

"Er…oh dear." Nora sympathised blankly, making a mental note to herself to Google what that was.

"I'm not completely dead yet, though." The woman assured with a dramatic sigh. "But the purification's started."

"Er…"

The woman stopped before the counter.

"Fortunately it's odourless."

"Oh. That's good." Nora smiled weakly.

"Hmm. But as none of us really exist it's not all bad." She insisted firmly.

Nora just blinked at her.

"We're a bookshop." Nora then said stupidly.

The woman stared.

"Yes. I know that. I'm looking for a book about pruning. Plants, not myself. We may all be inhabited by other beings but we still must eat, drink and prune our plants."

"Okay…" Nora cleared her throat. "Well, we have a section on gardening books."

"Wonderful. May I leave this here while I go and have a browse?" The woman asked, taking a small brown bag out of her handbag. "It's very delicate and I don't want to drop it around books."

"What is it?" Nora asked warily.

The woman just smiled and handed it to her.

"Which way to the gardening books?"

"Back there and up the stairs into the first front room."

"Thank you." The woman smiled and headed off.

Nora stared at the paper bag she held. After a long moment she peeked inside. She then shook her head and sighed, placing the bag of glass Christmas tree baubles onto the counter just as the phone began to ring.

"Good morning, The Secondhand Book….worm." Nora's voice trailed off as her ear was filled with loud, heavy breathing.

"Hello? Hello? Who's that?" Mr Hill's familiar voice asked.

Nora bit her lip.

"It's Nora, Mr Hill." Nora replied.

"Paula. It's Mr Hill." Mr Hill breathed.

"Hello, Mr Hill." Nora said, tightly.

"Nora. In your history section, would you happen to have a copy of '*Eleanor: April Queen of Aquitaine*' by Douglas Boyd?" He asked. "In the back room there."

Nora resisted saying she knew where both the book and the history section were located because he had asked her about them only two days ago.

"I'll have a look for you, Mr Hill." She said, regretting not having kept the book reserved for him after all.

"Fourth shelf down to the left of the door, in the middle of the shelf." He said quickly, followed by loud breathing.

Nora winced.

"Okay, I'll have a look." She said, feeling like she was in the 'Groundhog Day' movie, and headed into the back room.

The sound of the ripping and pulling of packaging tape accompanied by the kettle boiling could be heard coming from the kitchen. Nora imagined Cara inside making blue sand puddings.

"Can you see it there, lad?!" Mr Hill demanded in Nora's ear so she edged the receiver away, shaking her head.

She frowned at the history section, counted the four shelves down and saw the book that she herself had put away yesterday.

"Yes, I have it Mr Hill." Nora said, pulling it out.

"How much is it priced at?" He asked.

Nora needn't have opened the front cover. She knew the price off by heart.

"It's ten pounds Mr Hill." She replied.

"Ten pounds is it, Nora?" He shouted.

"Yes." Nora winced.

"Hmm, hmmm, ah, hmm. Well, it is a lovely book and I've been meaning to read it for some years." He deliberated.

Nora shook her head, bemused.

"Very well. I think I shall purchase the copy of '*Eleanor: April Queen of Aquitaine*' by Douglas Boyd. I am presently in Seatown so I shall come over this afternoon." He explained.

Nora's shoulders drooped.

"Okay, Mr Hill. It's *Shopping by Candlelight* this evening so it will be quite busy." She said in a futile endeavour of deterring him.

There was a confused silence. Followed by several coughs.

"I shall arrive in Castletown at about four o'clock this afternoon, Nora and complete my purchase. I have spoken to Georgina who said I can write a ten pound cheque for the book. I look forward to seeing you then, b-bye!" He said hastily and the line promptly went dead.

"So! You already knew the price? Of course you did." Nora sighed and headed off to the front room when she heard the front door close.

When she entered the room, Nora saw White-Lightning Joe standing at the counter, wide eyed and breathing rapidly.

"Oh, heee-loooo, Nora. Eeeeep!" He held up his white carrier bag. "Those books I said I wanted to sell."

"Oh. Yes." Nora nodded and dropped Mr Hill's book under the counter by the reserved section. "Shall I take a look?"

He shuffled uncomfortably and went red in the face.

"Ha-ha, yes sure, sure thing, here, let me." He flustered and drew out three Cole books.

Nora took them.

"The last few from my collection." Joe said, reddening. "I'm reluctant to let them go but…eeeeeee!"

"Oh dear. Yes, I understand." Nora opened the first one which was a red bound history of the Dukes of

Castletown. She glanced at the Cole section. "I think we already have one of these."

White-Lightning Joe made a strangling noise before coughing and spluttering.

"Oh! Oh but you could always do with one more, couldn't you?! Oh go on, Nora, it's quite rare."

"Yes I know it is. Of course we'll buy it from you." She saw that the previous pencil price inside had been rubbed out messily and seemed a little damp. With a small nagging feeling in the back of her mind she considered the other two, also books about Castletown, before nodding and looking at Joe who seemed to be holding his breath as he grasped the counter top before him, his knuckles white. "I can offer you twenty pounds for these." She said.

"Done!" He almost shouted and held out his hand.

Nora smiled uncertainly, opened the till and offered him a crisp twenty pound note.

"Thanks, Nora!" He ran for the door. "I'll come back later with some more! Bye!"

Nora stared as he disappeared into the street, slamming the door behind him. She then looked at the books just as Cara came into the front carrying two steaming mugs of tea.

"I've made the sand puddings so the postcard spinners will be safe." She announced cheerfully.

"Well done. Thank you." Nora watched the mug of tea plop in front of her. She picked up a pencil and headed for the Cole section to match the prices of White-Lightning Joe's books, ducking as Santa flew past. "Oh my goodness, I didn't even notice him the whole time I've been out here."

"That's because the batteries are running out and his voice is a lot quieter." Cara laughed, disappearing back to the kitchen to collect the sand puddings.

Nora searched for the duplicate Castletown books but couldn't locate them so she priced them up from memory, writing over the wet pencil smudges where the previous markings had been. She was frowning over them blankly when the phone began to ring again.

Nora ran around the counter and grabbed it.

"It's me!" Georgina's voice sailed out of the receiver, sounding bright and less bunged-up.

"Oh, hello!" Nora greeted, sitting down in the swivel seat.

"How's it going?"

"A little bit quiet." Nora confessed.

"To be expected. Hopefully it will pick up later. Fluffy, that's not edible! Now, I'm heading over to be there at about three. I've got the Penguin Mug rep coming to discuss stocking the Penguin book jacket mugs. Then I'll head off to Seatown and attempt to start salvaging the paperwork in the office. Could you please go over to the delicatessens and order me fifty mince pies? I'm afraid they might run out before I get there and I want to be able to pick them up on Christmas Eve."

"Okay." Nora agreed.

"Is Cara there?"

"She's just collecting her sand puddings."

"What?" Georgina sounded amused.

"It's a long story." Nora said.

"Okay well you can tell me about it this afternoon if you remember. Humphrey said he'll be over there for six. Hopefully the last hour of *Shopping by Candlelight* will be busy for the three of you; hence the extra man-power, but I doubt it."

"I'm going to be optimistic." Nora decided.

"That's the spirit." Georgina approved.

They said their goodbyes and hung up as Cara came back into the front.

"They're brilliant!" Nora exclaimed.

"Aren't they!" Cara agreed, holding up the two medium-sized blue lumps. "I'll put one each in front of the wheels of both spinners and then I'll be able to relax."

Nora chuckled, watching her open the door and set about positioning them carefully.

"By the way," Nora called, leaning on the counter as she watched Cara in the doorway. "Do you know what Cotard delusion is?"

"Oh that's a rare mental illness." Cara answered cheerfully.

"What?!"

She stepped back in, brushing sand from her hands and turning around to admire her work through the open door.

"Yes, it's when a person holds the delusional belief that they're already dead. Or they don't exist. Some think they are putrefying or have lost their internal organs. It's really quite awesome."

"How do you know such things?" Nora asked, amazed.

"I read." She shrugged, closing the door as the temperature plummeted below zero.

"There's a woman in who says she has it. She left her glass baubles here."

"Ooooh really!" Cara was excited. "In other news," she glanced back at Nora as she paused by the windows. "Your brother is heading this way."

Nora straightened up from lounging across the counter.

"Which one?"

"The middle one."

"Seymour?"

"That's the one." Cara smiled.

Nora joined her by the windows and they both peered out into the street, watching Seymour stroll across the cobbles, eyes fixed on the bookshop.

"He must be in town visiting Billy at the Antique's Centre before his theatre's opening night on Saturday." Nora said, but her eyes were narrowed with suspicion as she watched her younger brother heading towards them. He paused on the pavement outside, ran his hands back through his hair and ruffled it up, tested his breath against his left palm and then headed in just as the telephone began to ring.

Cara hurried behind the counter; her attention fixed on the door as Seymour cast it open and stepped inside. His gaze settled on Cara while he stepped down into the shop, closed the door behind him and smiled dashingly.

Nora cleared her throat so that he turned and noticed her standing by the window, one eyebrow raised knowingly.

"Oh hey, Nora." Seymour greeted.

Cara spoke to the caller while pondering Seymour and then began to rummage under the counter.

"Hello, Seymour. To what do we owe the pleasure of this visit?" Nora smiled.

"I was just passing and thought I'd drop in and have a browse." He said, glancing at Cara again.

"You're suddenly interested in books?" She asked and Seymour gave her a look.

He joined her next to the Folio Society section and pretended to examine the shelves with forced interest.

"What are you doing?" Nora whispered.

"Browsing." He replied and she snorted.

Seymour glanced at Cara again who was absorbed in her telephone conversation with what sounded like Mr Hill. She held up his book from where Nora had left it under the counter and told him the price again. Seymour winced when Nora pinched his arm.

CHRISTMAS AT THE SECONDHAND BOOKWORM

"I know why you're here." She whispered.

"You promised not to say anything." Seymour whispered back and trod on her foot so that Nora gave a yelp and smacked his arm.

"Children, children." Cara said laughing, returning the telephone receiver to its cradle.

Seymour turned and moved away from Nora who reached up to grab hold of the singing Father Christmas and switch him off.

"How do you put up with her all day?" Seymour threw a playful look back at his sister.

"Well, we're both mad." Cara chuckled. "How's everything going at the theatre?"

"Good." Seymour nodded, stopping before the counter.

"I'm looking forward to seeing the play."

Seymour smiled.

"I'm glad you're coming."

"Thanks." Cara smiled back knowingly and they stared at one another. "Nora said the owner is very benevolent."

"Well, she's right." He shrugged casually.

Cara studied him intensely. Nora looked between them while she pampered the spindly Christmas tree before the bay window.

Seymour then cleared his throat and glanced around the room.

"Where are your books about archaeology, fantasy and rock climbing?" He asked casually.

"Those are my favourite subjects!" Cara said, surprised.

"Really?" Seymour returned innocently, ignoring Nora's coughing that sounded suspiciously like she was covering up a laugh.

"Yes. What sort of archaeology?" Cara asked him.

"Erm…any sort." He said. "I find it all fascinating."

Cara looked pleased.

"Me too. Well, archaeology is in the back room, rock climbing would be on the top floor front room and there is a whole section of sci-fi, fantasy and horror books in the paperback room right up in the attic." She explained.

When Seymour looked blank Cara laughed.

"Would you like me to show you?" She offered cheerfully, wheeling back the swivel seat and standing up.

"That would be good." Seymour smiled and, glancing at Nora who was watching in astonishment, he winked at his sister and headed off with Cara, first to the back room and the archaeology section.

"I doubt he even knows how to spell archaeology." Nora shook her head and moved back to the counter as the door opened again.

Nora stared at White-Lightning Joe.

"Helllllooooo!" He greeted, standing in the doorway.

"Er…hello."

"I'll just have another browse." He said, almost fell in the shop and staggered to the Cole section, grinning. "Ha-ha, mind the step."

Nora watched him scan the shelves, glancing at her occasionally and grinning awkwardly. He still held his white carrier bag but it was empty of books and only seemed to contain one bottle of White-Lightning cider. When he looked at her again, seeing that she was still watching him, he went bright red.

Frowning, Nora turned to the computer when she heard a fanfare announcing a Skype message had arrived from Seatown. She had just finished reading it when she heard frantic shuffling behind her and turned to see White-Lightning Joe fleeing for the door again, which he threw open and left ajar as he ran out into the street and headed off up the hill.

Nora's stomach went cold with suspicion.

"No...he wouldn't..." She said to herself.

She stood up and walked over to the Cole section. It looked the same as she had left it. But she had a horrible feeling White-Lightning Joe was pinching books. He was desperate for money and acting very suspiciously, but surely he would realise it would become obvious if he acted so criminally.

Suddenly, the mystery of missing and returning Cole and Castletown books now made sense! Nora didn't have a chance to try and see if any titles were absent because the lady with Cotard delusion returned to the front, carrying a single book clasped in her gloved hands.

"This please." She said morosely.

"Thank you." Nora smiled, taking the book.

"How much for cash?"

Nora blinked.

"Oh. I'm afraid I can't change the prices. It isn't my shop."

"Humph." The woman took out her purse. "I used to be a top haggler in my old days. No point bothering now. What with the holographic moon in phase fifteen and the nanites in our Tropicana. It's all there on YouTube so we have to believe it!"

"Oh dear." Nora smiled politely and popped the price in the till. "Six pounds fifty, please."

With a sigh the woman passed Nora a ten pound note.

"Don't forget my package." The woman said. "I need those for filtering C60 water. Did you see the chemtrails across the sky this morning? Better get protecting ourselves before planet Nibiru crashes in the spring. Q-Anon tweeted about it this morning."

"Er...okay." Nora hastily gave the woman her change and the brown bag of glass Christmas decorations.

The woman smiled patronisingly, shaking her head at Nora.

"You *sheeple*." She sighed and set off to prune what Nora supposed were her *non-existent plants* with her own *dead* hands.

Nora wrote the sale down and then decided to examine the Cole section once more. She had been standing there for a few moments, spotting a couple of small gaps which she was beginning to suspect White-Lightning Joe had made through pilfering, when she heard the sound of footsteps coming down the staircase.

"I do think you'll enjoy it. And there are thirteen in the series." Cara was telling Seymour as they headed back for the counter.

"It sounds like a great title: The Eye of the World." Seymour said as he flicked through the pages of a paperback.

"Well, that's volume one so that'll start you off. It is very addictive." Cara said, sitting in the swivel chair behind the counter. "The author is a master story teller. There are sub-plots, love and hate relationships, twists and hints. The eternal evil enemy can be defeated but cannot be destroyed until the end of the world, which is fast approaching."

"Wow, sounds like my life." Seymour winked.

Cara laughed. She took a twenty pound note from him.

"You've read Robert Jordan haven't you, Nora?" Cara asked, handing Seymour his change.

"Sad to say I haven't." Nora admitted, glancing at the book in her brother's hand.

Seymour smiled at her smugly.

"Would you like a bag, Seymour?" Cara asked.

"No thanks." He popped his change into his wallet. "Thank you, Cara. I'll get started on this tonight."

"You can tell me what you think after '*The Surprise*' on Saturday night." Cara smiled.

"I certainly shall. I look forward to it."

"Me too."

Nora looked from one to the other.

When a Skype message arrived and Cara turned to read it, Seymour still remained gazing at her, holding his book. With a grin, Nora headed around the counter and grabbed her Parka.

"Georgina asked me to order her fifty mince pies. Do you mind if I do that now?" Nora asked Cara.

"Go ahead!" Cara agreed.

"You can be my chaperone, Seymour." She said, shrugging into her coat. When she reached him she prodded his arm to get him walking.

Seymour continued to look at Cara who glanced at him, smiled and said goodbye to him.

"Bye Cara." Seymour said, still looking at her while Nora pushed him to the door and steered him outside.

"You're over doing it! I think she's noticed you now after that charade!" Nora assured her brother once the door had closed.

"She definitely will when I quote Robert Jordan to her." He said, shoving the paperback into his coat pocket.

"You're too young for her." Nora pointed out as they waited for a car to pass.

"We're the same age!"

"Not mentally." Nora said and Seymour laughed.

"Thanks for paving the way and inviting her on Saturday." He appreciated.

"I thought you were playing it smooth and incognito."

"I was. But I got a little keen when you mentioned you were working together this morning."

They crossed the road, heading for the delicatessen door, Seymour grinning stupidly.

"Is she the only reason you came here?"

"Yes."

Nora chuckled, stopping before the delicatessen windows.

"You're crazy."

Seymour smiled.

"Humphrey's due over this afternoon then." He recalled.

"Yes. He's taking me for a meal in The Duke's Pie when we finish at the bookshop. Then we're going to watch the Christmas movies showing at the town hall."

"Sounds fun." He leaned in and kissed her cheek. "See you late tonight then."

"Enjoy your book." Nora gave him an affectionate hug.

Seymour saluted with it, winked and set off across the cobbled square, casting a look back at the bookshop and leaving Nora entering the delicatessen to order fifty mince pies for Georgina.

8 ROGER THE ELF

When Nora returned to the bookshop ten minutes later she noticed a small pile of Castletown books on the counter. She closed the door behind her and hurried over to grab them, ignoring Cara who paused in mid bite of a Lion Bar and stared at Nora.

"Did White-Lightning Joe just sell these to you?"

"Oh, yes." Cara grimaced, taking her bite of the chocolate bar. "Horrible little goblin."

Nora opened the front of one and saw that the pencil price was wet and smeared again. Her jaw tightened.

"I think he's stealing them and selling them back to us."

Cara choked on her Lion Bar.

"Whaaaaaaat?! The demonic little *hobgoblin*!" She exclaimed, upgrading him to a more menacing fairy creature.

"I know we definitely had one of these already." She took it over to the Cole section and scanned the shelves. "No it's not here so it must be this one. He must have grabbed it when I wasn't looking, gone off somewhere and wiped off the pricing and then come in and sold them. I bought three off him earlier that I recognised."

"The cheek! The cheeky little Grinch! We should call the police on him!" Cara exclaimed.

"Tempting." Nora agreed. "But Georgina's scarier than the police. We'll tell her and she can deal with him."

"Good idea." Cara glowered, shaking her head. "Little thief."

Nora was about to telephone Georgina and tell on White-Lightning Joe when the door opened and a man in a tweed suit with a trimmed red beard stepped down into the shop, accompanied by a woman in a white fur coat and white fur hat.

"Over here, over here. Look." The man said, leading her to the counter.

Nora stepped back, watching in surprise.

The man picked up a book that was displayed before the Shire Guides spinner.

"I saw it the other day. Look, it's a book about you. Your nickname: Moomin. Look!" He said and laughed a husky loud chortle.

The woman took the book from him.

"Moomin: The Complete Tove Jansson Comic Strip Book. Book two." The lady read aloud.

"We have all ten volumes of them. Brand new." Cara explained.

"Oh how horrible." The woman said and put it back.

"But it's your nickname, Moomin." The man laughed and took it up himself as the woman had a look around the front and then headed off, seemingly disgusted.

Cara and Nora stared at them.

"Don't you think it funny that it's her nickname?" The man asked Cara, laughing.

"Not really." She shrugged, turning back to the computer monitor.

The man's eyes narrowed.

"Well it is funny. What's your nickname?"

"I don't have one." Cara said without looking at him.

Nora saw him shake his head.

"Well you should get one. And while you're at it, get yourself a sense of humour too!" He said, laughed angrily and marched off with the woman.

"Come on. It's warm in here!" The man said and they left the shop, closing the door hard.

"Irritating pirate-beard." Cara glowered and stuck her tongue out at the door.

Nora laughed, picking up a pen.

"At least he gave us an '*it's warm in here*' tally."

"I thought you hated them."

"I do. But Humphrey has challenged me to make five hundred by Christmas day or forfeit a Christmas midnight swim in the outdoor pool by the car park."

"Whaaaaat!" Cara half-laughed, half-squealed.

"And we're only up to two hundred and forty nine."

"We'll have to start asking people how they're feeling."

"I tried that but Humphrey said it's cheating."

Cara chuckled.

The door opened to admit a pile of frozen slugs followed by Lady-Santa and Twinkle. Cara stared.

"Hi again! And Merry Christmas!" Lady-Santa greeted, armed with her assortment of coloured bags and followed by Twinkle.

"Hi." Cara returned, warily.

"Are you a mother?" Lady-Santa asked Cara.

"Huh?"

"Do you have children?" Lady-Santa rephrased. "As I told your colleague the other day, I am from Kiddies Boutique down Market Street and this week I am about town with some wonderful festive promotions on baby clothes."

Cara straightened up.

"Oh, actually I would be interested. My niece is thirteen months old." She said, eagerly.

"Fantastic! Would you like me to show you some wonderful items from our boutique? I have them here in my colourful bags."

"Yes please." Cara nodded.

Nora smiled, bending down to stroke Twinkle while Cara and Lady-Santa rummaged through her bags for some seasonal bargains. Cara bought some festive tops for her niece as well as a cute little Christmas hat.

"I shall be around town for the rest of the week including the weekend." Lady-Santa said, gathering up her bags again once Cara had paid. "If you want anything else, just grab me, or better still, come down to Kiddies Boutique for more festive bargains! Merry Christmas! Come on, Twinkle."

After Lady-Santa and Twinkle had left, Cara texted her sister to tell her she had some gifts for Violet for Christmas. Nora collected the frozen slugs (disgusting!) and other items of rubbish that had plopped inside and put the rubbish in the bin and the slugs in the yard, in case they were just hibernating. They had a few more customers before Nora was able to speak with Georgina.

Georgina was outraged about White-Lightning Joe's suspected thievery.

"When he comes in again, watch him! Try and catch him in the act or get some definite visual proof and then I'll confront him. The audacity. After all we've done for him, buying his smelly books and tolerating his smelly custom!"

Nora agreed.

"Yes, shame he's so desperate."

"Hmm. No excuse for robbery though." Georgina gritted.

"We could always get some CCTV cameras here. Then you might believe me about that customer who sounds like he does ballet in the room above, and the man I swear uses piles of our books for weight-lifting in the top room, as well as the hundreds of brigands stealing our posters and paperbacks, AND that oaf who sits in the paperback room eating pop tarts."

"No!" Georgina adamantly refused.

Nora pursed her lips.

"It's not as if we would spend all our time captivated by the security feed." She promised (half-heartedly).

"Yes you would. And I refuse to ruin the bookshop experience for people. It's bad enough feeling observed when *I* do my shopping in the local supermarket. It's not as though I'm going to put all my bottles of Prosecco down my trousers. No, no, no to CCTV!"

"Fine." Nora sighed, sticking her thumb down at Cara.

Cara pouted.

"Has Cara left for Seatown yet?" Georgina then asked.

"She's just getting ready." Nora said, seeing Cara pull on her hat.

"Oh good. It's busy over there and Jane and Betty could do with her help. Roger will be with you in a bit."

"I see him now!" Nora spotted her colleague walking past the window wearing what looked like every coat and scarf he owned.

"Good! See you later, Nora!"

"See you later!"

Nora hung up as Roger opened the door and stepped into The Secondhand Bookworm. He gave a glum wave with his padded, gloved hand.

"It's dire out there." He said, closing the door behind him. "We're in for a dreary old day. I'll put the kettle on."

He stopped dead as Santa parachuted past him singing 'Jingle Bells' and Nora and Cara burst out laughing at the expression on his face. Cara had switched Santa quickly on as a welcoming for Roger. Roger's lips twitched.

"*Him* I remember." He shook his head, starting to pull off his gloves.

"I'll turn him off." Nora reached up and grabbed Santa's black booted feet.

"We just wanted to see your face," Cara snorted, picking up a box of transfers to take with her to the Seatown shop.

"Funny!" Roger rolled his eyes. "Be careful on the roads. It's still icy."

"Will do!" Cara headed off out the door. "Have a nice day. Hope you sell lots. Byeeeee."

"Bye, Cara." Nora waved and watched Cara head off up the street.

"How's it been so far?" Roger asked, standing beside Nora and unravelling his first scarf.

"Weird and quiet."

"Not surprised." Roger shrugged with his usual pessimism. "Can't see this year's late night Thursday shopping will be any different from last year's. Pooh!"

"Well. You never know." Nora said.

"Is that your attempt as some festive cheer?" Roger spotted the Christmas tree.

"Yes, isn't it lovely?"

"If you're Scrooge." He sniffed.

The door opened and a very tall man stood on the threshold.

"Would you be interested in buying a unicycle?" He asked.

Nora and Roger stared at him.

"What for?" Roger asked.

"You could put it in your window display?"

"We sell books!"

"Don't say I didn't ask." The tall man said, turned around and left.

"That's set the theme for the rest of the day." Roger said morosely, turning and taking off his coat.

"You'd better make some tea then," Nora suggested.

"Give me a chance, woman!" Roger huffed, unzipping his enormous jacket.

Nora pondered him filling up the whole walkway under the stairs with his winter wear until he shuffled off to the kitchen to put the kettle on to boil.

"Got any Barbapapa books?" A woman asked, entering the shop with a handful of postcards.

"What are they about?" Nora asked.

"Barbapapa was born in a garden, just like a flower. He can take any form. He is very nice, everybody likes him." The woman said.

Nora stared blankly.

"These postcards, please. And do you sell stamps?"

"Yes. Where are they going?"

"To my friends." The woman said, taking out her purse.

Nora felt her left eye begin to twitch slightly.

Roger returned as the woman was leaving, having finally explained that Barbapapa was the character of a children's book and she wanted to post her cards to Australia. Nora stood up to take a look in the square in case anything interesting was beginning to happen. A young boy who could have been Tiny Tim hobbled past the bay window.

Roger put the cups of tea on the counter and had a nosey about.

"I get the strange feeling we're going to be graced with a fragrant visitor." Roger said, picking up the copy of '*Eleanor: April Queen of Aquitaine*' by Douglas Boyd put under the counter for Mr Hill.

"Hmm." Nora frowned. "Due in this afternoon."

"At least we'll have one customer." Roger grumbled.

Nora peered into the empty square, noticing that the Woman in Gold figurine outside 'Marbles' opposite was sporting a flamboyant pink fur coat and a blue ushanka hat. She wondered what the Duke of Cole would make of that! Her thoughts lingered on the Duke and she tried to guess what time he would come down from his castle, smiling with anticipation at seeing him again, though she doubted he would pay her any attention.

"What are you smiling at?" Roger asked suspiciously.

"Oh, nothing." She said and moved towards the counter. "Mind if I use the…*men's* room?" She asked, teasingly.

"It's gender free actually." Roger said seriously. "Get with the times, Ms Jolly."

Nora laughed and headed off, deciding to have a look about the shop and have a quick tidy up while she was upstairs.

When Nora returned to the front of The Secondhand Bookworm half an hour later, having shuffled along some books in the music section, sorted out the cake-making books in the cookery section, showed several customers to topics they requested, and stuck some shelf labels back onto their shelf fronts, Roger was reading a novel.

"We had a visit from the Cat-Man who spent three hundred pounds on 'The Three Little Kittens Painting Book' by Louis Wain." Roger said.

"You're joking!"

"Why would I joke about that?" Roger asked, although Nora could see he was pleased.

"He said he didn't want it when Georgina showed it to him last week." Nora recalled as she hung up the shop keys. "Cara and I were even thinking about colouring in the pictures."

"Well, he said he'd been having sleepless nights at the thought of anyone else owning it besides him."

Nora chuckled.

"People and their obsessions. Did you sell anything else while I was having a tidy up?"

"Two new Wordsworth editions, a Christmas book from the window, a Graham Greene Folio Society edition of 'The Power and the Glory' and twelve more postcards. Someone also asked if we had any free maps of Castletown."

"I may as well go home. You're doing so well on your own."

"But then I would miss your delightful company."

"True." Nora agreed and sat on the stool behind the till. "How's Seatown?"

"Cara arrived and said it's bedlam over there." Roger nodded to the monitor.

Nora leaned across Roger to read the Skype Chat messages, chuckling at a variety of complaints and comments from Betty and Jane.

The door opened and a woman stuck her head inside.

"Excuse me! Do you sell Blu-rays?" She asked loudly.

Roger had been in the process of sipping from a can of Tango and choked.

"No, sorry. We sell books." Nora replied.

"Oh. Anywhere in town that does?"

"There's a large case of DVDs in one of the 'Passageway Collectibles' rooms." Nora recalled. "They all seemed to be 18 rated but I saw a selection of romantic comedies on Blu-ray there once."

The woman blinked.

"Okaaaaaay. Well where's that?"

"I'll show you." Nora decided helpfully, grabbed her coat and set off with the lady, leaving Roger watching them drearily.

It was cold outside and Hugh was in the process of dragging his ROAD CLOSED signs down the hill from the Town Hall in anticipation of the one o'clock barricade.

"Down here." Nora said to the lady and they turned into a long winding passage between the bank and a jewellery shop.

Flashing Christmas lights lit up the whole length of the passage.

"I feel as though you're leading me off to be murdered." The woman laughed nervously.

The passage was lined, as usual, with large statues of Buddha, various fountains and numerous stone effigies. As usual, the door to the building stood wide open in welcome so Nora took the lady down a long hallway lined either side with tall glass cases filled mainly with stuffed animals and weapons and into the room ahead of them.

Pleasant oriental music was playing and cases containing items such as swords, pairs of vases, Shi-Shi dogs, daggers, religious idols, carved wooden boxes and other trinkets surrounded them.

"There they are." Nora indicated to the woman.

"Oh thank goodness for that!" The woman laughed and eagerly headed over to the large bookcase filled with DVDs and Blu-rays.

"Ah, you bring me more customers, Nora?" Jiao's smiling voice greeted from behind her.

Nora turned and saw the proprietor of the shop, Jiao, standing behind her counter, polishing an enormous Samurai sword.

"Yes. Oooh, what's that?"

"Ah, you like?"

"Well, I thought for Seymour's theatre but I guess he might lob his actors' heads off wielding that." Nora decided reluctantly.

"Ah yes. Very sharp." Jiao agreed. "You busy in bookshop?"

"Not too bad." Nora admitted.

"We look forward to Seymour's play on Saturday. We see you there, yes?" Jiao smiled, continuing to polish the sword.

"Absolutely." Nora nodded, glancing over her shoulder at the woman who already had an armful of Blu-rays. "Well, I'd better get back to the bookshop." She smiled.

"Goodbye, Nora." Jiao purred.

Nora said her goodbyes and hurried back before Roger missed her.

Back in the shop, Roger was dealing with several customers so Nora joined him. They spent the next hour serving a variety of people, bagging up books and dealing with phone calls as the sales picked up and Castletown became busier. By half past one, the traffic had stopped outside the shop with the road closure and it was blissfully peaceful.

"Go and have some lunch young lady." Roger suggested when her stomach growling ruined the tranquility.

"Okay. Thanks." Nora laughed, grabbed her bag, shrugged into her coat and set off to buy a hot sausage roll to munch as she had a look around Castletown preparing for *Shopping by Candlelight*.

Roger left for lunch at half past two and Nora was settling down behind the counter to wait for Georgina to arrive when one of her regular customers entered.

Fluffy-haired, bespectacled Eugene Harvey, a local author, entered The Secondhand Bookworm grasping a sheet of paper between his hands. He wrote books about empty fields all around the county of Cole where important historical structures had once stood.

"Hello." Nora greeted cheerfully.

"Hello on behalf of the LCAS." He said, his lips trembling excitedly.

Nora stared at him.

"Pardon?"

"I have your certificate here and wished to deliver it personally by hand." He explained.

"Oh!" Nora realised it was the result of her application to join the Little Cove Astronomical Society. Eugene Harvey was a member and very enthusiastic about the group's Star Parties. Nora had learned of the LCAS when she and Georgina had gone on a book call to a Mr Rigel who lived around the corner from Nora's parents and had an enormous telescope in his back garden.

Eugene stopped before her and held it out.

"Thank you." She said and took it.

"You can see where it has been dated and signed there." Eugene pointed.

"Oh yes. Thank you."

"As a member you are welcome to come to our regular Star Parties. We also meet on the third Tuesday of every month at Little Cove United Reformed Church, room B, for two hours. Refreshments provided." Eugene explained. "I have your welcome pack, here." He dug in his satchel and pulled out a brown envelope.

"Thank you, Eugene." Nora was pleased.

"Inside is a lot of literature and a monthly plan of events and meetings." He concluded, rubbing his hands together. "Will you be attending?"

"Can I bring friends?"

"We ask for a £1 donation for non-members attending meetings and Star Parties."

"Okay."

"Five planets are currently visible in December, with Jupiter being a brilliant fixture." He explained.

"Oh yes, I love to look at them."

"Do you have any more of my books that need signing?"

Nora blinked.

"Erm...no I don't think we do actually."

"Very well. Goodbye." He turned and headed off so Nora shrugged and examined her membership certificate.

Less than five minutes later the front door flew open to admit Georgina.

"I almost ran over three idiots trying to wave me back onto the ring road!" She exclaimed with a loud scowl. "I was driving the bookshop van for goodness sake, you would think the numbskulls would realise I was trying to get to my shop!"

"Oh dear." Nora hurried around to relieve Georgina of one of her boxes.

"It took me a long shouting explanation to convince them to let me through their blasted closed road to park outside the bank so I could unload. Imbecilic town, aaaaaachoooo!"

Georgina continued moaning, sneezing and growling as they unloaded the books, piled up the boxes, Georgina placed her handbag under the stairs and finally flattened her hair.

"Sorry, Nora. How are you?" She sighed.

"Very well. You look and sound so much better."

There was a trumpeting noise as Georgina blew her nose on a bright pink handkerchief.

"I am." She promised with a muffled voice. "Isn't this a lovely handkerchief? Troy bought me a pack."

Nora's lips twitched.

"Alright have a good chuckle." Georgina noticed the Christmas tree. "What on earth is *that*?"

"It's our Christmas tree." Nora defended.

"If you say so." She gave Nora an ironic look and stood scanning the cash book. "Oh well done. Some good sales. And Roger sold the Louis Wain." She recognised his tiny handwriting.

"To the Cat-Man."

"Really?!"

"Yes. Said he couldn't live with the thought of anyone else owning it."

"Hmm. Some people and their obsessions." Georgina shook her head. "Funny."

The door opened and a man in a heavy woollen coat unbuttoned over a black suit entered the shop. Nora and Georgina looked at him.

"Miss Georgina Picker-slim?" He asked politely, closing the door behind him as Roger attempted to follow.

Nora bit back a grin.

"Pickering." Georgina corrected, giving Nora a look as she walked around the counter. "That's me. And you've just shut the door in my colleague's face."

"Oh, did I? Sorry." The man apologised, turning to see Roger glaring grumpily between the 'Mind the step' sign and the 'Castletown Christmas Events' poster on the door window.

"Are you my three o'clock?" Georgina asked as Roger entered.

"Ford Calloway of Penguin." The man confirmed, holding out his hand.

"Wonderful. We already sell some of your Penguin book deckchairs and I'm looking to stock your Penguin book mugs." Georgina said, shaking his hand.

"We actually stock a variety of Penguin book related items such as umbrellas, notebooks, bags…"

"Let's start with mugs shall we?" Georgina suggested firmly.

"As you wish." Ford Calloway conceded with a polite smile.

"I'm afraid I don't have an office but I thought we could have a quick chat in the front of my shop here. Would you like a cup of tea or coffee?" Georgina asked.

Nora stood poised to oblige.

"No thank you. Do you need to see some samples? My car is parked over the river because the roads are closed but I'd be happy to go and get some."

"No that won't be necessary; I've seen your Penguin mugs. I would just like to discuss trade terms and then place my first order with you." Georgina assured him and turned to Nora before he could respond. "I would like a cup of tea, Nora if you're making one."

"Certainly." Nora nodded.

Roger was observing frowningly as he took off his coats.

"Tea?" Nora offered him.

"Yes please. And I brought a packet of biscuits with me today. They're on the side."

"I'll bring a plate of those through too." Nora headed off, leaving Ford Calloway obediently taking his trade order form from his briefcase as Georgina specified how many she would like to start off with and asking what titles sold best.

When she returned five minutes later, teeth chattering and hands numb from the kitchen, balancing three mugs of tea and a plate of biscuits, Nora saw that Georgina and Roger were the only people in the front.

"Where's Mr Penguin?" Nora asked, placing their mugs by the computer monitor.

"Long gone." Georgina said as she concentrated writing an email. "I told the silly man I wanted enough to stock both shops so it was easy when he had finally told me the trade terms. Several boxes of mugs will be arriving next week."

"That's exciting." Nora said.

Georgina took a sip of her tea, nodding gratefully to Nora.

"By the way. What's *this?!*" Georgina then asked and held up a tan coloured business card from the post file she had been sorting through.

"Oh! Him. Eugh. Cara and I had a visit from a man on Monday asking if we had any books bound in human skin. He left his business card for you in case you ever come across any." Nora explained.

Roger paused in mid bite of his jammy dodger.

"How delightful." Georgina said sarcastically. "Yes, I have heard of Anthropodermic bibliopegy. I'm not sure I want to contact someone interested in books bound in humans though. For a moment I was suspicious of the substance of his business card."

"I had the same thought." Nora admitted.

Roger had a look of revulsion. He returned his jammy dodger to the plate.

"Oh I suppose I should keep it. You never know. We might visit the house of a mass murderer one day who has bound all his books in the skins of his victims. There's always a customer for anything." Georgina muttered.

Nora spluttered on her tea, laughing.

"There are a few customers I'd consider using in book binding." Roger muttered glumly.

Georgina agreed.

While Georgina nibbled biscuits and drank her tea, Roger and Nora served several customers. Georgina ignored them as she sat at the computer and caught up on the emails, leaving Nora to direct several people to the paperback fiction room, look at a small bag of books for sale and, after purchasing a selection of craft books from the happy old lady, sell a set of thin, leather bound Dickens novels. Roger, meanwhile, sold handfuls of postcards, another Christmas book from the window, showed a grouchy old man an early edition of an Edgar Wallace novel and tidied up the Observer books.

With a final gulp of lukewarm tea, Georgina stood up ten minutes later and shuffled under the stairs.

Roger sat himself down in the swivel chair, pondering the empty street beyond the windows. Nora adjusted Singing Santa's gold trousers, noticing Roger's warning glare.

"I bought these!" Georgina's muffled voice then announced from under the stairs. Nora and Roger turned to see her pull three Christmas hats out of her bag.

"Wow!" Nora's eyes widened with delight.

Roger's face fell.

"Very festive." He said glumly.

"Oh don't be a humbug." Georgina passed one to Roger. It was a large Christmas turkey. Nora burst out laughing.

"You may well laugh, Miss Jolly." Roger glowered although his lips twitched slightly.

"Put it on." Nora pleaded.

Roger eased it over his slightly balding head.

"Wonderful." Georgina smiled and passed Nora a large Christmas tree hat.

"Oh thank you!" Nora accepted, pleased. She pulled it on.

"Very fetching." Roger observed gloomily.

Nora laughed again at his moody face beneath a large, quite realistic, Christmas turkey.

"This one is for Humphrey. Make sure he wears it." Georgina instructed, placing a green and red striped elf hat with large elf ears attached to it, on the overnight storage heater.

"I think the elf hat would suit Roger better." Nora decided.

Georgina shrugged.

"You can fight among yourselves about them." She took out a fresh pink handkerchief. "I'd best head over to Seatown."

Roger grimaced as Georgina blew her nose loudly before she gathered her things.

"I'm glad you're feeling better." Nora said.

"Me too!" Georgina squashed the handkerchief up her coat sleeve. "I've left you a box of Profile Publications, Nora. You and Betty can mark them up tomorrow. Pop them inside clear plastic wallets and label them with stickers on the outside, between three and five pounds each depending on condition. They're all aircraft magazines that will sell well."

"Okay." Nora nodded.

"Have a good afternoon and evening. Hopefully you'll sell loads of books!"

"Hmm, doubtful." Roger shrugged.

Georgina wrapped an enormous scarf around her neck and headed for the door.

"I'll be in Seatown until closing time if you need me." She said and was about to open the door when a figure loomed up to the window.

Nora paused from taking a bite of biscuit.

"Hello! May I come in?" A muffled, enthusiastic voice asked.

Georgina pulled open to the door and a very old man with a large shopper stepped down onto the flagstones.

"Ah. Yes. This is the bookshop. Tell me please, when is the owner in?" He asked.

"I am the owner." Georgina said, regarding him with suspicion.

Nora and Roger watched as the man stuck out his hand.

"Ah! Wonderful. Grand. My name is Mr Fink, I am very pleased to meet your acquaintance Ms….?"

"Pickering. Miss Georgina Pickering."

"A beautiful name. Now, I recently moved into Castletown and I am writing a book about the history of smuggling in the town. I already have a publisher and I am looking for stockists. Would you be interested?"

"I might be." Georgina said unenthusiastically.

"Oh, grand! Grand. Here, let me give you a card with my name and number on."

As he rummaged in his shopping trolley noisily.

"How much have you written so far?" Georgina asked, turning up her nose at him as he seemed to disappear into his shopper.

"Well I have it all drafted out now. I've been working with Castletown Museum, using a lot of their photographs and archives. I discovered some coins and a tunnel in the basement of my house at the end of Market Street that was once used for smuggling items from the river to the town. Wonderful history and very thrilling stuff!" He said and straightened up. "Here. My details should you wish to contact me."

"Thank you." Georgina said politely, taking a small white card.

"But I will pop in and keep you apprised of the progress."

"Do you know how much you will be selling your book for? Will it be in paperback or hardback?"

"Oh golly. I don't know all the fine details yet but those are very good points. When I find out I shall let you know." Mr Fink said, rubbing his hands together excitedly.

"Good." Georgina nodded and stepped up onto the pavement. "Bye!" She called to Roger and Nora and headed off with her small heels clicking and clacking on the snow-free pavement until they faded into the distance.

Nora bit back a grin.

"I won't have a look around as I am heading off to the museum but you have a lovely shop. Very nice." Mr Fink said enthusiastically.

"Thank you." Nora smiled, chewing her mouthful of biscuit.

"I hear the Duke will be down later on to turn on the Christmas lights. I hope to interview him for my book one day. What are your names?"

Nora swallowed her mouthful.

"I'm Nora. And this is Roger."

"Good to meet you both. I am sure we will become well acquainted. Best be going. Toodle-oo!" He waved, turned and dragged his trolley to the door, breaking wind loudly as he hoisted the shopper up the step and set off whistling.

Nora cleared her throat.

Roger blinked.

"Cheery fellow." Nora decided.

"Huh." Roger shook his head. "Bet he thought we were right idiots in these hats."

"Oh! I had forgotten I was wearing mine already. I really do think the elf hat would suit you better."

"Are you saying I look like an elf?!"

"A little." Nora laughed.

"Okay then. I'll swap it. It's better than looking like a prize turkey." He decided.

Nora watched him take off the turkey hat and pull on the elf hat. He modelled it for her glumly.

"Brilliant!" Nora snapped a photo of him with her iPhone.

"Humph. I'm sure we'll scare off what little customers we have." Roger shrugged.

As she put her phone back in her pocket, Nora noticed Mr Hill's book on the shelf.

"I think we should have another cup of tea. Before Mr Hill arrives." She decided.

"Agreed!" Roger nodded. "Allow me."

"Thanks." Nora sat down in the swivel chair, watching Roger the Elf head off into the kitchen to help prepare them for an unwelcome visit.

9 MR HILL'S UNDERPANTS, THE DUKE AND SHOPPING BY CANDLELIGHT

Mr Hill arrived promptly at four o'clock, having caught the bus from Seatown to Castletown and dragged his battered old suitcase down the hill to The Secondhand Bookworm. Roger was straightening up the shelves in the antiquarian section behind the counter after a group of people had had a thorough rummage and Nora was dusting the shelves in the window after having sold some Christmas books to a man with a flashing reindeer badge who complimented Nora on her hat, when Mr Hill burst into the shop.

"Hello, Laura!" Mr Hill greeted loudly.

Nora gave a start when she saw that he was speaking to her.

"Er…hello, Mr Hill."

He dragged his suitcase onto the carpet, wheezing loudly.

"I've arrived to purchase a copy of '*Eleanor: April Queen of Aquitaine*' by Douglas Boyd."

Nora watched him huff and puff to the counter, hauling his infamous large green case which looked as old as he did. Roger turned to face him and Mr Hill did a double take when he noticed Roger's elf hat. Roger noticed and glowered.

"I have your book right here, Mr Hill." Roger said, picking it up.

Nora joined Roger behind the counter and smiled politely at Mr Hill. He was an elderly man with a bristly beard, droopy eyes, thin grey hair under a dark red cord hat covered in medals and a very smelly raincoat. She screwed up her nose slightly.

"Lovely day today!" He said cheerfully.

"Yes it is." Roger nodded. "Very fresh."

"More snow is expected for Christmas." He said conversationally.

"I heard that too."

"Georgina said I could pay by cheque. Is that alright madam?" Mr Hill asked wheezily.

Nora wondered if he was calling Roger a lady but then realised he was looking at her.

"Oh, yes, she said that was fine." Nora nodded.

She watched as Mr Hill unbuttoned his raincoat and took out a cheque book and a ballpoint pen from an inside pocket. He wrote out the amount.

"And who do I make the cheque payable to?" He asked.

Nora and Roger stared.

"The Secondhand Bookworm, please." Roger said and shrugged at Nora.

Considering Mr Hill had written about a thousand cheques to the bookshop for nearly thirty years, back when Georgina's mother had owned the original 'The Secondhand Bookworm' in Piertown before selling the business to her daughter, Nora wondered if he was just toying with their sanity.

"We will need your cheque card to write the number on the back, Mr Hill." Roger said as he punched the price of the book into the till.

"Now…it's in 'ere somewhere." Mr Hill puffed and dug a card out of the pocket of his trousers.

As he lifted up his shirt, the front of his trousers was exposed. Nora stared when she saw a pair of dark red underpants sticking out the top. Roger quickly covered her eyes with his hand.

"Don't look!" Roger whispered hard.

Nora turned away, fighting the urge to burst out laughing.

Mr Hill was oblivious and handed Roger his cheque card.

"I think you will find it all in order." He said, coughing and spluttering as he put away his cheque book.

Roger edged back, smiled politely and picked a pen from the broken mug that served as a pen pot on the desk.

While Roger wrote the card number on the back of the cheque, Mr Hill puffed and panted as he unzipped his suitcase to put in his book. Nora did her best not to stare at his red underpants.

Roger passed Mr Hill his card back, gazing at his red knickers. Nora bit her bottom lip hard.

"Well, that's my business for today. I shall be returning back home now." Mr Hill said loudly, putting away his card. He tipped his stained cord cap so that the few medals on the brim glinted in the overhead lights. "B-bye. Merry Christmas and all the best, children. I'm most satisfied with the transaction."

"That's good, Mr Hill. Goodbye." Roger bade warily.

"B-bye, sir. B-bye young lady." He said to Nora.

"Happy Christmas, Mr Hill." Nora smiled politely and watched Mr Hill leave, hoisting his suitcase with much wheezing and groaning over the step, and heading out into the street.

"I bet one hour." Roger said, watching Mr Hill hurry off for the bus stop.

Nora glanced at the clock.

"Forty five minutes." Nora wagered in return. "There are a few phone booths along the route back to Longhill."

Roger's lips twitched and he wrote the sale down in the cash book.

Nora bent over one of the blue boxes that Georgina had left to rummage around the 'Profile Publication' magazines.

"Oh my goodness. There are millions!" She exclaimed, making Roger drop his pen.

"Millions of what?!" He demanded.

"Magazines. About silly old planes." Nora held up a handful, grimacing.

"Oh ho, ho, ho. I don't envy you and Betty marking those up tomorrow." He sniggered rudely, sounding like an uncharitable Father Christmas.

Nora sighed, popping them back into the box.

"As long as we have plenty of tea and cake."

"Speaking of which." Roger gestured with his head toward the kitchen.

"I thought elves were the helpful ones."

"I'm not a house elf."

"Free-elf are you?"

"Absolutely!" Roger insisted.

Nora relented and headed off to the kitchen to make them a round of tea.

When Nora returned to the front of the shop with two mugs of hot, steaming tea, Roger was staring morosely through the window into the town square.

"I gave the kitchen a clean, I can't help myself, but it's like a freezer in there." She said.

"Well it's like a morgue out there." Roger sighed drearily. "Mr Hill rang by the way."

Nora dropped the mugs onto the mouse mat with a thud.

"You're joking?!"

"Sadly not." He turned and plodded across the carpet to the counter. "Said he had some books for sale and asked if we were purchasing at the moment. I told him to phone Georgina in Seatown."

"He is insane!"

"That's why he fits in so well here." Roger pointed out.

"He can't have made it back to Longhill already."

"No. I expect he hopped off the bus and found a phone booth somewhere."

"I win the bet." Nora shook her head. "That was less than forty-five minutes."

"What do I owe you then?" Roger asked, plonking himself down onto the stool.

"One mince pie. Each. To go with our tea."

"Huh. Well don't expect me to wear this ridiculous hat out." He said, standing up.

"That's part of the forfeit." Nora decided.

Roger glared at her.

"My one consolation is that there doesn't seem to be anyone in Castletown, as predicted, so nobody will see me." He said, although Nora saw his eyes twinkling with humour.

"Thanks." She sat down in the swivel chair. "When you come back I may consider giving you an item of clothing and free you."

"I told you, I'm already a free elf!" Roger glared, wrapping several scarves around his neck.

Nora chuckled and he soon left to buy mince pies from the delicatessen dressed like an obese Eskimo with his many layers.

As soon as the door closed behind him, the telephone rang.

"Good afternoon, The Secondhand Bookworm." Nora greeted cheerfully.

"It's me." Georgina's voice sailed out of the receiver, followed by a sneeze.

"Oh dear. Are you okay?"

"Oh, yes. Cara's just dusting the shelves behind the counter here. Seatown is manic. I think Cara and I will stay open until seven here, too."

"Oh that's a good idea."

"I've never done it before in Seatown but it's worth a shot. Upstairs, madam. Yes, all of our books are for sale. Ahem, where was I. Ah yes. I just had a phone call from Mickey Lonardo." Georgina told Nora.

"A member of the Little Cove mafia!"

"Don't be daft, Nora." Georgina laughed and paused to blow her nose. "The pre-ISBN chap from Universe of Books."

"Exactly." Nora insisted.

Georgina snorted, recalling all too well their visit several weeks ago to a book charity organisation called 'Universe of Books', which Nora swore was a front for a mafia set-up.

"Anyway. He has a mountain of books for me to go through and I said we had been saving up some tat in the office here they can have, so I've added him to the calls day next week."

"Are we back doing calls then?"

"I think I can manage half a day. There's a backlog of people wishing to sell books; I'm sitting phoning them now."

"Why do I get the feeling I'm being invited on this call?"

"Because you're psychic."

"Wonderful."

"No grumbling. You have an eye for gems so I want you to come with me."

"Just to the mafia headquarters?"

"Yes."

"Okay." Nora grimaced.

"Just don't look at them as if they're going to put a hit out on us this time." Georgina warned.

"I'll try not to."

"Also, the Goat Lady phoned and left a message with Betty. Her mother-in-law is ill and when she goes to the other side would we be interested in buying her books."

"Whaaaaaat!"

"Hmm, I thought you'd like that."

"That's terrible. Plotting selling off the family inheritance in advance." Nora shook her head.

"They probably all smell of a paddock." Georgina sighed. "But I said we would be interested."

"Something else to look forward to then." Nora moaned.

The Goat-Lady grazed rare breed of goats and sheep on several fields around the county of Cole. She often told Nora all about how she *mob grazed* her herds in small fenced areas for a short time and then fenced them into a new pasture, thus allowing the grazed plants to grow back and thus win the favour of the current Duke of Cole, who was a fan of rewilding.

The Goat-Lady lived in a caravan with her husband Bill, a man with a scraggly beard who liked to pinch bottoms. The Goat-Lady also collected books about the county of Cole (although Nora never really saw her buy any, just browse through them while talking loudly about buying them). She claimed was a distant relative of the Duke of Cole as well as being related to Matthew Hopkins, a 17th century English witch-hunter whose career flourished during the English Civil War. He was known as the Witch Master General. Goat-Lady said she had his talent for detecting modern day witches. She smelt like a cow pat.

"No grumbling, remember." Georgina reminded Nora. "Oh great, a man is heading this way with a box of books. I'd better go. Aaaachhhoooooo! I think that's enough dusting now, Cara! Byeeeeeee, Nora."

"Bye-bye." Nora smiled and hung up as the door flew open, making her jump.

"I used to live here!" A woman exclaimed.

Nora stared as a large lady in an enormous patchwork coat to her ankles and a large pink tulip hat stepped down into the shop.

"Er…did you?" Nora replied warily.

She nodded vigorously.

"In the nineteen sixties. When I was a sprog. Mind if I take a look around? I haven't been back for twenty years."

"Sure." Nora nodded, watching her curiously.

"Ah, this was the front room. Behind you there's a chimney."

"So that's why I can hear pigeons as if they are in the wall."

"That'd be them sitting on the chimney pot. I used to hear them too. This is where my dad knocked my brother's front teeth out."

Nora arched an eyebrow, following the lady's finger to where she pointed at the art section.

"He was a lairy S.O.B." She chuckled. "Oh, you've removed the doors. The back room was the kitchen. My bedroom was on the next floor."

"Really?"

Roger returned at that moment, carrying a small white paper bag and looking annoyed. Nora suspected someone had laughed at his elf hat.

"Would you mind if I walked around with you?" Nora asked the lady. "I'd be interested to learn a little history about the building."

"That'd be great." The woman stuck her thumbs up.

"Thank you. Back in a minute, Roger." Nora set off with the woman.

The woman gave Nora a detailed tour of the shop, chuckling about the wallpaper in the children's room behind some of the fitted shelves, still there from when it had been her bedroom, and telling Nora of various rumours she had heard about a murder being committed in the attic a hundred years before.

"It became a tobacconist shop when my dad sold it." The lady said. "The old fellow who ran the tobacconist shop used to sell tobacco to J.R.R. Tolkien, the author."

"That's amazing!"

"Yeah. He sold sweets as well and lived in the other rooms with his mistress."

"Oh."

"I think she ran a brothel at some point."

Nora stared.

"There was a fire in this room." The lady explained. "And a baby fell out of this window."

Nora was beginning to think she didn't want to know any more history about the shop.

"Do you still get rats in here? They used to come into the house through there." She pointed to the bottom corner of the top front room. "One bit my gran and she died of the plague. Well, my dad insisted it was the plague anyway because they quarantined her."

"Er…"

"And my brother said he sometimes heard screaming, like this room had a ghost. Oh, you've opened up the attic. We found a dead cat in here. The yard hasn't changed much." She peered out of the window. "I remember falling over there and getting a large nail stuck in my wrist. I had septicaemia and almost died. Ah yeah, the outside toilet. I used to hate that. MASSIVE spiders! Do the pipes still freeze here?"

Nora tried to block out the woman's reminiscing as they made their way downstairs, ignoring several stories of relatives tumbling to their deaths down the rickety stairwells. Finally they were at the bottom where Roger could be heard chatting to someone. Nora noticed Harry standing at the counter. He stuck out his chest when he saw her.

"Well, thanks for the trip down memory lane." The lady smiled, heading for the door. "I'd better go and find my husband and kids."

"Goodbye." Nora said, grabbing her cup of tea.

The door closed and Roger looked at Nora.

"She didn't buy anything, then."

"No. She wasn't looking for a book; she used to live here. Gave me a traumatic tour of the history of the shop. I think I'd like to quit now."

"You could always work with me, Nora." Harry suggested.

"Er...thank you, Harry. I'm going to pop this in the microwave. It's gone cold." She turned around with her tea. "And see if we have any whisky to add." She muttered, heading off to the kitchen.

When Nora returned to the front, Harry had gone.

"I shooed him away when he started asking what size bikini you wore. Something about offering you a job as his personal assistant." Roger explained.

"The mind boggles!" Nora shook her head.

"His certainly does." Roger muttered.

They ate their mince pies, drank their tea and stood watching the Christmas tree preparations for the Duke. People were wandering around with hand-made lanterns (pleased with their results from the lantern-making stalls). The battery-powered lights danced and flickered like fireflies in their different coloured jars.

The town was filling up with visitors. Every shop that had joined in the event now had battery powered candles in their windows. The electric branch of candles in the bay window of The Secondhand Bookworm was part of the show and attracted several people who crouch down and took selfies with the book displays and candles in their backgrounds.

It was eerily quiet with the road shut and the absence of the sound of traffic. Roger moaned continuously about the lack of customers so Nora was pleased when she finally saw Humphrey heading towards the shop.

He wore a thick, dark brown sweater with a turtleneck collar, jeans, boots and a dark red tartan scarf, knotted simply in a reverse drape cross with a low-slung knot. The wispy eyelash trim of his scarf added an edge of rawness to his dark-coloured sweater. He looked handsome and lost in thought.

"What a sexy hat." Humphrey said, stepping down into the bookshop.

Nora turned slowly around to model it in all its Christmas glory.

"Wait until you see yours." She gestured.

"What has Georgina chosen for me?" He crossed the room to the counter. "Evening, Dobby." He greeted Roger.

"Humphrey." Roger held out the turkey hat.

Humphrey laughed.

"Prize turkey, eh?"

"Originally you were going to be an elf but I thought it suited Roger better." Nora explained, watching Humphrey cheerfully tug on his hat.

"It does, mate." Humphrey agreed.

He grinned dashingly when Nora snapped a picture of him with her iPhone.

"How about the Elf and the Turkey together?" Nora suggested.

"No." Roger retorted.

"Grinch." Nora sighed.

"Has it been busy?" Humphrey asked, running his blue gaze over the cash book.

"What do you think?" Roger moaned.

"I'll go into the street and drum up some business then." Humphrey decided and headed back for the door.

Roger and Nora looked at one another.

"What's he going to do? Drag people in and force them to buy books?" Roger asked, amazed.

"Use his charm I expect." Nora smiled, watching Humphrey head out.

Roger rolled his eyes, shook his head and set off to make them beverages.

Over the next half an hour, Humphrey stood by the door announcing the wonders of Christmas books and hidden literary delights in a mixture of humour and arm-waving dramatics. Nora considered putting him forward for one of Seymour's plays. It worked a treat for soon the bookshop was brimming with people buying last minute Christmas presents, or Christmas books, or a variety of titles, topics and subjects from throughout the shop (they were mostly women though, Nora noticed).

At half past six, the Duke of Cole and his entourage arrived in the town so everyone stopped shopping and filled up the square, craning their necks for a glimpse of Castletown's most famous new resident. Nora served a few customers while Roger and Humphrey stood outside the shop chatting and sipping mulled wine. Humphrey glanced back, pleased when Nora joined him with the last of their customers who wished them a merry Christmas and headed off into the crowds.

Once on the step, Humphrey passed Nora her glass of mulled wine. She took a sip, her gaze settling on the tall, handsome form of the Duke by the Christmas tree.

A carol was sung and a nativity procession arrived in the square, followed by children bearing their lanterns. The Duke spoke with the children and then the mayor gave a speech thanking his grace the Duke of Cole who had kindly donated the tree from his estate. The Duke turned on the lights, the square was filled with 'ooohs', 'aaaahs' followed by enthusiastic clapping as the tree lit up magnificently and the Duke smiled around at everyone.

His eyes then met with Nora's.

Nora straightened slightly and smiled back at him. The Duke remained staring at her, smiling warmly. He then pointedly tipped his hat at her, causing everyone who noticed to look in her direction.

"Ho, ho, ho!" Roger chuckled wickedly in his most realistic impression of '*Death*' in Terry Pratchett's novel '*The Hogfather*'.

Nora cleared her throat, glancing at Humphrey staring down at her.

"Ahem." She smiled, shrugged, and watched the Duke speaking with the Mayor before posing for photographs.

"And here's me looking like a prize turkey while the Duke of Cole makes eyes at my girlfriend." Humphrey frowned as they returned to the shop.

"He wasn't making eyes at me." Nora laughed.

Humphrey glowered.

"Thinking about giving you that private tour of his library, no doubt."

"What's this?" Roger's elf ears pricked up.

"Oh, nothing." Nora shrugged.

"Our new Duke has invited Nora to his library." Humphrey said.

"When did he do that?" Roger demanded, curious.

"Yesterday." Humphrey frowned.

"Secret liaisons with royalty, eh?" Roger winked broadly.

"Wouldn't you like to know?" Nora winked broadly back. She took hold of Humphrey's hand. "And Humphrey here thinks I'm going to run off to the castle with the Duke. He was just being friendly to one of his subjects."

"Really." Humphrey didn't sound convinced.

"It's warm in here!" A sudden voice said behind them.

Nora yelped.

"Are you still open?"

They turned to see a man wrapped in several knitted scarves that outdid Roger's winter getup. One was in the four-in-hand knot, an impressive technical feat and quite a raffish style.

Humphrey nodded.

"For another," he glanced at his watch, "fifteen minutes, sir."

"Mind if I have a browse?"

"Go ahead." Humphrey nodded.

Nora led Humphrey behind the counter and they sat down, leaving Roger tidying up.

"I think I currently only have eyes for turkeys." She told him as he passed her a pen.

Humphrey bit back a laugh.

"*Currently*, eh? Hmm, well, gobble, gobble, gobble." He agreed.

Nora pinched his cheek, fondly.

She was aware of him watching her intently as she added a line to her tally chart, hoping she wouldn't have to go swimming at midnight on Christmas Eve in the outside pool. Although. It *would* be with Humphrey. So it wouldn't all be bad.

She told him that as he cheekily pecked her neck.

While Roger locked the door on the dark bookshop, Nora and Humphrey stood on the street, admiring the large, twinkling Christmas tree in the square. Most people had gone home but a few groups were heading to restaurants or finishing off their mulled wine, chatting and singing Christmas songs or dancing around the war memorial, toasting the fallen heroes.

"I reserved a table at The Duke's Pie on my way down." Humphrey told Nora.

"Did you?" She grimaced slightly.

"You don't like it there?"

"I love it there. I just heard the Duke of Cole could possibly be there tonight."

Humphrey's eyes narrowed.

"I'll just have to make sure I use my cutlery correctly, then." He said, jealously.

"I hope you're not going to wear those idiot hats during your meal." Roger frowned.

"I suppose we should remove them." Humphrey pulled the turkey and mussed up his thick, tousled hair.

"It would be polite." Nora agreed, removing her hat, too.

"Millennials." Roger muttered, shaking his head. He set off. "See you tomorrow night."

"At the wonderful staff meal." Nora called after him.

"Looking forward to it." Humphrey stuck his thumbs up.

Roger waved glumly and set off, looking large and warm.

"Dinner with a Duke and then classic Christmas movies in the old town hall, my sweet?" Humphrey wrapped his arm around Nora's shoulders.

"Does this count as date number five?" She pondered his handsome profile, thoughtfully.

"I think it will." He met her eyes. "Perhaps afterwards you might consider calling me your boyfriend?"

"We shall see." Nora smiled and they set off up the hill towards The Duke's Pie after a successful '*Shopping by Candlelight*' in The Secondhand Bookworm.

10 THE DISGUISE IN CHRISTMAS TOWN

Betty Gracewing was doing her best not to bop her first customer over the head with the large blow-up candy cane Nora had arrived with that morning. He was an elderly man with loose false teeth and a dribbling scowl that made Betty's already-tender stomach heave. She stood smiling politely as the man insulted her and the bookshop for the umpteenth time, fighting the urge to pull his ugly brown beanie hat over his crinkly old face.

"And as I say, the service here has always been first rate and so I was very disappointed to receive the book in the post with the postage added to the payment." He repeated, shaking his head slowly and clicking his tongue so his front teeth almost fell out.

Betty winced. A feisty woman in her late seventies, Betty despised her generation, referring to them as evil *greyheads*. She tried to live as if she was still in her twenties, always had a shocking story to tell Nora, loved books, flirted with customers and sometimes transformed into a Gorgon if they mentioned her *age*. Georgina found her interesting and entertaining, sufficiently knowledgeable about books and an eclectic addition to her staff.

"I *never* pay postage because I have been such a loyal customer for so many years. I was most shocked and disappointed." The man sniffed.

"Dear, dear how very unfortunate for you." Betty sympathised sarcastically.

He stared at her suspiciously so Betty flashed a dazzling smile. Behind her, Nora choked on a smothered laugh, arranging the blow-up candy cane Seymour had given her in front of the antiquarian books.

"And so Ms Pickering assured me it was a young staff member who was newly employed and would not have realised and she has very kindly agreed to refund me the cost of the postage which is why I am here." He concluded and stuck out his hand expectantly.

Betty stared at his yellowing palm.

"I understand. How terrible for you. May I ask your name, sir?"

"Why?" He snapped sharply.

Betty stiffened.

"Well if everyone came into the shop claiming they had permission for me to hand them money without proof I would soon be out on the street." Betty replied tartly. "I will need to check your name."

"I can assure you I am not one for fibbing!" The man stated in affront.

"Neither am I!" Betty assured dangerously.

Nora stepped up to the counter.

"Ms Pickering told us to expect you sir but also to confirm your name. We get a lot of swindlers in here unfortunately." She explained, feeling Betty bristling next to her.

The man sucked his teeth, making a hideous squelchy noise as he did so.

Betty clutched her stomach.

"I see! Well. My name is Mr Pullan. Mr Gregory Pullan." He said aloofly.

Nora nodded with a polite smile.

"Thank you, Mr Pullan. I have your refund in an envelope here for you. If you could sign the book next to the pay-out figure we would be very grateful." Nora pointed.

Betty hissed and muttered expletives behind Nora's back at Mr Pullan. Nora fought hard not to laugh; watching as he signed his name, took the envelope, opened it, counted out the two pound coins and twenty five pence and shuffled off shaking his head.

The door closed behind him and Betty drew in a long breath.

"WHAT a pig!!!" She exclaimed, having checked no one else was close by to hear her.

"Very rude!" Nora agreed.

"All that hoity-toity fuss over a couple of quid. I should have jabbed him with the letter opener in the eye. The old *grey-head*! Always the same. Fussing over pennies. Can you imagine how much he paid to get over here to collect it? Probably twice as much! And he was so RUDE. So condescending. And I saw him looking at my boobs, the old letch."

"Whaaaaaat!" Nora gasped.

Betty's lips twitched.

"I know. I've still got it, haven't I. But as I told Georgina when she tried to set me up with that decrepit old Mr Marchland who collects books on fossils, I'm fed up not hard up. The very fact that he collects books on fossils was an insult."

Nora laughed, shaking her head.

"Well I think we deserve some hot soup as compensation. My treat." Nora decided, rubbing her hands together because of the cold.

"Oh Nora I couldn't possibly…"

"I insist!" Nora decided, picking up her woollen hat. "If Mr Pullan sets the trend for the day we're going to need fuel. Plus, we're going to go a little bit crazy marking up those magazines Georgina left us yesterday."

"Oh thanks ever so, Nora. Lovely. I could do with some nice settling soup after that *horrid* man's teeth set my already delicate stomach quivering." Betty smiled and watched Nora head off out of the door.

It was bitterly cold outside but Nora couldn't be bothered to put on her Parka just to nip to the delicatessen so she braced herself against the arctic blast as it howled down the hill, driving a few flakes of snow with it, and buffeted her across the empty road.

There was an odd, steady grinding sound in the street. Nora noticed Hugh sitting on top of a tiny gritting machine, spraying rock salt in all directions. A man crouched under his umbrella in shock.

Hugh manoeuvred the violent contraption around the corner from Market Street, where he had been gritting the road, and entered the square. Before he could notice her, Nora skidded into the delicatessen and almost fell into the shop.

"Alright there, Nora?" Philip asked from behind the main counter.

Nora straightened up.

"Good morning." She greeted sheepishly. "Ahem. Pardon the unladylike entrance."

Philip nodded, bemused.

Alice grinned from where she stood arranging expensive cigar boxes on a glass shelf.

"What are these?" Nora noticed a new pretty display of boxes of handmade chocolates.

"Rose and violet creams." Alice replied. "Pricey but tasty."

"Such lovely packaging. I'm here for some soup." Nora resisted.

"We have tomato and basil today."

"Delicious. Two cups please."

They chatted about the previous evening's '*Shopping by Candlelight*' and the Duke of Cole, having heard a rumour that the Duke had bought Nora and Humphrey drinks in The Duke's Pie.

"Well yes, it's true." Nora recalled. "He dropped in to sample some pasties and very generously paid for a round of drinks for all the diners. Seeing as it was only Humphrey and I enjoying a friendly meal together in the restaurant at the time it wasn't favouritism, just…happenstance." Nora glanced from side to side, suspiciously.

"You and Humphrey were dining just as friends, eh?" Alice winked.

"You're both dating though, aren't you?" Phil asked. Nora blinked.

"I'm beginning to think the goings on at The Secondhand Bookworm are a source of great local interest!"

"Only the love-life of the staff, Nora." Alice admitted.

Nora's mouth quirked.

"We all saw his grace tip his hat at you in the square." Philip pointed out.

"We're old friends." Nora shrugged, accepting the soup.

"I'm beginning to think there's more to it than that, Nora." Alice studied her keenly.

"Oh, a woman can but wish." Nora brushed off.

"Before you leave," Alice remembered and disappeared behind the counter, rummaging loudly.

Nora watched, bemused.

"For the bookshop." Alice re-emerged holding a single brown bauble with '*Merry Christmas from The*

Castletown Delicatessen' scrawled in gold lettering around the middle.

Nora held out her hand.

"Thank you!" She was genuinely pleased. "Our Christmas tree will be most grateful."

"And it will give us a bit of advertising, too." Alice winked.

Nora agreed.

"Have a good day." She set off, admiring the bauble carefully.

"Bye, Nora." Philip and Alice chorused and looked at each other as she left.

"Town gossips." Nora sighed and carried the bauble and soup carefully back to the bookshop where it was still as freezing and desolate inside as outside.

"Oh thanks ever so, Nora. It smells delicious." Betty took her cup.

"The soup is very hot though." Nora said, popping hers onto the mouse mat.

She walked over to the Christmas tree and carefully added the bauble.

"Wonderful, Nora." Betty admired.

Nora bowed.

The door swung open in a gust of wind.

"That's it. I'm not spending all day jumping up and down closing that door." Nora decided.

Betty watched, amused and interested as Nora fumbled around the stationery boxes under the counter for scissors, paper and packaging tape.

While their soup cooled, Nora made a thick rectangle wedge of paper which she taped to the door frame, tested the door against it, adjusted it several times and finally had a wodge that allowed for customers to open the door with a slight shove and prevent the wind from blowing it open.

"Perfect!" Nora nodded, pleased, and sat down to sip her soup.

"Who will be your plus one tonight, Nora?" Betty asked, delicately spooning the soup from her cup with a spoon she had magically acquired from her bag.

"At the staff meal?" Nora asked.

Before she could answer, the door opened after a man shoved it hard with his shoulder.

Betty and Nora stared.

"Got any stuffed animals?" He asked, standing on the doorstep.

Nora glared as the weak warm air from the oil heater was sucked out into the street.

"We only get a few books about taxidermy in to…" She began to explain.

"Not *books*…oh, is this a bookshop? I was looking for *actual* stuffed animals."

Nora and Betty screwed up their noses.

"No we don't have any."

"Didn't this used to be a stuffed animal museum?"

"No. There was an infamous Curiosity Museum here in the past but it was sold."

"What happened to the animals?"

"I'm afraid I'm not completely sure. I heard that The Funeral of Cock Robin, which contained about one hundred stuffed sparrows, was sold to an inn in Cornwall or Devon. But you could ask Bill Sykes…erm, I mean *Mr* Sykes. He used to own the museum. His girlfriend runs Lady Lanes Antiques just across the road and he is usually in there." Nora explained.

"That's great. Thanks." The man left, closing the door behind him so it remained firmly shut.

"Disgusting man." Betty said, shaking her head. "How would *he* like to be stuffed?!"

Nora sipped her soup, agreeing.

"I'm coming to the staff meal with Seymour tonight." She then said. "Humphrey is already invited as a member of staff but Seymour has a crush on Cara so I said he could come as my partner and gaze at her all evening."

"Oh how lovely." Betty smiled and winked.

"Who are you bringing?"

"My favourite son, Dave. Don't tell my other children he's my favourite, but he is. He was such a naughty little boy but I let him get away with murder. He's my youngest and works with jewellery, such a clever sweetheart."

"Is he married?"

"Yes but she's a…" Betty placed her hand to the side of her mouth. "…old battle-axe, a right old Carrie Nation."

"Carrie-who?"

"Oh Nora! You must have heard of Carrie Nation? She was a nineteenth century activist involved in the suffragette campaign for votes for women. She wielded a hatchet and lived in Hatchet Hall and published a magazine called *The Hatchet*." Betty explained. "They called her a battle-axe, a pejorative for an aggressive, domineering and forceful woman, but you already knew that last bit because you're so clever."

"And an aggressive, domineering, forceful woman; when it comes to rude customers." Nora chuckled.

"Well Beatrice, my Dave's wife, is a right old battle-axe."

"Does she wield a hatchet?"

"No. A rolling pin." Betty teased and they both laughed.

They finished their soup and then set about organising a large pile each of 'Profile Magazines' to place in clear protective bags, sellotape lightly down and price using small white stickers; a mind-numbing job especially when every single magazine was about a make of airplane.

"I'm not sure about this restaurant we're going to tonight." Betty mused aloud as she slipped a magazine about the *Avro Vulcan* into a bag. "Piertown is quite rough at night."

"I agree." Nora nodded. "Hopefully this Chinese restaurant will be civilised."

"I wish we were having something else." Betty sighed, folding the plastic top over the magazine and taping it down. "Chinese food can make my bowels a little loose."

"Oh dear." Nora sympathised.

The sound of a fanfare announced the arrival of a Skype chat message from Seatown. Nora leaned towards the monitor to read it.

'Just spoke to Georgina – she says to tell Betty about the THIEF – Cara xxx'

Nora read it and turned to Betty who was squinting at the monitor but unable to read it from where she sat.

'Ok x' Nora typed without looking.

"Cara said to tell you about the thief."

"Oh Nora, what thief?" Betty asked, aghast. "I heard about the posters going missing here. Did you catch the culprit?

"I don't believe that's related to this case, I'm sure we get an array of banditti, but this one however we know. Have you met White-Lightning Joe?"

"That plump little man who buys local guides?"

"Yes, him."

Betty turned up her nose.

"Is he a rotten old pickpocket?" She asked.

"Well, he's our current suspect in a specific scheme I think he's concocted."

"Oh, how terrible, Nora. What a wicked little git."

"We don't have any proof yet, so if he comes in and shuffles about by the Castletown and Cole section keep a sharp eye on him. We think he might be slipping books into his bag or up his coat, running out and going somewhere in the street to rub out the prices. He then brings them back to sell to us."

"What a terrible, evil pig!" Betty snarled. "We'll catch him in the act, Nora."

"He could well be in today."

"We will need a plan. How about, I put on a disguise, something from lost property, and stand outside as if I am window shopping, and when he runs out I follow him with my camera phone recording and catch him in the act."

Nora looked interested.

"That's a really good idea. But don't confront him because Georgina wants to do that. Just film him and we'll send her the evidence."

"Oh I like our plan!" Betty said, putting her wrapped and priced magazine onto the small, depressing pile of marked-up ones. "I'll go and find a disguise and keep it back here."

While Betty was in the kitchen rummaging through the lost property, a regular customer named Don popped his head in the door after using his knee to open it.

"Any regimental histories?" He asked predictably.

"No."

"I'll have a look though." He headed into the back room.

A couple entered, wearing neon pink bobble hats with neon green bobbles that made Nora blink.

"Good morning!" The man greeted loudly. He had enormous teeth that appeared to be too big for his mouth.

"Hello." Nora replied, putting down her pack of stickers.

"We're looking for some books. Do you list your books on your computer?" He asked, noticing the monitor on the desk.

"No, I'm afraid not."

"Really? I'm a piece of string! Ah-ha-ha-ha ha!" He guffawed.

Nora looked blank so the woman beside him shook her head.

"Oh it's his favourite joke. When someone says, '*I'm afraid not*' it sounds like '*I'm a frayed knot*'. So he calls himself a piece of string and thinks everyone will find it funny. Drives me mad, I could strangle him." She said and really did look as though she wanted to kill him.

"Oh. Ha-ha." Nora laughed politely.

"Oh get yourself a sense of humour, Iris." The man said to his wife, instantly sobering. He took out his wallet. "I'm looking for some novels. Do you have a section where you keep your novels?"

"Yes, we do. They're in the attic room." Nora explained.

"Are they really?" He looked around. "Do you have an elevator?"

"No but the staircase is back there."

"You don't really want to go into the attic do you, Rupert?" Iris frowned.

"I do. As a matter of fact." He said, hostile.

Iris shrugged.

"Well I'll stay down here."

"Fine." Rupert muttered and headed off.

When he had gone Nora looked at Iris who was staring at her steadily.

"Is there a purveyor of wines in town?"

"The delicatessen on the corner has a good stock of fine wines and…"

"Tell him I'm in there!" She said before Nora could even finish her sentence and in a moment she was gone.

Nora turned at the sound of footsteps behind her and almost fell off her chair. Betty was wearing enormous dark sunglasses, a deerstalker hat, a large holey red scarf and a horrid brown jacket that was at least three sizes too big for her.

Nora was about to comment when lo and behold the door opened with a loud jolt against Nora's wedge of paper and White-Lightning Joe entered. Nora turned and Betty picked up a random book from the art section and pretended to read it.

"Heee-loooo, Nora." White-Lightning Joe greeted.

"Oh, hello." She replied.

He smiled awkwardly, chuckled falsely and cleared his throat as he approached the Cole section opposite the door.

"I've got some books I'll bring in to sell. I'll just have a browse first." He said, his cheeks reddening.

"Okay." Nora said tightly, unable to help glaring at him.

He giggled nervously before pressing himself into the section, giving Nora shifty looks.

"Thank you for letting me browse, madam." A deep, low voice said, making Nora jump.

When she saw it had been Betty, who was now strolling towards the door, Nora desperately tried to keep a straight face.

"You're welcome. Have a lovely day."

"I will, madam." The low, deep voice replied and Betty's large, ridiculous form left.

White-Lightning Joe glanced over his shoulder at her, gave a small rude chuckle and returned to his fake browsing, casting looks at Nora.

Knowing they needed to catch him in the act of thievery, Nora reluctantly turned away to read a Skype message from Seatown. A moment later she heard a mad scrambling as White-Lightning Joe hurried for the door, struggled against the wodge for a moment, finally threw it open with a crash against the wall, and flew into the street. Nora shook her head angrily. Her outrage then transformed into amusement as she saw Betty immediately leave her pretended browse of the window and head after him.

It was only five minutes later that Betty returned, breathless and fuming.

"Oh he is a thief alright, the wicked man." She said, pulling off her sunglasses and unravelling the scarf.

"Did you film him?"

"I certainly did!" She held up her phone triumphantly. "I'll show you."

They bent over Betty's iPhone and watched the video. Betty had followed Joe at a distance while recording, turned the corner into Tree Lane and watched as he had crouched down by the closed Indian restaurant and taken two books out of his coat.

"Thief!" Nora exclaimed.

"Wretch!" Betty shouted.

The footage showed White-Lightning Joe lick his thumb and rub out the pencil marking on the frontispiece of each book and then place them into his carrier bag. He then set off sipping his cider for a stroll.

"Send it to Georgina." Nora suggested.

They spent a few minutes trying to send the video until it finally went. Georgina phoned the shop, fuming.

"The cheek of it!" Georgina growled angrily. "When he comes in to sell them, telephone me right away please."

"Okay." Nora agreed.

"Caught in the act on video. I feel like sending it to 'Crimestoppers'. Georgina said.

"Yes, even if it just shows the nation what he's doing." Nora agreed.

"He'll be sorry." Georgina seethed.

While Nora and Betty waited for White-Lightning Joe, Betty posed in her disguise for Nora to take a few photos and upload on Facebook and Instagram tagged as 'Sherlock Holmes' and 'Thief Hunter Extraordinaire' before Betty returned the items to the lost property box and made them a round of tea.

"Do you sell stamps?" A woman asked, almost falling into the shop as she pushed with all her might to open the wedged door.

Nora winced guiltily.

"Erm…yes we do."

"Large letter stamps?"

"Oh. No, we sell stamps for postcards."

"Never mind!" She exclaimed and stomped off only to be replaced by a burly black man wrapped up as if he was on a ski trip.

"Where are your art books?" He asked politely.

"Just there, sir." Nora indicated.

"Thanks. I'm looking for any books about Paul Cadden, a Scottish graphite artist." He explained.

"I don't recall ever seeing anything by him or about his work."

"They would be in your hyperrealism section."

"Oh. We don't have a section specifically for hyperrealism."

"No?" He shrugged. "Well, that would be useful."

"I don't think we ever have enough books on the subject to give it its own section."

"Shame. A real shame."

"You're welcome to browse."

"No, it's not worth my while if you don't think you have anything. Do you know his art?"

"I don't think I do."

"You should take a look. His phrase is 'to intensify the normal'. He produces mind-blowing pictures. Paul Cadden. Google him. You'll be impressed."

"Okay, thanks. I will." Nora nodded.

Betty returned with tea and eyed the man with interest, who paused to consider a book about barometers on the counter. She turned to Nora and winked, nodding her head towards him. Nora bit back a grin, picking up a Profile Magazine to price. She almost dropped it when the door opened with an enormous crash and White-Lightning Joe hung on the door handle.

"Whew! Eeeeep! Flippin' eck!" He exclaimed, followed by giggling. "What's happened to the door?"

Nora and Betty stared at him. The man who had enquired about Paul Cadden headed off into the back of the shop to browse.

"Sooo-rriiii." Joe apologised with a large, fake grin, closing the door. "I don't know my own strength." He pattered across the room to the counter. "I have a couple of books for sale."

Nora resisted saying 'I bet you do!' in an angry voice and reached for the phone.

"I'll need to telephone Georgina, the owner, about them." She said, pressing speed dial for the Seatown number.

"Oh. Okay." White-Lightning Joe said nervously.

He glanced at Betty who was glaring at him witheringly over the top of her reading glasses.

"He-he-he." He giggled, taking a book about the history of the South Downs and a book about Castletown from his white carrier bag and placing them on the counter.

"Hello, Georgina. I have Joe here wishing to sell some books." Nora said, watching him. "Of course." She passed Joe the phone and he took it with a grin.

Betty and Nora watched him steadily.

"Heee-loooo, Georgina." He greeted.

Nora wondered what Georgina was saying because gradually White-Lightning Joe's smile faded. He blinked repetitively but said nothing. Gradually his face reddened to the shade of a beetroot as he stood listening. He gave a few nervous, guilty chuckles, his bottom lip began to quiver and his eyes filled with tears.

"Okay." He finally said and handed the phone back to Nora.

Betty and Nora still stared at him until he took a great shuddering breath, waved frantically in Nora's face and turned.

"Byeeeeeeeeeee." He wailed and flew from the shop as fast as he possibly could.

"Good riddance!" Betty called after him and made a rude gesture with her hand.

"What did you say?" Nora asked Georgina.

"I told him we knew he was stealing our books and selling them back to us. And that I could go to the police. But I would let it go this one time. And he is banned from the shop and is NOT to set foot in either of my branches again. He didn't deny it."

"No. He turned and ran." Nora nodded.

"Hopefully that will be the last we see of him!"

"He left the two books he took off the shelf earlier. I'll reprice them and put them back on the shelf."

"Don't ever let him into the shop again, Nora. I'll send a staff memo around informing everyone he is banned."

"Such a wally to do that."

"Yes. Silly man."

Betty used a variety of stronger descriptions for him. When Nora had hung up they reminisced over the whole event, finally glad it was over, and settling down to continue the monotonous job of pricing the box of Profile Magazines.

After lunch, Nora hung a selection of magazines in their plastic wallets in the window by the Christmas books, the latter of which were gradually reducing to one shelf after most of the titles had sold. The door opened as she was sticking a magazine about '*The Roland CII*' next to a magazine about '*The Dorner Do 17 and 215*' and let in a howl of arctic wind.

"Three floors of books?! I may be some time!" A man in a large blue knitted hat exclaimed.

"It's warm in here!" The lady with him grumbled.

"Yes, it's warm in here!" The man agreed.

Betty picked up a pen and added several lines to a tally on Nora's chart while Nora picked up a magazine about '*The Hawker-Hunter Two-Seaters*'.

"You there. Can you hear me?" The man asked Betty.

Betty slowly looked up.

"Can your old grandma here me?" The man asked Nora, loudly.

Nora grimaced, feeling Betty bristle with affront and take a long, angry breath.

"I can hear you! I happen to have both my hearing aids in but unfortunately both my ear horns are currently being polished." Betty said sarcastically.

The man stared.

"Well, can you check your computer and see if you have a certain book in stock?" The man asked Betty. "You can use the computer, can't you?"

Betty gave him a contemptuous glare. Nora was surprised the man didn't turn to stone.

"Just about." She said, tightly. "But we don't list the titles of our books on our computer."

"How silly." The woman with the man scoffed.

Betty's eyes flashed red.

"It would be an impossible task. All of our delightful books are in topical sections if you would like to browse." She said primly.

"Where do you keep books about pottery?" The woman asked her.

"On the top floor, front room."

"FOOTBALL BOOKS?" The man shouted.

"IN THE SAME ROOM!" Betty shouted back.

"Right you are. Up we go." He said and they set off through the walkway.

The man's elbow knocked a book off the side shelf as he passed but he and the woman ignored it crashing to the floor. Betty picked it up and stuck her fingers up at them as they disappeared up the creaking staircase.

"What a *beast*." Betty whispered resentfully.

Nora agreed.

Betty was muttering expletives so Nora quickly changed the subject.

"Oh. The Woman in Gold has a new hat." She said, pointing across the street at the gold statue of a woman that stood outside the entrance to a shop called 'Marbles' every day. "Although, it looks a little out of place in this weather."

"What is it?" Betty asked, joining Nora by the window.

They pondered the bright yellow beehive fascinator hat, complete with elaborate honey-coloured mesh and what they assumed to be bees or flowers on wires sticking out at many angles. Betty snickered.

"I may buy that." Nora then said seriously.

"Really? Oh Nora, you should, you would look beautiful in it." Betty encouraged.

"I have a wedding to go to in the summer and I have a yellow, silk dress. It would be such fun to wear that!"

"Oh how elegant and fascinating you would look!" Betty agreed.

"Thanks." Nora laughed.

"Go and see how much it is." Betty said.

"Would that be okay? It looks amazing from here and would likely be snapped up by a Castletown diva."

"I'll cover base." Betty volunteered.

"Okay. Thank you. I'll grab my coat and head over for a look."

"And if you buy it you can model it for me and it will be like a breath of summer." Betty sighed dreamily.

Nora liked the sound of that! She threw on her coat, zipped it up and headed off into the light blizzard, leaving Betty flying towards the counter to answer the telephone.

11 THE RAVENS AND THE STAFF CHRISTMAS MEAL

When Nora returned to The Secondhand Bookworm carrying a large, yellow hat box, she almost dropped it when she saw two notorious ladies huddled by the art section, conversing rapidly in whispers. Betty was seated on the stool behind the counter slipping another pink Profile Magazine into a plastic wallet.

"We already have that one, Poppet!" Miss Raven was whispering hard as Nora squeezed past.

"Don't you...don't you...don't you want a better edition?" Mrs Raven whispered back breathlessly.

"No, Poppet. Ours is just as good. It would be a waste of money."

"Well, if you're sure."

"I am!" Miss Raven snapped.

Mrs and Miss Raven were two notorious regulars who collected children's books, carried hundreds of carrier bags and insisted on a ten percent discount every time they purchased a book from The Secondhand Bookworm.

"Arrrgh!" Nora exclaimed as she almost tripped on the deluge of carrier bags behind the counter.

"Oh sorry, Nora. Goodness, are you okay?" Betty asked.

Nora steadied herself and sighed; glad she hadn't inadvertently popped the blow-up candy cane.

"Yes. Fine." She placed the hat box on the counter top.

"Hopefully those witches will be gone soon." Betty whispered out of the side of her mouth.

Nora doubted it.

"Oh let me see it, Nora. What a lovely millinery box. The colour is beautiful." Betty admired.

"The box was separately priced, even though it was the original for the hat, so I thought that was a cheeky rip off. But Stan said it was a collector's item in itself. He's right; it is a beautiful box, lined with yellow satin." Nora explained and opened the lid.

"Oh Nora, yes, a millinery box is a must." Betty agreed. "How stunning! A magnificent hat. What a beautiful shape, so clever, like a real beehive, and yet such a classy hat style. Put it on."

Nora took off her Parka and carefully removed the fascinator hat from the box. She put it on and modelled it for Betty who clapped her hands with admiration and enthusiasm.

"Oh can't you wear it tonight to the staff meal? Humphrey would drool all over his sweet and sour."

"No. I'll save it for the wedding." Nora decided.

Betty agreed that would be best.

Miss Raven glided to the counter. She paused pointedly, watching Nora steadily, so Nora removed the hat and placed it in her box.

"Yes, we would like to purchase these but we would like to leave this one as it isn't in as good condition as the copy we already have." Miss Raven said.

"Don't forget….don't forget…the discount." Mrs Raven whispered behind her daughter's back.

Miss Raven ignored her.

"The Sleeping Beauty Ladybird is priced too high at three pounds. Would you take two?" She asked Betty, blue eyes flashing.

Betty gritted her teeth.

"Oh I'm terribly sorry but the prices are fixed." Betty refused.

Miss Raven clenched her jaw.

"Oh they're not always fixed, especially in our case, because we are such good customers. Could you get Georgina on the line? She would give us a discount."

Betty began to tremble with rage.

"Georgina has given us strict instructions not to change the prices on any books. We can give you your usual discount…"

"Our usual discount would not be enough." Miss Raven said, smiling threateningly. "If you could phone her, I would be much obliged."

Nora stepped in.

"May I have a look at the book, please?" She asked Miss Raven, politely.

Miss Raven looked at her sharply, her knuckles whitening as she held it tighter.

"It is one I am very familiar with and am aware of its value."

"But I would like to check it as I have a trained eye." Nora insisted firmly.

It looked for a moment as though Miss Raven was about to throw a tantrum, while Mrs Raven stood behind her daughter breathing like a choo-choo train. Finally, she handed over the book.

"Hmm. Yes." Nora over-exaggerated her examination. "Hmm. One moment please." She rummaged under the counter until she found a small

magnifying glass kept in a stationery basket. Betty
watched, delighted, as Nora peered through it,
examining the ladybird book. "Some slight foxing.
Clean pages, no dog-earing. Complete with jacket. A
slight tear but that's to be expected. Hmmm. An early
copy." She looked up after ages, keeping the magnifying
glass to her eye. Miss Raven jumped. "It is priced very
fairly, Miss Raven. You would be able to have a ten
percent discount but the price remains at three pounds."

Miss Raven turned and conversed with her mother in
whispers. When she turned back, Nora kept the
magnifying glass up, this time over her mouth.

"We'll take it." She said, smiling sweetly, distracted
and intimidated slightly by Nora's large, straight lips.

"Lovely." Nora said brightly, returned the
magnifying glass and rang the prices of the books
through the till.

"And the usual discount please." Miss Raven
reminded Nora.

"Certainly." Nora nodded.

"Ask her…ask her….ask her…ask her for a bag."
Mrs Raven whispered.

"I will!" Miss Raven snapped and flashed a sweet
smile. "May we have them in a bag, please?"

Nora was tempted to charge the Ravens five pence
for the bag but instead nodded and Betty unhooked one.

"TWO bags please. To double them up." Miss Raven
snapped.

"For the love of…" Betty began but stopped and
unhooked another one.

"We are returning by taxi." Miss Raven explained
defensively. "And they have to be strong."

"Six pounds and twenty pence please." Nora said.

"Is that with our discount?" Miss Raven asked
dangerously.

"Yes." Nora smiled tightly.

Betty slipped the books in the bag, placed that bag into another bag and resisted throwing them at the Ravens.

"Thank you." Miss Raven said, accepting the bag and passing it to her mother. She then emptied a small, crumpled bank bag of twenty pence pieces onto the counter and counted out the amount.

"Shall I…shall I double check it…?" Mrs Raven whispered hard.

"I've got this thank you Poppet!" Miss Raven hissed.

Nora accepted the handful of coins, printed a receipt and watched the Ravens gather up their carrier bags, two black sacks and two rucksacks and then head off whispering. When they had gone Betty looked at Nora. She pursed her lips, pretended to lock them and throw away the key.

Nora laughed.

"I think we should have some tea and cake to see us through to the end of the day."

"Shame we don't have anything stronger." Betty muttered and glided off to put the kettle on.

At the end of the day, Betty counted up the sales while Nora cashed up and Skyped the final takings through to Georgina in Seatown. A woman with a grin like the Cheshire cat had been their last customer of the day, but she had only asked if they sell dice.

All the Profile Magazines were marked up and those not hanging in the window were placed in the aviation section. The shop was tidied, emptied of customers, the Christmas tree plug pulled out its socket in the next floor front room, the branch of candles in the window switched off, front ceiling lights turned off, door locked and once Georgina had skyped through: '*Well done. See you later!*' they turned off the computer, wrapped up, grabbed their belongings, set the alarm and left.

Betty and Nora had both parked up the hill so they crossed the road and passed the Woman in Gold who was now wearing a foam dome flight helmet. The sound of clip-clopping drew their attention to the figure of Lady-Santa, followed by Twinkle, crossing the road in her tiny customary Santa dress, red leggings, red high heels, Santa hat and myriad of coloured bags, now a familiar sight about the town.

"I'm reading a wonderful biography about Margaret Thatcher." Betty shared, pulling the collar of her coat about her tighter. "Shame we've got this staff meal tonight, I was really getting my teeth into it."

"Well it shouldn't be too long. It usually finishes at about nine."

"Oh that's very civilised. I can put my hair in curlers and get a good couple of hours reading in." Betty said, eyes twinkling.

"Hey Nora. Had any books about Passchendaele in?" Albert from the print shop asked as they neared.

"Oh that was one of the worst battles of both world wars." Betty said sadly.

"I don't recall seeing anything recently." Nora pondered.

"I'll pop down for a look at some point." Albert promised and watched them pass his doorway.

"Are there many people coming tonight?" Betty asked Nora as they approached their cars.

"I think there are quite a few including Georgina's niece Elizabeth, who worked in the shops until she went to Oxford University, and her boyfriend Jason. Jason is going to work over the summer because he's studying at Port Town University and will be coming home for the holidays. Also Felicity, who used to manage the Seatown branch before she became an accountant, is coming with her house lodger Rick, whom she is currently dating. Terri is coming; she left to go into agriculture, Georgina invited her even though she no longer works here; and a few Saturday people we don't get to see much, like Steve, who used to be a Goth, and Sophia, who left to work in hospital management because she was living on baked beans and needed more money, but who might come back to work with books one day. My cousin Felix is coming even though his first day of work is tomorrow."

"Sounds diverse." Betty praised. "I'm looking forward to it."

"It's usually quite eventful." Nora recalled.

They reached their cars, scraped away some ice that was already forming on the windscreens, Nora carefully placed her yellow millinery box onto the back seat, they said their goodbyes and set off home to prepare for 'The Secondhand Bookworm Christmas Staff Meal'.

The Fortune Palace of Piertown was a large, ground floor restaurant located opposite the pier on the seafront. Humphrey and Nora stopped on the way to pick up Terri who wore a tiny black leather skirt, heeled knee-high boots and a boob tube visible beneath her opened raincoat that made Humphrey's eyes pop. She clambered into the back of Humphrey's car and spent the drive into town talking about sheep dipping and cow foot fungus until they pulled into an icy car park by the theatre and met Seymour, Felix, Heather and Milton.

Heather, Nora's sister, often worked *ad hoc* for Georgina on some weekends. Her date was their brother Milton who didn't want to be left out of his kindred's night on the town. Seymour wore a black suit, waistcoat and tie beneath his black ski coat. He had a Christmas card for Cara. Felix had come alone and was nervous about meeting everyone as well as starting work at The Secondhand Bookshop the following day.

"Oh golly. I hope I don't give anyone a disgust of me." Felix worried, straightening his tie and tucking his beanie hat over his cold ears. "I often say silly things when I'm nervous."

"You'll be fine. It's you getting a disgust of everyone else I'm concerned about. Staff meals can be a little outrageous." Nora grimaced.

"Eeek. 'Anxious emoji'." Felix grimaced and hung back for Heather and Milton.

"Thanks for asking me this morning." Seymour smiled at Nora.

"I thought you would need a change of scenery before the theatre opens tomorrow night, pardon the pun." Nora said.

"I do need a breather." Seymour chuckled. "I've been driving everyone mad. One of my actresses almost quit."

"Try to be more like P.T. Barnum, the greatest showman." Nora suggested.

"I don't own a circus and we are not performing a musical." Seymour said, offended.

The staff of The Secondhand Bookworm had arranged to meet in The Melon Ball, a cocktail bar a few doors from the restaurant. When they entered, Jane and her date, Ian, had just arrived and were ordering martinis.

Jane worked part-time at The Secondhand Bookworm. Recently divorced, she spent her time working at the bookshop, managing her three teenage children and studying towards opening a dance school. During quiet times at The Secondhand Bookworm, Jane had taught Nora the tango.

"Over here, worms." A young man's voice hailed.

Nora recognised Jason Dale whose arm was around Elizabeth's shoulders as they stood by the bar talking to Georgina, Troy, Mrs Pickering and Mrs Pickering's almost-deaf brother Orville.

Georgina wore a vintage corset, having arranged with Felicity to dress in matching get-ups. Felicity arrived in a black and green steampunk corset under her feather-and-down winter coat. She and Georgina spent ten minutes discussing waist cinching. Troy listened with great fascination as he held a box of Christmas presents.

The group soon swelled to over twenty people with everyone gradually arriving. Roger telephoned to say he was picking up Sophia and her boyfriend and that they would meet them at the restaurant, so they all headed off down the road.

It was cold but very busy in Piertown. Recently there had been an influx of homeless people in the town, so there were mountains of sleeping bags in most of the doorways of the shops. Humphrey and Nora soon lagged behind, handing out change and asking how people were. Humphrey kept hold of Nora's hand while they listened to a toothless girl tell them her woes. When Humphrey gave her five pounds to get the bus to her boyfriend's house in Wall Town, the girl threw her arms around him and called him '*boootiful*'.

"Just make sure you get someone warm." Humphrey urged her, worried.

"I will. God bless ya, James Bond." The girl shouted.

Nora smothered a smile. Humphrey certainly did look like Ian Fleming's suave and sophisticated fictional British Secret Service agent, appearing especially debonair in his navy blue wool suit, white shirt and black tie for The Secondhand Bookworm Staff Christmas Meal.

"I was reading about The Duke of Cole's homeless charity. It has a special focus now on Piertown so all these people should be getting extra help soon." Nora told Humphrey as they caught up to the bookshop group.

Terri and Jane were loudly dancing the conga.

"That's good news." Humphrey nodded. He frowned. "Your new Duke is quite the do-gooder."

"He's not *my* new Duke." Nora blushed.

Humphrey's stare landed on her cheek.

"If you say so." He remarked with a slight smile.

Nora chuckled and nudged his arm.

"Good evening. Welcome to Fortune Palace. You booked?" The lady at the door greeted the front of the mob.

"The Secondhand Bookworm party." Georgina announced. "There are twenty-eight of us."

"Ah yes. We busy tonight with other party too. You on right hand of restaurant, they on left." The woman said, picking up an armful of menus and then screaming in Chinese at two waiters who were watching two fish fighting in a large fish tank.

"Thank you." Georgina nodded and stood with Troy in the doorway welcoming each person until everyone from The Secondhand Bookworm had entered and they filled up their table by the dance floor and a DJ who had a black screen set up behind his music gear.

Nora sat next to Humphrey on her left and on her right Cara, who had brought her sister, Ella, as her guest. Seymour bribed Ella with theatre tickets so she would let him sit next to Cara.

Betty and her son Dave sat opposite and Nora watched as Felicity, Rick, Jason, Elizabeth, Georgina, Troy, Mrs Pickering, uncle Orville, Jane and Ian settled at the top end of the table, laughing loudly and causing a scene that attracted the attention of the other party.

Roger arrived, looking harassed, with what little hair he had sticking up on the top of his head, followed by Sophia and her boyfriend Harrison who both looked tipsy.

Milton and Heather sat with Terri, Agnes and Agnes' boyfriend Neale at the other end of the table, observed by Betty who was pleased to be in the middle so she could hear everyone's conversations. Steve, the former Goth, had brought his pretty girlfriend Jenny, who had her tongue pierced, and sat next to Betty who looked happy and in hope of some thrilling gossip.

Once everyone was seated, Georgina stood up, upset her chair and howled with laughter as she and Troy bashed heads to pick it up. Roger looked unimpressed.

"Before we order our meal we will order drinks and then I have some awards to give out." She announced loudly.

"I think George's a little sloshed." Humphrey murmured in Nora's ear. "She had two cocktails on an empty stomach in The Melon Ball and is still taking her flu medicine."

"Oh dear." Nora looked alarmed.

A chicken wing sailed through the air and landed on the table. Everyone looked at it.

"Keep it down!" A man on the other table hollered.

"Yeah pipe down will 'ya." A woman shouted.

Georgina stared at the party on the left of the restaurant for a long moment, cleared her throat and, ignoring them, loudly suggested that they all order drinks. She sat down with a scowl which finished with a hiccup as The Bookworm Party exchanged glares and stares with the other party.

"They from local building company." The waitress explained when Betty asked. "They called 'Grott and Co'."

Steve, Seymour, Cara, Ella and Felix sniggered at the name.

"I've heard of them." Humphrey said warily. "They're quite rough."

"Oo-eer!" Felix whispered, alarmed.

They looked over to the other table. The occupants were staring at them, drinking beer and gobbling their food. Two vacant-looking young men were hunched over plates of ribs and chicken wings, munching slowly and almost threateningly, like dogs.

Drinks were ordered and Georgina rebelliously stood up and began her speech.

"Another bookshop year has passed. Takings were up and all of our customers were pleased with how you dealt with them, despite the difficulties. HILL!" She said and burst out laughing.

Humphrey shook his head.

"This year, Troy and I decided to hand out awards for all your hard work as a thank you and to show our appreciation." Georgina explained.

"*Our* appreciation? She's only been dating Troy a few weeks!" Humphrey whispered hard.

"They seem inseparable." Nora observed.

Humphrey rolled his eyes.

"Americans." He muttered.

Troy stood up and placed the box of presents onto the table. A barbeque rib hit the side of his face.

"What the…" He stammered.

Mrs Pickering tutted in disgust and uncle Orville cupped a hand to his ear.

"Pardon?" He asked.

"No throw food! No throw food!" A man who appeared to be the manager cried, running towards the other table with his arms flailing about.

"Sorry, mate. Don't mind them. Ha-ha, it was just a joke." A beefy man with a beard and tattooed face apologised, glancing at the two dog-men who continued munching slowly, staring ahead.

"Any more food throwing and you'll regret it." Jason called out.

The bearded man looked alarmed and glanced at his companions who looked at Jason in unison, chewing slowly.

"THE AWARD for the person who can sell anything goes to…" Georgina interrupted loudly.

Everyone looked at her.

"NORA JOLLY!" Georgina declared, holding up a present.

"Oh." Nora blinked.

Everyone clapped so she stood up and walked to the end of the table.

"Nora seems to be able to sell any book that comes into The Secondhand Bookworm." Georgina told everyone proudly. "From a piece of tat to the most expensive book I have in stock."

"Well done, Nora." Felicity praised.

"Congratulations!" Elizabeth smiled, sticking her thumbs up.

Nora shook Georgina's hand and took the present, pausing to shake Troy's hand too when he grabbed hold of hers.

"What is it?" Humphrey asked, reclining his elbow on the back of his chair.

"Oh do show us, Nora." Betty said.

"Open it!" Cara demanded.

Nora tore off the paper and held up two small bath and shower gel bottles. They passed them around for a sniff.

"The award for…" Georgina started to announce but was cut off as the DJ started a loud record that almost blew Mrs Pickering off her chair.

"Ooooh Lady Gaga!" Felix enthused and began to sing along, dancing and wiggling in his chair much to Ella and Milton's amusement.

"Excuse me!" Georgina exclaimed.

Troy leapt onto the dance floor, as if to start dancing, but instead told the DJ to turn it down until his girlfriend had finished handing out awards. He slipped some dollars into the DJ's jacket pocket and headed back to the table. Nora and Humphrey laughed together as they watched and the DJ shook his head, lowering the volume.

"As I was saying. Aaaachoooo!" Georgina said loudly.

Cara giggled.

"The award for the Most Punctual Sales Assistant goes to…"

Everyone waited curiously.

"ROGER!" Georgina announced and everyone clapped.

Roger stood up glumly. A spare rib sailed over his head and between Jane and Ian who jumped. Jason stood up but Elizabeth pulled him down.

"Ignore them!" Mrs Pickering declared after giving 'Grott and Co' a withering look that achieved nothing.

Roger received his present, unwrapped some shampoo and conditioner, frowned moodily and looked impatiently over to the bar for his lager and lime.

Fortunately the drinks began to arrive. Georgina gulped down several mouthfuls of Prosecco. Humphrey arched an eyebrow.

Over the next ten minutes, Jane won an award for 'Most Friendly and Happiest Member of Staff', Betty won an award for 'Most Glamorous Salesperson', Agnes won an award for 'Person Most Likely To Locate A Book', Cara won the award for 'Person most likely to spot a rare edition', Troy awarded Georgina 'Fastest van driver', Felix won the award for 'Newest member of staff' and Heather 'Most Helpful Ad Hoc'. Everyone else received gifts with a general 'Wonderful Staff Member' announcement, presented by a giggling and very loud Georgina.

Starters were ordered and delivered while 'Grott and Co' moved onto their main meal, casting surly and threatening looks over at The Secondhand Bookworm party.

"Do you think we'll make it out of here alive?" Terri asked, noticing the menacing glares they were getting.

"Who knows." Roger said grimly, studying the dessert menu.

"Have you seen Steve's party piece?" Felicity called down to Betty.

"Oooh no. Do show." Betty pleaded.

"Please don't." Nora grimaced, suspecting what was coming.

Steve stood up.

"I have a hole in my chest. Look." He said and stuck his finger into a point somewhere around his ribcage, where most of it disappeared with his t-shirt material up to his knuckle.

"Aaaaaagh!" Felix exclaimed in horror.

Betty looked delighted but everyone else paled.

"That is shocking!" Dave admitted.

Steve sat down laughing.

"I've had it since I was a kid. One day I can have an operation to build some rib."

Nora shuddered, taking a sip of her wine.

"Not sure I can eat my starters now." Humphrey grimaced, staring down at his plate of barbeque spare ribs.

"Steve used to have hair past his waist." Nora told Felix.

"Crumbs. Really?"

"Yeah, I had it all chopped off just before I started working at The Secondhand Bookworm." Steve joined in. "Figured Georgina wouldn't appreciate me turning up with jet black long hair, black nail varnish and black eye make-up. Even though I only do the occasional Saturday."

Felix stared.

"What was that, Felicity?" Cara asked with an alarmed tone, having caught a few words from a conversation further down the table.

"Oh I was just telling Sophia that Rick and I have new piercings." Felicity explained.

"You don't want to know where!" Jane promised with wide eyes, having been party to the discussion.

"We got them done together, didn't we Donkey!" Rick said, kissing Felicity's hand.

"It was very romantic." Felicity boasted.

"The mind boggles." Cara muttered to Nora.

Nora winced, alarmed.

"Who is Rick calling Donkey?" Humphrey asked Nora in a low voice.

"That's his pet name for Felicity." Nora shrugged.

"They have a very different idea of romance to me." He decided.

Nora agreed, casting him a look out the corner of her eye.

Humphrey noticed and winked.

As their food arrived and people began to eat, the DJ cranked up the music. Another Lady Gaga song began, pounding in their ears.

"Ooooh can I get up and dance? I so want to!" Felix said through his mouthful of prawn toast.

"No!" Seymour forbade.

They then watched as several women from 'Grott and Co' scrambled from their chairs and began to dance. One girl's behind kept nudging uncle Orville's shoulder and he looked around confused. Georgina stood up and announced that they should pull their crackers so they could all wear Christmas hats for the main meal. They all crossed arms and took hold of the end of the cracker held by the person either side of them.

"THREE. TWO. ONE. PULL!!!" Georgina cried and everyone obeyed.

It sounded like an explosion in a box of firecrackers. There was a scramble around chairs and under the table for parts of crackers and soon everyone was wearing a coloured Christmas hat and reading out jokes.

"What did Cinderella say when her photos didn't arrive on time?" Cara read.

"Erm…"

"Don't know."

"Give up."

"One day my prints will come." Cara concluded.

Nora burst out laughing.

Humphrey held up his joke.

"A sandwich walks into a bar. The barman says, 'sorry we don't serve food in here'."

Nora, Heather, Cara, Dave and Terri laughed.

"True or false?" Steve asked.

"Whaaaaaaat?" Cara interrupted.

"I don't have a joke; I have a true or false." He held up his bit of paper.

"Weeeeird!" Cara shook her head.

"A group of peacocks is called a parliament?" Steve read.

"False!" Seymour exclaimed. "It's a muster."

"Correct." Steve nodded.

"Clever boy." Cara praised.

Seymour smiled smugly.

"He can't have googled the answer that fast." Milton frowned.

"Seems like he does have brains." Heather teased.

"What did the police officer say to the stomach? You are under a vest." Jenny read.

Nora was the only one who laughed.

Humphrey smiled and toasted her with his glass of larger; loving that she found ridiculous jokes amusing.

"I have a true or false!" Agnes announced. "In the film Fantasia, the sorcerer's name was Yensid?"

There were lots of 'erms' and 'errrrs' before everyone gave up.

"True!" Agnes declared. "It is Disney spelled backwards."

"Oh I never knew that." Neale said.

"What do you call men waiting to have their hair cut?" Felix read.

"Give up." Betty said.

"A *Barber Queue*." Felix howled and everyone groaned or chuckled.

"I have a true or false." Nora said.

"Where did they get these crackers?!" Cara demanded.

"Donald Duck's middle name is Fauntleroy?"

"Yes!" Milton exclaimed.

Everyone looked at him.

"A wild guess."

"Cheater." Cara pointed.

"He's right though." Nora said.

They moved from the jokes and true or false questions to the toys in their crackers until they ordered another round of drinks.

"Are you going to ever work for us, Ella?" Betty asked Cara's sister.

Ella bit into a spring roll.

"Maybe one day. I'm interested in architecture and would like to go abroad to study."

"Oh how wonderful." Betty admired. "I wish I was young again. But I am so old. Perhaps with a face lift and some Botox I could pass for twenty one again."

Dave pronged a dim-sum, looking perplexed.

"Have you ever been abroad, Ella?" Betty then asked.

"Ella just got back from Brussels." Cara answered for her sister.

"Did you enjoy it?" Dave asked.

"It was eye-opening." Ella admitted. "Especially when we found ourselves in the red light district and had to pass down a street with naked men standing in all the windows."

"Oh my goodness!" Heather gasped.

"I'll have to book up." Betty said with a wicked glint in her eye.

There was a commotion down the end of the table where Georgina, uncle Orville, Mrs Pickering and Elizabeth had grown tired of large bottoms pressing into their chairs and arms and were asking the 'Grott and Co' ladies to take their dancing further away.

It looked as though there could be a fistfight but the manager and several waiters hurried over and jumped between the groups with flailing arms again. It was agreed that dancing should not take place next to people's chairs, but a handful of Thai curried chicken pieces pummelled The Secondhand Bookworm table from the dog-men who were watching steadily as they gobbled.

"I think I should have a few words with them!" Jason stood, rolling up his sleeves.

Elizabeth pulled him down again and distracted his retribution by telling everyone how no one could best her aunt Georgina in an arm-wrestling match.

"Uh-oh." Humphrey winced.

"Sounds interesting." Nora watched as Georgina shouted for more Prosecco, grabbed Jason's arm and began to wrestle him.

"Come on, darling! Come on, darling!" Georgina goaded loudly.

Jason looked alarmed that he couldn't push her arm down.

"Bookshop muscles, darling!" Georgina laughed and pinned Jason's arm to the table.

"I can't believe it!" Jason was shocked.

Roger stood up and stormed off to the toilet, shaking his head, unimpressed by the rowdy dramatics. His chair fell backwards and his coat flew into the middle of the dance floor but he ignored both. Harrison and Sophia laughed hysterically, pointing as a woman's heels became tangled in Roger's jacket, she staggered and flew into a man eating ice cream at her table. His face dipped forward into his dish and he stood up, furious, with chocolate ice cream on the end of his nose. More Thai curried chicken pieces buffeted the table, one landing in Jane's noodles and another hitting the back of Jenny's head.

"This doesn't look good." Nora observed warily.

"No throw food! No throw food!" The manager returned again, waving his arms like a windmill.

"Sorry, mate. Won't happen again." The bearded man glanced at his companions.

A handful of rice showered '*Grott and Co's* table, landing in people's hair, pudding plates and glasses, courtesy of Jason who was grabbing some more.

"Na, na, don't mate, don't." The bearded man advised, worried, as the two men who had done all the food lobbing stopped eating in unison and straightened up. "It was just a bit of fun. Don't wind them up, mate. Let it go."

"Jason." Humphrey called and shook his head, warningly.

Jason wavered for a long moment, considering the building company group who were all hissing and swearing and complaining as they brushed away the rice. Finally, he returned his handful to his plate.

"Fine. But try and control your dogs." Jason advised the bearded man.

The bearded man's eyes flashed dangerously but he laughed it off and filled up his companions glasses with more beer, placating what looked like a murderous wrath brewing from two dangerously unhinged sociopaths.

"I'm beginning to fear getting knifed in the back." Heather admitted, casting a worried look over her shoulder.

"We'll leave after pudding." Seymour said, winked at her reassuringly and continued his intricate discussion about Robert Jordan with Cara.

When Roger returned from the toilet he saw his trampled jacket in the middle of the dance floor.

"What the heck!" He exclaimed.

Troy and Mrs Pickering convinced Roger not to press charges about the defilement of his coat. Roger sat down with pursed lips and bristling eyebrows.

"Oh I haven't had this much fun in years." Betty admitted.

There was a faint smell of muddy smoke.

"I think it's the DJ." Ella gestured. "He keeps disappearing behind his screen and a plume of smoke drifts up to the ceiling every time."

Milton sniggered.

"Probably has some weed behind there."

"And a couple of bottles of wine." Agnes added as they watched the DJ emerge holding a full-up glass of red liquor.

He cranked up the music and Mrs Pickering covered her ears. Conversation had to be conducted by shouting for the rest of the meal, while 'Grott and Co' finished up and more people took to the dance floor.

"Ugh. It's almost hypnotic." Dave said, referring to the women's lumps and bumps as they wiggled about near them.

There was a scream of laughter and two couples fell into the DJ's screen.

A handful of strawberries pummelled the table, courtesy of the dog-men.

"I think I'd like to skip pudding." Heather announced loudly.

Felicity stood up.

"When we're finished here, a group of us are going on to 'Waves' nightclub at the end of the pier. Everyone is welcome!" She said, held up her glass and made a toasting gesture.

Agnes, Terri, Sophia, Neale, Steve, Jenny and Betty cheered.

"I must be an old lady at heart. I'd rather go home and read." Nora told Humphrey.

"That's why I love you." He said.

Nora stared.

Humphrey cleared his throat, the tops of his cheeks suddenly flushing. He ran both hands of splayed fingers quickly through his hair, leaned forward, picked up his larger and took a large gulp, meeting Nora's eyes.

She winked, covering one of his hands with hers, deciding *that* was going to be a conversation for another time!

While Dave tried to convince Betty he didn't think it wise or appropriate his mother go off nightclubbing at the end of the pier, the plates and dishes from the main course were collected.

The pudding menus were passed around but Troy and Georgina, Jane and Ian were now on the dance floor, claiming territory from 'Grott and Co' who, seeing Georgina's determination, surrendered space to her frantic jig along to 'It's raining men'.

"I'm going home." Roger announced, shrugging into his heel-stomped jacket.

"Aw, that's a shame, Roger." Betty pouted.

"We won't be long behind you." Humphrey told him grimly.

Sophia told Roger she and Harrison would go on clubbing so would get a taxi home. He stormed off without saying goodbye to anyone.

Nora grimaced.

"Can't I stay? I'll get a taxi home." Felix asked eagerly, eyeing the dance floor.

"No." Nora refused. "I want you well-rested and sensible on your first day of work tomorrow."

Felix shrugged and pondered the pudding menu, swaying in his seat to the music.

Only uncle Orville, Agnes, Dave and Milton ordered pudding. While they waited for it to arrive, Nora nipped to the ladies and then thanked Georgina as she passed her on the dance floor.

"Oh you're welcome sweetheart!" Georgina shouted and hugged Nora tightly.

Nora finally managed to untangle herself to join Humphrey who was helping Heather on with her coat.

"Eeeeew!" Heather exclaimed, holding up her scarf.

Several spare ribs hung from it.

"Oafs." Milton glowered, picking them off and considering lobbing them at the dog-men.

"I'll grab a taxi back, Nora." Terri said. "I'd like to go on to 'Waves'."

"Okay. Merry Christmas." Nora smiled, admiring the younger generation who were still able to dance all night!

Those who were bailing out remembered to remove their Christmas cracker hats before they left, bade goodbye to the people who were bravely staying, dragged Felix away, who was heading for the dance floor as another Lady Gaga song began, and eventually left the restaurant.

It was brisk and sleety outside.

"How about we all go along to Starbucks for a nice civilised coffee before heading home?" Cara suggested as she stood with Seymour on the slightly icy pavement.

"That would be lovely." Nora agreed, securing her award bottles in her bag as well as a few Christmas cracker toys she had collected for her niece and nephew.

"Sounds good." Humphrey nodded.

Milton, Felix, Heather and Ella concurred.

"Let's hope nobody from 'Grott and Co' has the same idea." Humphrey added.

"Indeed." Nora agreed and with a wry smile back at The Fortune Palace they all set off down the street, reminiscing over another year's typical Christmas Staff Meal for The Secondhand Bookworm!

12 FELIX AND THE CHRISTMAS FARMERS TURKEY MARKET

Nora picked her cousin Felix up from his house in Little Cove, not far from her parents' home, and they drove to Castletown in a light blizzard the following morning. Although the weather was poor, in the distance they could see the town square full of brightly coloured, twinkle-light-bedecked stalls piled high and brimming with the Christmas Farmers Turkey Market wares.

They parked in the small car park Nora had used on Wednesday when the town had been closed; having heard the weather forecast was for snow that afternoon. Felix gripped the dashboard as she manoeuvred into an icy space and he let out a relieved breath when the car finally stopped.

"I'll just grab a ticket for the day's parking." Nora said and almost skidded over.

Felix sniggered and chuckled as she righted herself, hanging onto her door, and walked warily to the Pay Here machine.

"Cripes. All day free outdoor swimming on Christmas Eve and Christmas Day?!" Felix exclaimed, reading a poster as they walked across the car park.

"Remind me to show you my tally chart. It's very important." Nora said.

"Oh okay."

"We'll go this way today. It goes over a small metal footbridge across the river and into the other car park, past the back gardens of some houses and a pub. A scenic tour." Nora decided.

"I wouldn't mind the mundane route." Felix winced at the thought of crossing a small bridge over the fast flowing river.

"I'm in charge." Nora reminded him.

He followed her to a walkway between the Castletown Lido and some houses.

Felix enjoyed his tour, despite closing his eyes the entire time they crossed the river. Nora pointed out the beginning of a walk into the hills that was believed to have been part of the route King Charles II took when escaping the Battle of Worcester. They peered nosily into people's back gardens, wandered around the vintage amusements and rides that had been set up for the day in the old abbey ruin by the river, considered signing up for the paper lantern making workshop, crept along secret passageways behind shops where little slices of forgotten history dwelt in the forms of ancient doors, 16th century windows, iron water pumps and plaques marking archaeological discoveries; hurried behind the post office and took a short cut onto Tree Lane, scowled at the Indian restaurant, almost collided with Lady-Santa, whom Felix stared after slack-jawed until Nora dragged him along, inhaled the scenes of roasted chestnuts, mulled wine and hog roasts in the square and finally reached The Secondhand Bookworm, ten minutes late.

"Now for future reference, being late is a firing offense." Nora explained as she unlocked the door.

"Understood." Felix followed her inside. "What's that?!"

"The alarm. I'll show you how to disarm it."

"Oooo-er!" Felix hurried after his cousin and watched as she punched in a four digit number and pressed 'enter' so it stopped beeping.

"You won't need to remember that yet but I thought I'd show you." Nora said.

"Thanks." Felix nodded.

"Oh dear. Well that's the end of that, then." Nora noticed a heap of red and white striped plastic on the floor which had been the blow up candy cane but which must have slowly deflated overnight.

"What's *that*?" Felix gawped.

"It *was* a Christmas decoration." Nora said, picking it up and throwing it unceremoniously under the stairs.

Felix sniggered.

There was a movement outside the window so Nora flew back to the door and shut it before anyone could come in. She locked it behind her. Felix stared.

"I want to show you the kitchen and how to turn on the shop lights before we have any customers." She explained.

"Okay."

Felix followed Nora into the back room; they unlocked the kitchen door, shrieked at how cold it was inside, closed the door behind them and locked it again. As they climbed the staircase, Nora explained the function of each shop key on the ring she had grabbed, showed Felix the light switch located behind an old Russian travel guide on the shelves at the top of the stairs, showed him where to turn the Christmas lights on for the outside Christmas tree, showed him where the toilet was and which key opened the door and made him promise never to let customers use it, especially not transvestites.

"Why single them out?" Felix asked, smothering a laugh.

"I let a transvestite use the toilet once and Georgina had a terrible experience afterwards with a diarrhoea-clean-up. She's prejudiced on those grounds."

"I don't think it's a given fact that every transvestite would soil the toilet." Felix sniggered.

"No, but it's not worth risking the wrath of Georgina. Anyway, it's against health and safety to let the public use it. We keep bleach in there. They could sue us if they accidently drank some."

Felix sniggered and chuckled all the way down to the ground floor.

Back in the front room, Nora noticed the grim face of a bobble-hatted man peering in through the front door window.

"We'll open up and put some bits and pieces out onto the street. Did Georgina show you how to use the till?"

"Yep. She said to use a different till button to yours."

"You can use Elizabeth's seeing as she no longer works here."

"Can I change it to my name?"

"Keen aren't you?"

"I don't want people to think I'm called Elizabeth." Nora laughed.

"We'll change it in a minute." She said and unlocked the door. "Good morning." Nora greeted the customer.

"If you like freezing your fingers off!" The man retorted, stepping down into the shop. "Do you buy books?"

"Yes we do." Nora nodded.

Felix watched the man peer around, peer at him, peer at Nora and remove his bobble hat. They both gave a start at his perfectly bald, shining head, which looked like a peeled egg.

"I have a small library I have inherited. I live on a boat house and I don't want them to get all damp so I thought I'd sell them on. Would you be interested?"

"It's possible. It would depend upon their subjects and condition."

"I can email you a list and some photographs of them." The man proposed.

"That would be good." Nora indicated for Felix to grab a blue business card from a small plastic holder on the counter. He did so and handed it to the man.

"Thanks. While I'm here, I need a present for my fat sister who's on a diet. Do you have any?"

Felix smothered a laugh so pretended to tidy the free maps. Nora tried to ignore him hunched over with his shoulders shaking.

"We have a health section and a cookery section upstairs." She said.

"I'll have a browse." The man decided and strolled off into the depths of the shop.

"Fat sister!" Felix gasped, straightening up with the map box. "He can talk."

Nora's lips twitched.

"Some people are quite rude. You'll come to see that." She said.

They put the free maps out as well as two postcard spinners with Cara's sand puddings as weights to stop them rolling into the road. Then they clipped the cheap paperback boxes to the wall, catching several books as they almost slid off their shelves onto Felix's head.

Once back inside, Nora turned on the oil heater and Felix turned on the fake branch of candles in the window. They still didn't fancy removing their coats.

"Personal belongings are kept back here." Nora explained, throwing their bags under the stairs with a crash. "Hope you didn't bring anything fragile." She then grimaced.

"Some household china." Felix joked.

They filled up the till with the cash float and Nora explained about the cash book.

"Basically just try to remember to write everything you sell down. Here's how you do a discount." She demonstrated.

"Can I make my own key name?"

"Alright then." Nora sighed and turned on the computer.

Felix spent the next ten minutes designing a miniature representation of himself in Manga style with his name underneath on a small square of paper to fit in the till key. They sold some postcards to three American tourists, a Christmas book out of the window, gave directions to the museum and Nora bought a small bag of crisp, clean crime novels.

"You will be able to start buying books after a while."

"Oh I hope not!" Felix worried.

"You'll get the hang of it. Oh, while I remember. If anyone steps into the shop and say's 'it's warm in here!' please add a line to this tally chart."

Felix leaned over and read Nora's chart and then spent the next ten minutes sniggering and chuckling about it until Nora sent him off to make tea.

By midday, the shop had warmed up enough for Nora and Felix to remove their coats. Nora kept on her fingerless gloves and Felix lamented that he didn't think to bring his. When the infamous regular Map-Boy made an appearance, Felix was astonished to watch as the secondhand Ordnance Survey maps through the walkway into the stairwell were systematically rummaged through and muddled up over the next half an hour and the Map-Boy sat himself on the floor in the way of everyone, unfolding various maps, examining them with 'oooohs' and 'aaaaah's before leaping up and running away.

"That reminds me." Nora was replying to a Skype message from Cara in Seatown. "Did you get Georgina's email about White-Lightning Joe being banned?"

"Oh yes. Crumbs. Shocking stuff." Felix nodded, dropping onto the swivel chair.

"Do you know what he looks like?"

"Nope."

Nora dug out her mobile.

"As well as having made millions spending ten years running an international corporate business in London, Humphrey also happens to be very good at art."

Felix shrugged, mildly impressed.

"I asked him to do a crime sketch of White-Lightning Joe I could put on a mug shot background for our bookshop wall."

Felix doubled up laughing so Nora waited until he had finished before showing him her iPhone.

"Gulp! That looks scary. Does he look like that?"

"It's uncanny how much." Nora nodded. "I'll forward it to Georgina. She should be able to focus now, hopefully, after the cracking hangover she probably has this morning."

Felix doubled up laughing again, clutching his stomach, so Nora left him to it as she forwarded Humphrey's facial composite to Georgina and then served a customer who looked like a penguin in a bobble hat.

Because of the Christmas Farmers Turkey Market, most of the people visiting Castletown remained outside. The weather was fresh and biting, but pleasant when the sun came out from behind the snow clouds. At one point a light snow flurry dusted the market. Felix found the constant sound of gobbling turkeys highly amusing.

"They don't sell them. They're for the children to look at." Nora explained, watching Father Christmas and a group of roaming musicians pass by. "They're in a pen by the war memorial."

The sound of a fanfare announced the arrival of a Skype message. Felix rolled forward in the swivel chair to read it.

"It says *'Pls print and put on wall - Cara'*." Felix relayed.

He clicked the attachment and a page opened up in Word. He then doubled over laughing.

"What is it?" Nora asked.

"Cara had the same idea as you!" Felix snorted, pointing to the screen.

Nora saw the sketched face of White-Lightning Joe staring back at her, his silhouette super imposed upon a police line-up background. The words 'DO NOT SERVE THIS THIEF' were along the bottom as well as some random information that read: 'Name: Joe. Height: 5ft 5 (approx.). Weight: plump. Eye colour: blue. Distinguishing marks: Greasy hair, smells of cider.' Felix laughed until tears blurred his eyes.

"We'll put it on the wall here, so the customers don't see it." Nora decided, indicating to the wall running under the stairs.

Felix printed it out and tacked it up.

"Gosh, I hope I never cross The Secondhand Bookworm."

"Yeah, if you do you'll end up with a mug shot on our wall." Nora chuckled.

The door opened and a man stuck his head in.

"Any Muffin the Moo?!" He asked.

Felix dived behind the counter, laughing.

"No, sorry." Nora replied. "We haven't come across any yet."

"No, no, no that's okay; one day though, one day!" The man sang and his head disappeared, followed by the door closing, getting stuck a little in Nora's make-shift door wedge.

"This is our accident book." Nora then remembered once Felix had re-emerged.

"Do people have accidents?"

"One man caught his walking stick in a small gap in the wooden floor in the back room and fell flat on his face. Another man tripped on a step upstairs and fell flat on his face. A woman fell down the last few stairs back there and landed flat on her face. One lady tripped over the free map box outside and scraped her elbow. Georgina likes a record kept of anything like that. We write it in here." She showed him a book that was kept in the electric meter cupboard.

"I hope I don't witness anything like that." Felix grimaced.

"One time someone had a heart attack on the pavement outside. I wasn't present for that though." Nora shared.

"Oh dear. 'Anxious emoji'." Felix said.

The telephone rang so Nora made Felix answer it while she went to look for some books in the transport section just through the walkway. When she returned, Felix had written a telephone message down.

"A Mr Reeve has some books for sale. He sounded like an ogre. He spoke with a thunderous, non-stop roar." Felix shared.

Nora laughed.

"Well done, yes just write the information on the message pad and use a highlighter so Georgina sees it. She arranges the calls day. I hope she takes you on one soon."

"I hope *not*." Felix lamented.

Nora sent Felix off around the shop to tidy up any shelves and familiarise himself with the stock. She gave him a walkie-talkie and once he had overcome his fear of the sudden shouting of taxi drivers blaring out, he set off happily. He soon returned with several books that had taken his fancy.

"I know I shall probably spend all my wages on books!" He lamented.

"What do you like to read?" Nora asked.

"Oh anything! I would like to collect those one day." He pointed to several early Andrew Lang fairy tale books in the antiquarian section. "I adore the illustrations."

"They are nice." Nora agreed. "You should definitely pick something to start collecting."

"I like your collection currently at auntie and uncle's house. It was awesome in your old flat in your big white bookcase. Before the building started to subside and you were forced to leave and return to your parents' house."

"I would have been quite upset to lose my first edition Tove Janson Moomin' books down a sinkhole." Nora nodded, grimly.

"And your 'Mumfie' books." Felix smirked.

"They are very rare. *The wanderings of Mumfie the Elephant*. So sweet." She sighed, dreamily. "I acquired them on a call with Felicity."

"Felicity with the questionable piercing?" Felix asked.

"Yes, her. The books had a little bookworm munching in the end paper but the culprit had long since died. I paid thirty pounds for one book and fifty for another. I grabbed them before Felicity even knew what they were."

"Did you fight over them?"

"No. She collected Folio Society books. But she sold her entire collection when she became an accountant."

"Ohhhhh." Felix pondered the market through the window. "When do we have lunch breaks here?"

"Whenever you like. Within reason of course."

"Do you think it would be alright to buy some boar flesh and eat it back there?"

Nora's lips twitched.

"Of course. You can go soon if you want. The hog roast is very popular."

"Okay. If that's alright?"

"Sure." Nora nodded.

Felix leapt off the swivel chair, grabbed his coat and rucksack and set off happily to explore the market and buy some pig.

Nora left Felix for ten minutes soon after one thirty to do a little Christmas shopping herself in the market. She took the walkie-talkie with her in case he had an emergency, and as a back up to her iPhone. The paper lantern display was stunning, filled with different coloured battery-powered tea lights and lining the old Cole flint walls along the river. There were fresh and locally sourced festive and seasoned foods on the many market stalls. Nora bought some Christmas chutneys, bags of strawberry marshmallows, a tin of lollies and a Christmas tree made out of green buttons for presents, as well as a sausage roll for her lunch.

She glared at the rival bookstalls, pausing to browse the items they were selling, reluctantly impressed to see they had marked them up correctly and were obviously selling them well. With a glance about her, Nora purchased a book about 'Fungi' for her sister Heather, a book about 'Irish Wolfhounds' for her eldest brother Wilbur who had three in his Northumberland farmhouse, and a copy of 'Perfume: The story of a murderer' by

Patrick Suskind in a beautiful Penguin Essentials edition. Georgina had recommended it to her when she had first started and Nora fancied reading it again. She paid and stuffed them in her bag before anyone noticed.

"Busy at the bookshop, Nora?" A familiar voice asked as she browsed a craft stall.

"Hello Tobey!" Nora smiled.

Tobey worked in the bank and often bumped into Nora on their lunchbreaks in the 'Secret Garden' by the river. He had a crush on Imogene from the Organic shop, even though she was quite obsessed with Humphrey.

"Hi." He nodded.

"Not as busy as I would like." Nora picked up a pine needle scented candle. "Hopefully it will pick up this afternoon."

"I've finished for the day. I'm meeting Imogene so we can watch the Rock Choir together."

"The Rock Choir?" Nora winced as she next sniffed some strong cranberry, citrus and sage wax. She felt suddenly light-headed

"Yes. Sounds intriguing, doesn't it. I wonder if they'll be singing rock versions of traditional Christmas carols."

"You'll have to let me know what they're like." Nora was amused.

"I will."

Nora saw him hold still and stare and then heard the now familiar clip-clop of heels behind her. She knew without looking that it was Lady-Santa and Twinkle, the latter causing a stir among the men who posed with her for some selfies.

Nora and Tobey chatted for a while until Nora decided to head back and see how Felix was doing. In the front of the shop, Felix was listening to a customer educate him on the history of the Shire books displayed on the counter. A regular customer of the bookshop was browsing the antiquarian books behind him.

Nora wondered if Mr Clegg would use his 'secret weapon' that day to deter people venturing too close to him. She hoped so, just to see Felix's face. Sure enough, as she pointed a group of people to the staircase so they could climb up to the paperback fiction room, a man sidled close to Mr Clegg and started to examine a run of leather books. Mr Clegg scowled and used his 'secret weapon'.

Felix almost fell over at the loud and long drawn out sound of flatulence behind him. Biting her lip, Nora watched the man next to Mr Clegg stare in shock, turn away and head off into the back room, leaving Mr Clegg muttering.

Felix desperately tried to keep a straight face as his customer pretended not to have heard anything and continued talking about the Shire Library editions of 'Wigs, Hairdressing and Shaving Bygones' and 'Old Letterboxes', until he paid for his books.

"Would you like a bag, sir?" Felix offered in a strained voice.

"No thank you. Save the planet and all that." The man refused.

"Merry Christmas, sir." Felix bade, his lips quivering with supressed laughter.

"Oh. Hello Nora." Mr Clegg said, turning around with a book in his hands.

"Hello, Mr Clegg." Nora smiled, watching him walk to the front of the counter.

Felix stared at him.

"Forgot the bloody farmers market was on today. Shouldn't have come. So damned busy." He moaned savagely and sneered. "But I found this gem. Just come in, did it?"

Nora placed her bag and shopping under the stairs before receiving it from him. She read the title.

"Unforgettable Fire: Pictures Drawn By Atomic Bomb Survivors." Nora read aloud. "Oh. Yes I remember buying this one last week."

"It doesn't have a dust wrapper but I'll still take it. I see you priced it at £25."

"Yes. I can check online and make sure it's a competitive price for you."

"No need. I trust you. It's a must have." He popped his black man purse onto the counter. "Did you look through it?"

"I did." Nora recalled.

"Hmm. A harrowing collection of artwork done by survivors of the Hiroshima bombing, with accompanying information in English. Incredible. Thought-provoking stuff, especially if, like me, you worked on the atomic bomb."

Felix stared. Nora nudged him and pointed to her pencil price marking for him to put it in the till.

"I trust you'll give me my usual discount."

"Certainly." Nora assured and reminded Felix how to take ten percent off.

"By the way, I see the decorating elves have been in." Mr Clegg said.

"Oh. Yes. We had to have a new carpet so Georgina had the walls and ceiling painted to match it." Nora explained.

"And she chose pink?" He asked ironically.

"Hmm."

"Women." Mr Clegg scoffed, shaking his head.

He paid by card, popped the book into his bag and shuffled off, swearing under his breath as he left.

"What an unpleasant fellow." Felix decided. He then snorted with laughter. "I can't believe he farted. Do you really think he worked on the atomic bomb?"

"No." Nora admitted.

"Maybe he did. And it made his anus loose." Felix suggested and then doubled up in hysterical laughter.

Nora shook her head, deciding Felix would probably enjoy working at The Secondhand Bookworm after all.

13 THE SURPRISE AT THE JOLLY CHRISTMAS THEATRE

By the time they were ready to close The Secondhand Bookworm for the day, Nora and Felix had added an incredible twenty-three tallies to the '*It's warm in here*' chart, taken over six hundred pounds in sales, dealt with the toothless Father Christmas and his terrible guitar playing, sent the Singing Santa around the ceiling for a few circuits and even tidied the shop.

"Well, it didn't snow in the end." Nora said as they locked the front door on the darkened shop.

"That's good news. Fun times." Felix said.

They walked towards the bridge, pausing to look at a display of Russian nesting dolls in the charity shop window. The smallest one was the size of a pea.

"Georgina has put you down to work next Saturday." Nora recalled.

"Oooh that's right. 'Happy emoji'." Felix said.

"Did you enjoy today?"

Felix nodded, sniggering to himself. Nora assumed it was about Mr Clegg's secret weapon.

"Good. I think you'll get on great."

"Thanks!" Felix appreciated.

"So you're coming to the play tonight?"

"Wouldn't miss it. Seymour's invited me to audition for his next play."

"That's great."

"Yeah, it should…" His words trailed off and Nora saw Felix staring ahead. "That looks very much like Humphrey's forensic sketch…only in real-life 3D."

Nora followed his line of sight and groaned.

"Yep. It's real alright." She said, watching White-Lightning Joe plodding gloomily towards them over the bridge. It seemed a doomed place in which to guarantee meeting him.

White-Lightning Joe suddenly spotted Nora, jolted, looked around desperately for an escape route and then stood with slumped shoulders.

"Heee-loooo, Nora. And friend." He greeted morosely.

"Hello." Nora said in a disapproving tone.

"Nora. Am I really banned from the bookshop? Really, *actually* banned?" He asked, his bottom lip trembling.

"I am afraid so. That's what happens when you steal books." Nora said firmly.

He sighed, long and drearily.

"I understand." He said, his eyes full of tears. "Do you think Georgina will reverse it?"

"No."

"Life sucks." He said, kicked an empty can of coke into the road and it hit the hubcap of a passing car with an almighty thwack. "Oh bugger. See you." White-Lightning Joe said and legged it, running almost comically down the road and into the vintage fair.

Felix just stared, dumbfounded.

"Nitwit." Nora decided, prodded Felix and they continued on towards the car park.

"I really am going to have to rethink my preconceived ideas about the world of secondhand books." Felix decided thoughtfully.

Nora grinned.

"And welcome to my world!" She declared triumphantly and linked her arm with his, grateful for the end of a long and truly book-wormy week.

The Jolly Theatre was a tall Jacobean building which Seymour Jolly, the new owner, had boldly schemed in purple. The façade was impressive, with the ground floor comprising of a row of elegant glass doors and the upper floors boasting flood-lit arched windows, some with leaded light and others with the stained glass figures of playwrights and characters from famous plays.

Although The Jolly Theatre was located on the edge of Little Cove, which was renowned for being a sleepy little picturesque seaside village, the theatre itself was in a popular location that boasted restaurants, an Art Deco cinema, wine bars and clubs. Wooden polished walkways led down to Little Cove harbour where yachts and motorboats were moored, their lights glittering in the darkness and reflecting upon the sea.

The light from the chandelier in the foyer of The Jolly Theatre had its own twinkle as it fell upon Nora, Humphrey, Cara, Milton, Heather and Felix when they arrived *en masse* at The Jolly Theatre and stood in the street, listening to the excited chatter of the people queuing up outside.

"Don't we get to bypass this rabble?" Milton asked loudly as he stopped behind Nora at the door.

A lady in a large brown fur coat turned and tutted at his comment.

"Seymour asked us to soak up the atmosphere and listen to the people so as to pass any comments on to him." Nora told her brother, brushing snow from Humphrey's coat.

"So get listening, Milton." Humphrey said, smiling warmly at Nora.

Milton rolled his eyes and checked his watch.

"Here's my comment. '*Get a move on!*'" He said and the Fur-Lady's partner joined in with the tutting.

"Well, I am hugely impressed." Cara declared, poking her tongue out at Milton. "You can tell Seymour that."

Heather chuckled.

"That's probably the only comment he'll really be interested in." She deduced.

Cara looked pleased and blushed slightly.

When Cara had arrived at Nora's parents' house earlier, Nora had been amused to see that Cara was actually keen to look nice for Seymour. She had modelled the green dress she now wore under her heavy winter coat; having chosen it to accentuate the colour of her eyes and to compliment her short blond hair. Nora just hoped she didn't distract Seymour on stage.

"We're moving." Felix pointed out.

Milton stuck his thumbs up and their group passed through the doors into the bustling grand foyer.

"Aren't they two of your bookworm customers?" Humphrey's voice then sounded close to Nora's ear.

"What?" Nora froze.

"Over there." Humphrey indicated, watching Nora's expression when she saw Mrs Raven and Miss Raven huddled together by the bar. "Ouch!" He winced when Nora clutched his arm.

"Cara! It's The Ravens!" Nora whispered hard.

"Where?!" Cara asked in shock.

Heather craned her neck to see and Felix stood on tiptoes.

Mrs Raven wore her usual duffle coat but wore a black hat with an ostrich feather poking out of the band circling the brim. Miss Raven was in an oversized white jacket with enormous shoulder pads, a puffy pastel green skirt and her usual white socks and plimsolls. Both where arguing about payment for the glasses of wine they were holding and Heather saw that Mrs Raven was holding a crumpled clear money bag.

"Right, we avoid the bar!" Cara decided.

"Are you kidding?!" Milton objected.

"You're only seventeen anyway!" Nora said.

"I'll get you your milkshake Milton, don't worry." Humphrey said.

"I've changed my mind about the queue. Come on; let's just get to our box." Nora decided. "Seymour can conduct his own research."

"Who are the Ravens?" Felix asked Heather as they left the queue to the ticket collection box and walked on the plush, purple carpet.

She went to reply when she came up short behind Cara who had stopped behind Nora with a yelp.

"What is it?" Cara asked with a laugh.

"You wouldn't believe me if you didn't see for yourself!" Nora said, amazed, and indicated towards a familiar figure standing with a battered green suitcase at his feet.

"Mr Hill!" Cara exclaimed in a loud whisper.

"Do you mean Mr *Sell-my-books-and-buy-them-back-again*?" Humphrey was amused.

"Yes." Nora groaned. "He's standing by the staircase that leads to the boxes. We'll have to lay low until the doors open and he disappears."

"Oh, I don't know. The old fellow looks like he might enjoy a chat." Humphrey nodded.

"Now would be a good time for Felix to get to know some of the regular customers of The Secondhand Bookworm." Heather suggested playfully.

"Oh crumbs. He looks a little eccentric." Felix grimaced.

"That's an understatement." Cara grinned.

Holding Nora's hand, Humphrey led the party through the crowd to where a large framed poster of Hamlet adorned the plush crimson silver walls of the foyer. Next to it, one of three graceful staircases ran up to two black doors leading to the seats on the first and upper levels. It provided perfect shelter, but also an excellent view of the lobby. Humphrey positioned Nora in front of Hamlet and waited for the others to join them.

"You all stay here and I'll beat off the Ravens at the bar as I get us drinks." He decided.

"I'll come with you." Milton offered and they set off through the amassing crowd.

Once alone, Heather started laughing into her hands.

Nora, Cara and Felix stared at her. She covered her mouth, snorting loudly.

"Oh no." She laughed. "It's just that I've spotted the farting man."

"What?!" Cara exclaimed with a laugh.

"Oh *him* I know!" Felix said.

Nora scanned the crowd. Sure enough, Mr Clegg had indeed just stepped through the entrance doors to The Jolly Theatre wearing a suit with a white bowtie. He was accompanied by a woman.

"Isn't that his ex-wife?" Cara noticed.

"Georgina said they still go on dates together." Nora recalled.

"I'm so glad we have our own box. Imagine being stuck behind him throughout the whole play." Heather said.

They all grimaced.

"This is turning into an afterhours *Bookworm Saga*." Nora sighed.

"Yes, and don't look now but I think Humphrey might have some competition." Cara nodded.

"What do you mean?" Nora asked warily.

"The Terminator has just strolled in."

"Please tell me you're joking!" Nora whispered desperately, but Cara pointed to the revolving door.

Nora stood on tiptoes and spotted Harry, scanning the interior for someone Nora hoped dearly wasn't her.

"I think this development calls for drastic measures." Nora took out her iPhone.

"Gosh. You're not calling the police are you, cousin?" Felix asked, although his tone indicated he rather hoped Nora was.

"No." Nora laughed.

"The men are coming back with our drinks." Heather then noticed.

Humphrey was walking through the crowd with a tray of wine glasses held high above his head, trailed by Milton carrying two glasses of coke.

"Any chance you can come to the framed Hamlet poster and show us a secret way to our box?" Nora asked her phone. "We're being surrounded by bookworms out here."

The sound of Seymour's husky laughter came through the receiver and Heather grinned.

"Thanks." Nora nodded a moment later and ended her call. "Seymour's on his way."

Cara adjusted her hair and looked eagerly around for the sudden emergence of Nora's brother, just as Humphrey arrived.

"Miss Raven sends her regards." He said as he lowered the tray, took a wine glass off and handed it to Nora. "And is looking forward to sharing the box with us."

"Humphrey!" Nora rebuked, taking the glass from him.

He gave Cara her glass, gave Heather hers and picked up his own. He then handed the tray to a passing usher who took it politely. Milton passed Felix his coke.

"You've got some competition." Cara said to Humphrey.

"What?"

"One of Nora's admirers is here." Cara said.

Humphrey straightened up and turned sharply.

"Who?" He demanded.

"The Terminator." Cara pointed out.

Milton snorted into his coke as Humphrey scanned the foyer for Harry.

"Well you're not going to have much luck up against a robotic assassin from the future, Humphrey." Milton said. "Wow Nora, you really do attract some interesting people."

Felix sniggered into his coke and almost choked when Heather let out a small scream. She clutched onto Milton's sleeve and he turned as something pressed against his back, making him jump too.

"Argh!" Cara gasped and stepped away as her elbow was nudged from behind.

Nora edged aside too and Heather stared when the framed poster of Hamlet swung open and a hand with a finger beckoning them forward emerged through the opening.

"What the…" Humphrey stared but Nora took his arm.

"This is our way out of here." She edged around under the stairs.

The hand led to the plush purple velvet sleeve of a prince's coat and the body of a costumed man that ended in the grinning face of Seymour, almost unrecognisable with a black moustache and goatee and a gold,

bejewelled crown on top of his head. Nora took hold of
her brother's hand and stepped behind the poster,
followed closely by Humphrey and then Cara.

"This is amazing, Seymour!" Nora was impressed,
moving along so everyone could enter.

The group found themselves in a narrow passageway.

"Isn't it!" Seymour agreed. "And please call me
Prince Phoebus, King of Garfagnana. Come in, madam."
He took Cara's hand and she stepped into the passage,
smiling at him.

"King of *where*?"

"You'll see."

"You never showed us this before!" Milton
exclaimed in affront once he and Heather were through
the hidden opening.

Seymour closed the door, which was the same size as
the framed poster of Hamlet, and stood before them.

"My theatre has many secrets." He said mysteriously.
Milton thumped his velvet purple arm. "Ouch! I need my
arm for the performance tonight."

"Seymour this is brilliant. Where does it lead to?"
Nora asked, peering behind her and then ahead.

"It goes all around the internal walls of the structure
and opens through various parts of the foyers on the
upper levels and throughout the whole theatre. I think it
was used by performers in the past to come out in
various locations during their plays." He explained and
indicated for Nora to lead the way. "Just keep walking
forward and up the rickety old stairs at the end of this
passage. We'll go straight to where your box is. So. You
saw loads of bookshop customers did you?" He asked
gestured Cara ahead of him.

"At least five." Cara nodded as Nora led with
Humphrey behind her.

"That is so cool."

"I don't think *cool* is the word I would use, little brother." Nora said, admiring the old panelled walls surrounding them and the little electric candle bulbs at various intervals along the route.

They listened to Cara telling Seymour the bookworms they had spotted, climbed an old staircase and continued along the passage as it veered left.

"This is fun." Humphrey admitted.

She glanced back at him and smiled. Seymour called at her to stop walking.

Her brother then squashed his way to the front and pushed on a panel. It swung wide open to reveal a luxurious foyer with a deep green carpet and fine décor. They stepped out and Nora recognised it as the location near to the boxes. Cara gazed around impressed. Once everyone was out Seymour called to an usher waiting at the top of the staircase cordoned off by a rich black cord.

"Hey Seymour. And gang." The man greeted, walking over. "Oh, hi Milton. Nora. Heather." He recognised.

"Hello." Nora and Heather chorused back.

"Yo, Danny." Milton nodded.

"Can you show them into their box please, Danny." Seymour said. "And also fetch them some programmes."

"Right, boss." Danny said and indicated for them to follow him.

"You sound like you could be a crime lord, *boss*." Cara said to Seymour.

Seymour looked delighted.

"I hope you enjoy the performance." He said to her.

"I'm sure I will." She nodded and watched him bow his head and then step back into the passageway. "Wait in the main foyer after the play. I'll come down once I'm changed."

"Good luck!" Heather called and they set off behind Danny.

The usher informed then that the Mayor, the Chief of Police and the Duke of Cole were due for the opening performance.

"The Duke of Cole?" Nora asked, trying not to sound interested.

Humphrey glanced at her.

"His Grace heard about the opening of The Jolly Theatre. Seymour has placed him in the box opposite yours." Danny explained.

"Let's hope we don't get distracted." Cara grinned at Nora.

"Let's hope *he* doesn't get distracted." Humphrey corrected.

"What would distract him?" Cara asked, frowning.

"Ooof!" Humphrey replied as Nora jabbed him in the ribs.

Cara looked at them with suspicion but her attention was diverted when Danny opened the door to their private box.

It was a plush room immediately at the front of the magnificent auditorium, to the left side and above the level of the stage which spread beneath them clearly for the perfect view. There were eight private boxes, four each side. The Jolly's and their guests had been given the first on the left. Danny indicated to the first private box opposite, reserved as the royal box, on the right hand side of the theatre, explaining that it was always reserved for royalty. He said that when the Duke of Cole's secretary had contacted the theatre to enquire about a ticket for the Duke, Seymour had been amazed the royal box would actually be used on the opening night. It was considered a very lucky omen.

Danny pointed to the box next door and explained that the Mayor of Piertown, the Chief of Police and Mr and Mrs Jolly would be sitting next door to His Grace. Nora considered the royal box briefly before turning to examine the eight plush seats, assortment of footstools and little oak tables which could all be moved about in their own box. The opening that looked onto the auditorium was framed by thick red velvet curtains with gold tassels.

"Golly! Are you sure *this* isn't the state box or royal box provided for dignitaries?!" Felix stood in awe at the front, peered down over the large empty auditorium.

"This is box number two." Heather explained. "One box down from the royal box. And Seymour gave it to us above the Mayor and Chief of Police. The Duke will be sitting opposite us."

"Wow. 'Impressed emoji'." Felix admired.

Cara stood at the opening too and scanned the area. She held up her iPhone and took a few photographs. She then snapped everyone choosing their seats and uploaded them to her Instagram account, until Danny arrived with the programmes and also some nibbles.

"Enjoy the performance." He said. "If you need anything I'll be outside along the hallway."

"Thank you." Nora smiled.

The door closed.

Nora and Humphrey settled in chairs to read the programme. Humphrey rested his feet on a footstool, crossed his legs at the ankles and sipped his wine, looking very much like Harvey Spector from the TV show *Suits*!

Nora read the introduction and the plot of the play aloud.

"Four years before his death in 1936, G. K. Chesterton wrote a play for the community theatre in his hometown of Beaconsfield, England." She read.

"I thought he only wrote two plays." Cara joined in.

"He had two plays produced: *Magic* and *The Judgment of Dr Johnson*, both of which were very successful." Nora read. "But it was only in 1936 that he penned another and he thought it needed revising and never got around to it so never saw it performed in his lifetime."

"Gosh." Felix mused, helping himself to a handful of peanuts.

"That's sad." Heather said.

"The play 'The Surprise' is part fairy tale and part allegory." Nora read. "It tells us the story of an author who claims he has written the perfect play. Although there are no villains in his play, it has a very dramatic tension. The author even has the perfect actors that are lifelike puppets he has created just for it. When a wandering monk passes by, the author puts on a performance for him, but is unsatisfied even with everything perfect, for he wants his characters to have free will…"

"Ah. I see the allegory." Humphrey smiled.

"G. K. Chesterton was a Catholic, like J. R. R. Tolkien." Nora explained. "Seymour studied both authors at university, especially the theology in their writings." She looked down and continued to read. 'The Surprise is an appropriate title for this play because nothing can prepare the audience for what will happen, especially at the end…"

A voice interrupted over the PA system to announce the doors were now open and the performance would start in fifteen minutes.

"Sounds like it will be good." Humphrey sipped his wine.

"I'm sure it will be. I've seen numerous characters in rehearsals. The princess is very amusing." Nora nodded.

She closed the programme and watched the people filling up the main house below.

"Let's see if we can spot any more bookworms." Cara grinned, glancing back at Nora.

"Please no." Nora laughed but leaned forward with her glass of wine and gazed out over the auditorium.

There were lots of people now and Nora was pleased for her brother. The tickets had been a sell-out and it was going to be a full house.

"There are Mrs and Miss Raven." Cara spotted, peering through a pair of opera glasses.

"Where did you get those?" Nora asked.

"I sometimes go to the ballet in London with Ella. We can only afford the cheap seats at the back to I bought these." Cara grinned. "I brought Ella's lorgnette for you."

"Really?"

"Here." Cara said and handed Nora a pair of spectacles on a stick from her bag.

"Thank you, Cara." Nora held them up.

They had a times three magnification power so Nora got a shock when she saw an old lady's wart closer than expected. Humphrey thought Nora looked very sophisticated as she held them before her eyes and sipped her wine.

Alongside watching the Ravens weave their way through the crowds to reach their seats they spotted Mr Hill settling into his place not far from them, leaving his battered green case in the aisle. Mr Clegg and his ex-wife were on the other side of the hall much to Nora's relief and then Cara spotted Billy and Jiao from Passageway Antiques followed by Eugene Harvey. Eugene sat himself down and took out a pair of binoculars so they all ducked when they swung in their direction.

"There's Annabelle from the charity shop in Castletown. That must be her husband with her." Nora noticed, leaning with her chin on the wooden edge of their box.

"I can see The Terminator." Cara said.

Felix choked on his coke, laughing.

"The *Terminator*." He repeated, snorting with amusement again at the moniker.

"He's with a woman. That's a relief." Nora breathed.

Harry glanced in their direction but didn't seem to recognise them so Nora and Cara felt safe to spy on him. Nora then did a double take when she saw Spencer Brown and his wife walking towards the front of the auditorium to take their seats.

"Hooray, there's Georgina and Troy. Oh, and Mrs Pickering and uncle Orville." Heather said.

"I suppose we can't shout down to them can we?" Cara joked.

"I can wolf-whistle." Nora suggested playfully.

Cara laughed.

In the end, Cara sent a text to Georgina who received it as she was about to turn off her phone. They watched her read it before looking up at their box and when she saw them she waved.

Felix choked again when Cara pointed out a woman who had come into the Seatown shop a few weeks earlier and browsed around the front while holding a pair of knickers.

Mr and Mrs Jolly arrived and waved over at the group from their box, joined by the Mayor and his wife and the Chief of Police. Finally, when every seat in the theatre seemed to be occupied, the lights dimmed and the air of excitement and anticipation grew.

Nora kept glancing towards the royal box and finally noticed the Duke of Cole enter in the darkness. He was accompanied by a man. Nora recognised him as Edward, a butler who worked in a large house just outside Castletown in the service of Lady Augusta Dribble, the Duke of Cole's twelfth cousin, twice removed. It appeared he now also worked for the Duke. The butler went to stand behind the Duke's chair but at the Duke's insistence finally conceded to sit down next to His Grace.

Nora smiled when the Duke's gaze scanned the auditorium, skimming over them in their box, before swinging back to her. He took a small pair of black theatre glasses from his pocket and levelled them upon Nora. Nora watched him smile warmly and dip his head in acknowledgement. Nora smiled back before looking hastily away, blushing.

Cara turned and stared at her.

"Something you're not telling me?" She asked.

"The Duke of Cole has a crush on Nora." Humphrey said flatly from behind them.

Nora cleared her throat, turning back to sit with him.

His elbow was leaning on the arm of his chair, his dark brows lowered thoughtfully. He rubbed his chin, blue eyes trailing Nora into the chair at his side.

"I've only met him once." She smiled.

Humphrey shrugged.

"I wouldn't begrudge you snagging a Duke."

"Neither would I!" Nora shook her head, amused at the far-fetched possibility. "But as it currently stands, I think I may have a crush on someone else."

Humphrey didn't look convinced, but his mouth quirked when she held up the lorgnette.

"*May*?" He repeated, flatly.

"I only have *four* eyes for you, Humphrey." She smiled, wiggling the eye piece.

Humphrey took hold of her other hand, lifted it to his mouth and covered her knuckles with a kiss.

"We shall see." He said, his own eyes slightly narrowed.

"The play's starting." Milton threw a look back at them, shaking his head.

Nora settled back in her chair, watching as the heavy curtains lifted to reveal a magnificent fairy tale setting. It

showed a great striped marquee in the centre, bright
bunting, flags, banners and a puppet theatre. A lone
soldier held a spear, standing in the centre of the stage
with his back to the audience.

Complete silence fell.

The audience watched as a brown robed friar strolled
onto the stage. Nora snuck one last look around the
auditorium, thinking of all the bookshop customers
below as the play began.

Her gaze was drawn once more to the royal box
opposite. She blinked and then smiled when she met a
now familiar pair of eyes.

"Heaven be with us, is the *king* here that he should
have a sentry posted?" The friar declared loudly,
indicating to the motionless, silent guard.

"Not a king." Nora murmured, forcing herself to look
away and back down to the stage. "But a Duke."

"What was that?" Humphrey whispered suspiciously.

"Oh, nothing." Nora smiled.

She placed her finger to her lips and hummed
thoughtfully.

"Just the future possibility of a surprise." She
whispered to herself and grinned.

THE END

ALSO IN THE SERIES

'The Secondhand Bookworm'
'Nora and The Secondhand Bookworm'
'Summer at The Secondhand Bookworm'
'Halloween at The Secondhand Bookworm'
'Black Friday at The secondhand Bookworm'
Book Club at The Secondhand Bookworm'
'Valentine's Day at The Secondhand Bookworm'
'Lockdown at The Secondhand Bookworm'
'Strange Things at The Secondhand Bookworm'
'Winterland at The Secondhand Bookworm'

Available in paperback and Kindle

Watch for more novels in the Bookworm series

Also by the author

'House of Villains'
Available now from Amazon

ABOUT THE AUTHOR

Emily Jane Bevans lives on the south coast of England. For ten years she worked in, and helped to manage, a family chain of antiquarian bookshops in Worthing, Arundel and Chichester in Sussex. She is the co-founder and co-director of a UK based Catholic film production apostolate 'Mary's Dowry Productions'. She writes, edits, produces, directs, narrates and sometimes acts for the company's numerous historical and religious films on the lives of the Saints and English Martyrs. She also likes to write fiction mainly based upon her bookselling memories.

EMILY JANE BEVANS

MARY'S DOWRY PRODUCTIONS

Mary's Dowry Productions is a Catholic Film
Production Apostolate founded in 2007 to bring the lives
of the Saints and English Martyrs, English Catholic
heritage and history to film and DVD. Mary's Dowry
Productions' unique film production style has been
internationally praised for not only presenting facts,
biographical information and historical details but a
prayerful and spiritual film experience. Many of the
films of Mary's Dowry Productions have been broadcast
on EWTN, BBC and SKY.
For a full listing of films and more information visit:

www.marysdowryproductions.org

CHRISTMAS AT THE SECONDHAND BOOKWORM

Made in United States
North Haven, CT
11 September 2023

41420835R00171